Bob Boyton has been a writer and performer for over 25 years. For much of that time he has also worked with single homeless people. Bob lives in Camden Town, where he is a council tenant. Bomber Jackson is his first novel.

First published in 2012 by
heavy-bag books
83A college place
London NW1 0DR

Printed and bound in Great Britain by
CPI UNITED KINGDOM
108 – 110 Beddington Lane
Croydon
Surrey CR0 4YY

A CIP record of this book is available from the British Library

ISBN 978-0-9572174-0-9
Cover and typesetting by Becky Morrison

BOMBER JACKSON DOES SOME

By Bob Boyton

For Jane and Tali and in memory of Jim Cronin who took his shot at redemption.

Boxing always ends in sadness. Every fighter has a story that could break your heart. We lose, we get hurt and everything comes apart.

Barry McGuigan (in Boxing News, May 2011)

PART ONE

Chapter One

Sitting in the back I feel as nervous as a kitten for the first few minutes.

The cab driver keeps trying to talk to me, but he's such a carrot cruncher I can't be bothered.

Just after the town starts to be houses on both sides of the road, we pass the hall where I went to AA meetings.

I didn't mind the meetings, as it goes. First it was handy getting out two hours a week, then I began to get into it, even though most of them didn't think a convict should be allowed in the same room. The way I looked at it, the trouble was that compared to me half of them never had a drink problem, they only went to stop themselves getting nagged to death by their old man or old woman.

Best one there was my sponsor Cynthia, although going by her severe looks and the way she spoke like a magistrate, you wouldn't book her as being kind.

I didn't let on to Cynthia that I'm finished with meetings now I'm out. She'd have only gone into me. I made out I'd be looking for one to go to as soon as I got back to London, but really I figure they can all get on with their recovery and I'll get on with mine.

The cab drops me at the station and I've got a half-hour wait for the train.

I've got the discharge grant intact and enough smash to get a Mirror for the wait and a Telegraph for the journey, because I'm really into the reading habit. There's a Boxing News in amongst the magazines, but reading that always weighs a bit heavy on the heart, and I'm feeling rough without anything else upsetting me.

I have a look through the window of the buffet but the tea place is all one with the bar. Getting a drink in nick is more trouble than it's worth, so this is my first temptation, and it's found me half-wobbly, so I decide I'm better off plotting up on a bench on the platform.

I sit down and really I fancy diving into the Telegraph, bathing myself in all that news, but I stick to what I decided and leave the Telegraph for later, in case there's a bar on the train.

In the old days I'd get on a train sometimes when I'd had a little touch, just to have a beer, not bothered where I was going. You're anonymous drinking on a train. No one's going to be looking at you to notice you're suddenly holding dough, or wondering who the geezer is offering strangers a drink.

The front of the Mirror says the new prime minister Tony Blair's doing a marvellous job and on the back West Ham have lost again, but they would have – it was Saturday.

Inside there's boxing, if you can call it that, heavyweights, an old boy and a no-hoper fighting for a world title no one gives a monkey's about, except for the two managers and anyone else who's taking money from it.

The no-hoper's a Spanish Yank, Johnny Guiterriez – Johnny Guitar. It makes me restless thinking about him, wondering if he knows it's all gone away from him or if he doesn't care because he's still got the need, wants a taste one more time before he has to admit he'll never know anything like it ever again.

I turn over to the crossword, hoping it'll stop me thinking about him, stop Johnny Guitar playing the blues in my head.

Yellow fruit found in the Caribbean, six letters.

Three more clues and I give up, disgusted with myself. Forty three years of age and I'm doing a crossword for muppets, all because some fighter I'm never going to meet is making me want to have a drink.

This is one of those times I could phone Cynthia, tell her I'm drifting near trouble, but I know the first thing she'll do is try to drag me back into it all, start making herself busy, looking for a meeting for me to go to.

Instead I do one of the other things they recommend, think about my last meeting and try to draw strength from that, except it ain't a good memory.

When it was my turn to speak I told them they'd help me realise wanting to be world middleweight champion was what turned me into world champion drinker, so now I'm going to be just ordinary because I know I'm worth more when I'm not trying to be someone, and they all sat there looking at me as if they didn't get it at all, not even Cynthia, who just gave me that cold little smile.

Thinking about how they let me down like that decides me. From now on I'm definitely on my own, but sitting there in the weather I can't help thinking about walking through that buffet door behind me and the couple of little scotches I'd have, to help kill that prat feeling that's still running about in my gut.

Next I start wondering whether the news stand has got a biro and an exercise book, because I'm looking over my shoulder at the buffet window and I can almost taste the yellow warmth of the light I can see shining down onto the optics. In my head I've got this great description going, of standing at the counter ordering a drink and the whole thing feeling like laying my head between an accommodating pair of tits.

Only I don't mean some woman and me, naked and all sexed up. In my idea it's more like a few stages before. The two of us are both still dressed, it's Saturday night in Poplar in the old days, not long before chucking out time. We've both been sitting down but she must be coming back from having a piss or something because she's standing up next to my seat, and then she laughs as I reach out and pull her towards me, so my head's resting against her breasts through her jumper and she's a big girl so they're squashing my ears. You can tell from her laugh both of us know it's going to happen, me knowing she'll be all wet and warm and hoping I haven't had so much I can't do it, or if I fall asleep, that she'll be one who likes it in the morning. Maybe this ain't even our first time, but she's one of those who don't mind it being every now and then, thinks it's tasty knocking about with a boxer but doesn't want to go through all the training and the blood and guts, just likes me when I'm spruced up and relaxed.

As I come to the end of the daydream I uncross my

legs to stand up but I stay sitting. I feel like I'm soaking in sadness at all the years it's been since I had a decent girl and I think what's the point of writing anything, because how would I explain everything that's happened since I was even with an old sort, and I certainly ain't going to put down that the best kindness I've had was three months two'd up with a little wifey in the Scrubs because the top man on the wing remembered seeing me fight once.

Then I do stand up and walk over to the edge of the platform, looking down at the dirty hardness of the ballast because I want to distract myself with something I can write about, but I've worked on the permanent way and I know all I'm looking at is heartache and shit wages, although I almost smile to myself because that would make a great title for a country song.

Then I think about the train that nearly had the lot of us out near Watford, which decides me I might as well test myself out in the buffet because if that Intercity 125 had done me none of it would matter.

I walk over to the refreshments room but the cautious side of me is still holding me back, telling me that if the Fellowship's let me down I ought to give the writing a go, even on the out, get focused on that instead, in case I can't help having a brandy to go with that hot chocolate.

As a compromise I don't go in at first, but look through the window, studying the only punter in there.

He's got a pink face, with white hair at the sides and a bald patch on top, which is pink as well. He looks as if he works in an office where all the men are called Johnson or Perkins and all they ever drink is half a pint of bitter down the club and a sherry with the old woman before lunch on Sunday. Except this is half nine Thursday morning and he's pouring a can of John Smith's, which used to be one of my beers, into a thin half-pint glass.

His John Smith's doesn't look like it's changed much since I had one, still got that dark rich colour that lets you know just how sweet it tastes and how much better you're going to feel.

This bloke knows all about the taste. As he lifts the glass up the tip of his tongue's poking out onto his bottom lip, lying in wait for the beer.

I'm loving watching him, like he's going to have that first mouthful for both of us, waiting for his first sip. I'm even thinking maybe I won't bother going in, only just before the glass reaches his mouth I notice the old girl behind the bar staring at me as if I'm a nut nut. There's so much hatred on that putrid face of hers I can feel it in my chest. Now I'm going to have to go in to front her up, show her she can't go around like that, spraying poison everywhere.

She's still giving me x-rays as I open the door but after about fifteen seconds I don't care because I've got that alcohol smell stroking my face like a warm flannel.

I feel half-pissed just breathing it in and I must have looked it, because Perkins looks like he's got half a mind to have it away but he doesn't know who scares him most, me or Boadicea who's standing there wafting me the death wish from behind the counter, alternating it with giving him the I'm-desperate-save-me look, though soon as I put a tenner on the counter she shapes up.

'Two cans of John Smith's and a large scotch, love.'

It's so easy to say, I can't believe I've given myself all that ag.

I've let her put my change down in front of me, too busy with all that flavour to count it. Then I have half the scotch to warm myself up.

I put the short glass back on the counter.

I decide I'll pack it in again tomorrow before I get myself in bother.

Chapter Two

This bloke comes over the loudspeaker but I can't understand what he says. He must be as drunk as I am.

'Is that your train then, Bomber,' asks Iris behind the bar.

We're all friends now. We know each other's names

'Don't need a train, I'm fucking flying already,' and I hold my arms out like an aeroplane. 'Zoom zoom.'

I think that's funny, but Iris says, 'Language, please.'

She doesn't really look like she's got the hike though, just looks a bit tired.

Then Sidney starts laughing, but she gives him a look like Mummy's telling him off for playing out with the bad boys.

I'm still trying to make my mind up whether they're on the vinegar stroke. It's down to her if they are. He wouldn't have the strength to put it to her.

I've seen plenty like him inside. There's no harm in them, but they get pushed around from the first day of their sentence until the last, unless they find someone to look after them, or sometimes they take the easy way out and top themselves.

Looking at the two of them I reckon they must be having it, only I don't know if he's just hanging around for the beer or because he likes the jollies as well.

It is a bit hard to imagine, but she has got a sparkle in her blue eyes even though the blonde barnet's beginning to look worn out, bit like leaves on a pot plant that needs watering.

She hasn't got a lot inside her blouse either, but I reckon he has a dive.

She sussed I was a fighter straight off, I've felt her looking at the scars on my boat then clocking the big lumpy hands and two broken knuckles as I'm finishing my first beer.

I didn't let on I've noticed her looking, but she had me in suspense as I was draining the beer, wondering was she going to sell me another one, knowing I had to be an ex-con. It wasn't the sort of town you'd find a boxer there for any other reason.

The way it turned out I didn't have to worry, I'm just sipping my third scotch chaser when she's said something about how boxers must be very brave, and it's come out that Sidney's a bit of a fight fan himself and thinks he might have seen me win a fight at Belle Vue Manchester, even though I never fought there. But I still fancied a drink and didn't want to upset either of them so I let him shake my hand anyway and feel how big it is.

Not long after that the announcer comes on. That's when she drops her little hint that I ought to be on my way, which does hurt a little, although I don't mean to upset her by swearing.

Perhaps I ought to try to make it right, but I'm nearly empty again so I'm busy feeling in my pocket for notes, trying to count up what I've spent so far, and work out can I buy my new pals a drink.

I can't remember her prices at all so I grip both the

notes I've got left and bung 'em down on the counter without looking at them.

Then I glimpse down at two fivers. I feel like a gambler looking at his cards.

I say, 'Not a royal flush, Iris, but not crap either.'

She gives me an old-fashioned look as if she don't know what I'm on about.

I blank her look, because suddenly this feels like poker with money on the table.

'Same again, Iris, and one for my mate Sidney, who despite...' I can't think of a word... I say, 'Despite whatsits has come to stand next to me.'

I put my arm round Sidney who leans into me in a very pally way.

Then I realise what I've forgotten. 'And one for yourself, Iris.'

She must have got the hump again. She makes out she hasn't heard me offer her a drink.

'Seven pounds please, Bomber.'

I want to tell her she's having a laugh with her prices but I'm not so drunk I don't know that would be the end of it, so I give her the money instead.

Sidney moves away from me and gives me my arm back.

'Just going to find a bar stool, Bomber.'

Sidney pats my forearm. I reckon he talks to the dog like that, perhaps it's on the fierce side. He probably shits himself on account of the dog as well.

Personally I don't mind because we're all having a good time.

While he's gone round the corner to get his stool Iris turns her back on me, starts arranging packets of crisps on the back shelf.

From the back she hasn't got any shape at all in that nylon coat. You can't even see her sag, but I haven't seen her legs yet, and the drink's making me feel fruity, so I could do with them being worth looking at.

I take my chance and stretch forward on the stool to have a peek.

Even with her tights you can see they aren't special. I've just finishing looking when she turns round and almost catches me.

I don't think she cops on, but I make out I'm looking around the bar anyway. Next to where Sidney was standing I notice an old briefcase sitting on the floor.

I nod towards it. 'Sidney starts later, does he?'

Iris says, 'That's Sidney's business. You'll have to ask him about that.'

The way she says it gives me the hump.

I look at her because I don't get it at all, why she has to sigh when she tells me that, like I've upset her again. All I've done is ask her what time Sidney starts. She gives me one of her disappointed looks back, then looks away. I take a big mouthful of beer and try to forget it.

I'm beginning to think she's murder to have about when you want to have a drink. You just start enjoying yourself when she makes an atmosphere.

I've been getting on top form up until now but she's beginning to bring me down and Sidney's been gone so long he must be having a constipated shit, although just then he comes back round the corner.

He must have heard the two of us talking because as he puts his bar stool down next to mine he looks up at me and says, 'They had to let me go, Bomber.'

Then he sits on the stool still looking at me as if he's afraid I'm going to take the piss.

I shake my head as if I'm going to say something serious. 'They had to let me go and all.'

That cracks us both up and I slap him on the back. Although I make sure I don't do it so hard he'll fall off, I can feel Iris wanting to throw me out.

Now I've made him laugh I want to ask him what's in the briefcase, although I think I've guessed the strength of it anyway.

Sidney picks up the short I bought him before he went to the khazi. 'Cheers, Bomber.'

I let the briefcase go, say, 'Cheers,' back, even though I'm more than halfway through my pint and I've got to start going slower because of the money situation.

'You know Bomber, it is most certainly good to…'

It's coming to me how pissed he is, because I'm still waiting for him to finish what he's saying when he gestures to Iris with his empty brandy glass and mouths to her, 'Large one,' then hands her a ten-pound note.

I'm expecting 'And one for Bomber?' from Iris, but she just says, 'Thank you, Sidney,' and takes his money.

That's it cold. They've done me.

Iris doesn't surprise me but I can't believe Sidney. He's got to guess I'm potless even if he doesn't know it. I sit there, looking in the other direction, thinking,

'You cheap little cunt.'

I'm thinking it so hard I almost think I must have said it out loud, the way it echoes around my nut, but I can't have because just then Sidney takes me by surprise and ends up saying something sensible, although he takes about a million years to get it out.

'You know, my friend, even though we've only just met, I really do think, it's you middleweights who deserve a lot more of that glamour that some of these heavyweights get. I mean, it's you who take the bigger risk.'

I turn to agree with him, but my head suddenly feels heavy and I have to put both hands on the bar to stop myself falling.

'You alright there, Bomber?'

I nod that I'm okay instead of talking.

'Thought you were taking a dive in the second for a moment there.'

He thinks that's funny, gives a little laugh and puts a hand on my arm. He's probably only trying to steady me, but for a second I forget where I am and move back, making myself narrow, my right arm coming up because he's that side of me. Then I'm back in the real world and see Sidney's face looking as if he's shit all the colour out of it.

I look down at the counter, rest my hands flat on it as I shake my head.

'It's alright. Carry on about the middles.'

Sidney's leaning over looking up into my face, like he's trying to work me out. I don't want him seeing how

I close I was. I want to tell him he's making me feel like a goldfish.

'I said I'm alright. Carry on – you're good as gold.'

He doesn't know whether to believe me or not and for a minute it's just been me and him but then he can't hold it on his own any longer, has to look for Mummy to see what she thinks.

Iris is halfway down the bar polishing glasses.

She shrugs her shoulders at him, carries on polishing. I can see her meaning as clear as he can.

She does me a favour, looking at her face brings me back to normal. I want to tell her she's got it all wrong, explain I'm just a bloke having a beer, but I can't be bothered with her deaf ears.

I turn back to look at Sidney, who must be on the mend by now because he only half-looks as if he wants to puke up.

My last mouthful of beer goes sour on the way down, which doesn't make me feel so clever, but I manage to wink at him to say hello.

I want Sidney to start talking about boxing again, so we can carry on having a conversation, with me telling him he's right or wrong depending on what he says, but he's got to start, because after all the months I've been on the dry the drink's hit my brain like a dose of chloroform. I can't get thinking again without him doing his bit.

Sidney looks down at his glass without saying anything. In the silence it all feels gone again.

I'm gutted. It feels as if I haven't really been sitting

here, one normal bloke chatting to another, the way I used to before I became a bum, but then I think of a funny that might pull things round.

'People think I'm punch drunk, but I'm not. I'm just drunk.'

When Sidney laughs it feels like we're pals again and I give his shoulder a little squeeze.

As I take my hand away I almost whisper, 'Didn't frighten you did I, Sidney. Knew I was only teasing, didn't you.'

'Of course, Bomber.'

I give my head and shoulders a funny shake to let him know we're mates.

'Tell me about the heroic fighting middleweights, then.'

'Just meant to say this, Bomber. You boys, I mean you boys, I've got to say you are the unsung heroes, the middleweights, that's who I mean, hitting hard enough – you know what I mean – hitting hard enough to do a lot of damage, but often not enough to knock each other out, you take a lot more punishment, fight for fight, than the heavies, and you're fitter, punches that can snap.'

I want to tell Sidney he's bang on, even if it does take him a long time to say it, but now he's on one he's not stopping.

'...Rumble in the Jungle, Rumble in the Jungle – heavyweights, Bomber, but more like middleweights. Foreman couldn't put Ali away, got to be where Ali picked up his... What do you call it, Bomber, you know when you get punched too often, hurts the brain? Oh come on Bomb, you must know, you must know...'

Sidney stops but I hardly notice. I've watched that film so often, when I remember it it's like watching it again. It's so clear I could be looking at it on the telly above the bar, seeing Ali telling big George to hit him again – an old favourite of mine that was, winding up the opponent until he lost his temper and his judgement.

I used it a lot. 'Come on then – hit me, you cunt,' screaming it at the other bloke. 'Your old woman's had half your neighbours – come on, hit me, you cunt.' Except I didn't let the other guy connect, didn't have to prove I could take a punch.

Sidney must've got the hump that I'm away in a daze. You'd think he'd know better, but he tries to squeeze my arm. 'You know what is it, what's it…'

I come out of it about half way for a couple of seconds, realise it's only Sidney but then I really go, the way I do sometimes when I have a drink. I'm back in my last big fight, I can feel Terry Cooke holding me while he's hitting me in the kidneys, he's pouring the poison into my ear, instead of the other way round. I'm so unfit I can hardly move my feet. He keeps catching me low with his right.

He never ran out of breath, the whole fight, never had to stop talking to save himself, knew he was hurting me from halfway through the second, even kept on with verbals when he knew he'd done me, suffocating me with words that felt as if they were tumbling down on me like rocks, making sure I'd remember it was personal, remember who'd hurt me worse than I thought it could get.

As he's holding onto me I can't believe he's followed me here. I'm trying to have a drink but he's stopping me picking up my glass. This time I want to hear what he's saying but I can't, because I'm screaming at him to fuck off and leave me alone.

Then I hear my corner stabbing me in the back. 'Stop it, stop it.'

'Get out, Bomber, get out,' Iris is shouting at me, must be from ringside.

Then I come round, see Iris behind the bar, holding the shillelagh that was hanging on a hook by one of the beer taps. I'm standing where I was but as I turn round to look for Sidney I'm crunching glass underfoot. There's pieces of it all over the floor like the tears of a big glass doll that someone smashed up.

I begin to get an idea of what's happened.

Sidney's over against the wall, trying to shrink out of sight behind a bar stool that's lying on its side.

As I look at him I can hear Iris making these breathing sounds more like an animal than a human, and I know she's going to get me nicked. All I can think of is that I want another drink before it happens.

I turn back and step closer to the bar. 'Give us a bottle of scotch,' I growl at her as if I'm doing a robbery, so she won't mess about.

Iris flinches and drops the shillelagh so it clatters on the floor.

She bends down and starts scrambling under the counter with her hands.

As she straightens up she says, 'Here, I've only got a

bottle of vodka,' in a quivery voice and I can see her eyes filling up.

I take it from her. 'Ta.'

Half of me wants to tell her sorry but I know better because that might break through her shock, and the longer that lasts the more time I've got before she makes the call.

I go out of the door and onto the platform, then I take the top off the bottle and get about a third of it down my throat. As I do I get a flash of being in the Scrubs, having the little wifey's Hampton in my mouth.

Chapter Three

I get taken off the train by transport police and slung into the back of a van. At first I manage to get a few in but once they smother me I'm in for some.

After the ride round they dump me on some wet mud in between a ditch and the road.

It must be the pain from what they've given me that brings me around again because their boots crashing into me is the first thing that comes back, then after that I begin to remember the little Scots steward, with all the bunny, in the empty restaurant car, and realising he was risking getting me nicked by breaking open bottles of brandy for the pair of us after we'd done all the half-empty wine bottles.

Somehow he must have seen I was going to come across the table at him and called up the Keystones.

I stop worrying about any of that because I can smell the turd even before I've opened my eyes. It's about six inches in front of my face, three lumps sticking up through the runny stuff. My stomach gives half a heave because I think it looks like the sauce on chocolate pudding.

I push myself back a foot and my legs are okay. I reckon it's broken ribs filling me up with pain, plus my head must have stopped a few when they really got going and started enjoying themselves.

I pull myself up, hanging onto a road sign that's handy,

Looking at the light in the morning sky I reckon it's something like half five or six.

I'm wet down one side of my jacket and shirt. Then I remember waking up with one of them pissing over me as they pulled me out of the van before I went unconscious again. If it didn't hurt so much I'd have time to wonder what he tells his kids he does for a living.

Going by the sign I'm only about twenty miles from the nick. Below the main board there's another sign pointing to a turning to a hospital in three hundred yards, which is where I'm going to have to go to get my ribs tied up and with a bit of luck a nice big scrip for painkillers, as long as the doctors don't realise I'm halfway to rattling from needing a drink and tell me to fuck off and suffer because it's self-inflicted, which I've certainly had from a couple of merciless cunts.

About ten yards along there's a wire fence between me and the road which I can hold onto without having to bend, but even with that the pain slows me. Then in and out of the pain I'm beginning to feel a bit like a spaceman and I'm half grateful for the agony because I know I'm having thoughts that aren't right. At first I notice a couple of dirty old pick-up trucks going past, but then I start thinking all the cars going past are shiny, and I know all the people in them are all old grannies with nice warm clothes for when they get out and they've all got a pound of boiled sweets in a paper bag waiting for them at home. Then I get another shot of pain and I can't think about anything except I know I've noticed an Old Bill car slow down as it comes past twice now and I can feel a collar coming, which I reckon has to be about as unfair as it gets. Then I start thinking about the sweets again. The Fellowship says always keep some in your pocket, something sugary to suck in case you fancy a drink, because a sweet taste in your mouth is always going put you off the idea.

This pain's good, almost makes me spew when it hits but stops me thinking about all the different kind of sweets you used to get: liquorice cuttings, Everton Mints, Fox's Glacier, Butterscotch, then penny satellites and all the different chews, Fruit Salads, Black Jacks, Refreshers, Love Hearts. Benny sold them in his shop in Devon's Road, and when we didn't have money we used to go in try to empty him out. Everyone said he was a nonce but he wasn't.

I know that's a nick for sure, if I start asking the people in the cars for a sweetie.

More pain, and just as it comes I think I've seen Old Bill come past me for the third time. I'm flying into a different scene, looking at Jesus up on the cross, stuck up there for really trying to be something, and Peter denied him three times in the garden the night before, just like my old man disowned me, told the East London Advertiser he'd got a bet on Terry Cooke, said I was finished.

The fence ends at a telephone box. I think I'm going to lie down in it, but instead I ring Cynthia, my last chance, ask her to stop the fight, get me out of the ring, take me down from the cross. Cynthia, save me.

I'm almost right about the collar. I'm outside the phone box, leaning against the door letting it hold me up, when the car comes back.

At first only one of them gets out and comes over. He doesn't look more than twenty one. Underneath his peaked cap there's a baby face. I'm worn out the first look I take at him, my pain's gone to sleep for a minute and I want to follow it, but I can see the busyness in those blue eyes, know I've got to duck and weave a bit.

'Been in a fight, have we?'

He thinks he's got it sorted, puts plenty of needle in, so I'll give him an excuse to make himself happy.

I nod hard enough to let him know I've heard him but not so much it looks like a yes.

'You must have done something.'

I'm about three inches taller than him and he decides to stretch up as he says it. He's telegraphing all over the place without knowing it, telling me he's running out of dialogue already.

Maybe I let him know and I don't see his right hand, because suddenly I get a burst of pain that bends me over and knocks me out.

I can't be out for long. I come to still leaning against the phone box, only a bit lower down and the pain still echoing inside me.

I look up and by now the other one's there as well.

'Would you like to stand up, mate.' It doesn't sound like a question, only he doesn't know it but we've got a problem, because I don't know if I can.

I think myself into trying, and put my hands behind me for extra leverage, but I'm not sharp anymore, and his face doesn't look clear.

31

All the same I move my head away from the phone box and straighten up a little. Maybe I don't do it fast enough because he slaps my face with the palm of his hand, which is a non-scoring punch but I feel it down below anyway, jumping around inside me like a new silver bullet.

I try to look at him because he's saying something, but suddenly I don't care, I'm looking down at the three of us.

This is better than the opium tea you can get hold of in the nick sometimes. I see him looking puzzled and then he aims his left at my crotch. My old reflexes float into action, I twist right to left, catch it on the thigh, bang. 'The only punch that hurts is the one you don't see,' Cassius Clay said, but not with broken ribs it ain't. I'm floating in agony, waiting for the next one like a dog with a broken spirit, then I see Cynthia.

'This gentleman is a friend of mine, officer.'

They hear her BBC voice and move back, change the way they stand.

'I'm afraid he's fallen on very hard times, haven't you, Anthony.'

The younger one starts talking about an ambulance. I'm half-dead but I'm still going to remember the panic in his voice.

Cynthia looks at me with her clever face, sees 'no' in my eyes and says 'no' to them.

Cynthia walks ahead. They're holding me up helping me to her car.

The one who hit me's whispering threats, but it's all over.

Cynthia opens the passenger door, and they get me into the seat.

'Thank you, gentlemen.'

'Glad to be of service, Madam.'

They slam the door and I shudder.

'I've got a private doctor, Bomber. He'll get you better.'

Cynthia's sweet voice puts me to sleep.

The doctor comes to see me, gives me a shot, pain-killers and Valium. He comes every day, and most of the time I stay in the fog, he says it's extensive bruising, nothing broken.

Then one day I'm properly conscious again, and the thing that hurts most is wondering what Cynthia thinks of the bum she's brought home with her.

I lie there letting it torture me for a couple of hours and then I half sit up. Everything still stings a bit but not enough to drive my thoughts away, so I look round the room to distract myself. The walls need repapering and the woodwork's chipped in a couple of places, so maybe she'd like me to do a spot of redecorating.

That's what they said in one of the therapy groups in nick. 'Try to repay a kindness, don't get so you feel guilty, guilt's a fine excuse for having a drink.'

Although stuck in Cynthia's little box room, with her old-fashioned two sheets and a blanket holding me in, I'm not worried about wanting a drink. I feel safe, almost like a little boy waiting to start my life again, before I've made any mistakes.

Except these sheets with a little hint of starch make me think of the white on a nurse's uniform as she bends over me, positioning herself so my hand slips up her black tights, and suddenly a little dreaming and I've got an erection, which lets me know how careful I've got to be not let Cynthia know I'm like that, because I don't want her to, not after everything she's doing for me.

I go back to the nurse anyway. I let my hand get as far as finding she's willing then I stop it, looking round at all the furniture Cynthia's got stuffed in here for rescue.

'Afraid I'll have to put you in my junk room. It really is a bit of an old glory hole, full of odds and ends I haven't got around to throwing away yet.'

That was when she was helping me up the stairs, panting as she said it. The slim slight shape of her we must have looked like a giant held up by a butterfly.

I've got to have smelled like licking a dog's arse, and she was the one doing the apologising. I reckon that's how it is with those sorts of people, always terrified a row's going to break out, so they keep saying sorry.

She's right about throwing it out. I wouldn't bother with the furniture and the two pewter mugs, and the clock don't look worth nicking. It could be that's why she's put me in here, afraid if she puts me in with the decent stuff, I'll clean her out.

Maybe that's what the Fellowship advises sponsors, because they've had toerags do that before. That's one of the things they teach you, that there's nothing new in being a drunk.

Just then there's a knock on the door. I wait for her to come in.

'Thought you might be awake in there.' But not too

kindly, in her magistrate's voice.

'Hello Cynthia. I'm awake. Come in.' Except it comes out shy because I'm feeling a prat for not realising it's manners, she'd been waiting for me to tell her to come in.

The door opens but I'm not ready for it. The bell's gone but I can't get off the stool.

Cynthia's holding a tray with a cup of tea and a plate of biscuits. She looks at me with those blue eyes of hers, more friendly than her voice, but not missing anything. I look straight back.

Hiding my nerves, the old thief's trick when you think you've been sussed, I don't miss much either. Her hair's blonder again, like it used to be some weeks at the group.

'Thought you might feel up to a cup of tea.'

She gives me the tray and backs away towards the door.

'That's lovely of you. Never got this in nick.'

Cynthia looks at me, nothing on her face.

I feel like I've got nothing in my brain, expecting someone like Cynthia to find that funny.

She nods her head. 'The bathroom's just down the hallway.'

Cynthia gives half a smile. 'Doctor said there might be things you don't remember. I'll see you later.'

I drink the best cup of tea in the world, or at least the best for going on ten years, which is about how long it's been since a woman made me one.

Tasting it and then feeling it trickle down to my gut is

better than that nurse could have felt, except now I know I'm going to have to have a shit, which starts me hoping I didn't have to have one when I didn't know what I was doing, with Cynthia having to help me.

A little bit later she comes back with a dressing gown that used to belong to her husband and tells me my clothes were a goner, but if I tell her my sizes she'll get me some in town.

Chapter Four

I'm still in bed, half-tired out and half daydreaming. There's nothing I've got to think about, when she comes back, about half past four. She doesn't bother knocking this time, comes straight in and gives me this tracksuit she's bought in the town.

'Thought you might find this comfortable around the house.' She twinkles as she holds it up for me to look at.

Even I know it's the kind of thing that hasn't been in fashion for about twenty years but I put on a this-must-be-my-birthday kind of face because I haven't got any money to pay her for it and I don't know what else to do, besides 'comfortable around the house' makes it sound as if I haven't got to leave yet.

Then she puts the local paper on the bed.

'A bit of an exaggeration I expect, Bomber. They'll do anything to sell newspapers, these journalists, I should know – I was married to one.'

Then she turns to go out. 'Dinner's at six, I thought I'd do one of my specials now you're well enough to have a proper meal. Telly's in the lounge if you feel like coming down before that. I don't much like being talked-to while I'm cooking, so feel free.'

She closes the door and I look down at a picture of Iris on the front page of the paper, standing on the station platform in front of a broken window, looking as if she's just been kicked up the cunt by a horse.

37

I make Cynthia right about them exaggerating. I don't remember smashing the window and if I did the till where's the hundred quid I'm supposed to have nicked? But paranoia creeps up on me all the same as bits and pieces start to come back.

I manage to damp that down and try to work out how Cynthia's going to go.

I can't see her handing me up, not after she's come this far, although I'm going to have to see how she sounds. If she thinks I've got to pay the price like the Fellowship would think I'll have to appeal to her sense of fair play as an Englishwoman, try to get her to give me a chance to creep away.

The newspaper doesn't give my name but after what Sidney and Iris must have told them Old Bill must know who I am.

One thing's sure, I know I'm not going the Fellowship way, volunteering to get myself nutted off by some country judge. Owning up to the consequences is alright for bank managers and dentists, all they're going to get is a slap on the back of the wrist.

I can still feel my fear lurking in the corner of the room so I try to concentrate on page two onwards, but most of it's local stuff, and the nearest professional football club plays in a league I've never heard of.

Five minutes later I sling the paper on the floor and lie back with my head on the pillow. I start by feeling myself through the duvet until I'm not thinking about anything else except that nurse with the black tights.

Afterwards I doze off for about half an hour, then I

get up and put on the track suit, nervous about having to get half-clever with Cynthia and trying to pretend I hadn't imagined it was her in the nurse's uniform.

I make myself forget all that and what I did to Iris's bar as I go downstairs and find the front room.

The telly's over in one corner but I don't bother to begin with, I'm happy sitting in an armchair taking in the décor.

It's not like some villains' houses I've been in, where even the wallpaper's got to tell you how much he can pull up if he has to. Instead everything's done with taste.

There's a rug in front of the gas fire that makes you feel cozy just to look at it and the green of the carpet goes with the green in the wallpaper without being flash, and matching exactly.

I begin to notice voices on a radio turned to low volume and every now and then, from the same direction, the sound of what must be Cynthia moving about in the kitchen.

But it's all so quiet that I can still hear birds singing outside.

That's when it comes to me. Cynthia's reminds of these houses I burgled, years ago, with a mate, Peter.

The two of us used to drive out to Essex in this van. Barking, Upminster, places like that, we even went as far as Leigh-on-Sea, next to Southend. Pete never reckoned it, he wanted to do places that were big money jobs, out in the stockbroker belt, said people in these kinds of houses didn't have enough stuff. It wore me out showing him, you just had to look for the gear, plus in those days houses like Cynthia's didn't have an alarm. We were doing alright until Pete got caught for something else.

I used to like those houses. Even then, you could always smell the floor polish, and I loved the quiet. You knew these people didn't have kids that needed clumping all the time. They weren't houses that heard a lot of shouting or screaming.

Cynthia's house is like one of them brought up to date, the colour scheme is a little bit different from what it would have been and in those days there weren't CD players or video machines to nick, but nothing else feels as if it's changed much.

I go into a little dream about being the man of the house, telling her the best window locks to buy and fitting them for her, then I remember the picture of Iris.

I switch on the news and it says an opinion poll has just made Tony Blair the most popular prime minister in peacetime.

After that there's a big works closing down in Wales. It just gets onto the sport when Cynthia calls me in.

As I get out of the chair I decide I won't talk to her about the Iris business until after we've had grub.

The kitchen gives straight on to a dining area that looks as if it used to be a separate room. Cynthia's still standing in the kitchen part doing something on the work surface.

As I sit down ready at the table, I give her a quick look while she's still busy and see her legs for the first time because I've never known her wear a skirt before. I don't keep my eyes there very long but I can't help thinking her legs look a bit tasty.

Cynthia sits down at the table and we have smoked salmon with little slices of toast to start. She says sorry about three times for it not being brown bread because according to her that's what it should be.

Her going on like that almost spoils it. I can't work it out. The woman's slid between me and two Bill who wanted to nick me but she's carrying on as if she's in pieces over putting the wrong kind of bread in the toaster.

I feel like telling her growing up in Poplar we had other things to worry about. I wonder what she'd say if I told her she's making me feel as if I'm back with the foster family.

Instead I play the good boy, tell her not to worry.

I help her clear the plates away and then we have a chicken casserole, which has to be one of the best things I've eaten, ever.

Even Cynthia can't find anything wrong with it and I'm on second helpings when suddenly she says, 'Oh Anthony,' giving me my proper name, which I always like from a woman, but sounding as if she's just heard about a baby dying. 'I've been sitting at the table all this time with my apron on.'

I haven't even noticed. When I was looking at her I was too busy glomming her legs. Anyway, who gives a monkey's?

I say, 'Didn't notice, Cynthia. Your cooking's too good to think about anything else.'

Only I look her in the eyes and I don't see any babies

dying, instead I half-wonder if this is a bit more than just a rescue job, but I think I keep that hidden and she just gives me another little look, not as strong as the first.

If she was an East End girl I'd think she was showing out to me, but with Cynthia I can't tell. One thing's definite, I'm not making a move unless I'm bang on certain.

I look round the room and say, 'Lovely colour scheme in here, Cynthia. Blinding.'

She says, 'Thank you, Bomber', back to her magistrate's voice, which lets me know I've said something wrong again.

Much later I think maybe she doesn't know what I mean by blinding.

'Why don't I put everything in the dishwasher and bring coffee through to you in the lounge.'

She's got the same worn-out tone my old woman used to get when I said I was going down the pub, but my old woman had good reason.

I reckon if this is what her moodiness is like I ain't surprised her and her old man were on the drink a lot.

I say, 'Yeah that would be lovely, thank you, Cynthia,' and get up from the table.

I ought to offer to help but I walk out of the room instead, because she's got me back to feeling I'm whacking myself over the head every time I open my mouth.

When she comes in with the coffee about five minutes later she's taken off her apron but the state she puts my nerves in I'm not in the mood to enjoy her legs.

'Would you move that small table over to in front of the sofa, Bomber. I'm afraid this tray's rather heavy for me to do it as well.'

I get busy being the butler on his final warning, before he gets the elbow for neglecting his duties. Cynthia stands there while I sort out the tray and the coffee table the way she wants, between the sofa and the armchair.

Then we move around each other for about a minute other working out where we're going to sit.

I feel like I'm up against a southpaw in round one.

I end up next to her on the sofa and looking at her I get the vibe that ordering me about with the coffee table has put her back on the sunny side of the street.

Cynthia clears her throat like a lady. 'Umm, I don't suppose, Bomber, it would be very wise for you to come to Fellowship tomorrow, not what with the law after you and all.'

The way she laughs you can tell she thinks she's Morecambe and Wise.

I try to give a little shrug and a smile as if she's been as funny as she thinks she has, because she's letting me know I'm off the hook, even if it slaughters me the way she talks to me.

I nearly go, 'I'm a name, not a number,' but that's only an old prison joke she isn't going to get.

'In a few days, Bomber, when you're really better, you make your mind up when, I can drive you somewhere.'

She laughs. 'I expect over the state line would be good.'

Then she says softly, 'We'll be like Bonnie and Clyde,' and pats my hand and leaves hers there, on top of mine. I don't bother saying Bonnie and Clyde both got shot, because she's got my head going round again.

I look down at our two hands and have a glance further down at her legs, which are definitely exciting, but I can feel her tensing up again and I can't see how I'm ever going to relax her enough for me to have half a chance.

I half-hold Cynthia's hand but she pulls away, says, 'No, I don't think so, Bomber,' which could be me blown out, but then again, with Cynthia, maybe it isn't.

'Do you watch Coronation Street too, Bomber?'

Like most of what she says I haven't got an answer to that, so I sit there like a double lemon.

Watching telly with Cynthia isn't like watching with a normal person. She just sits there looking straight ahead without saying anything, doesn't even ask me if I want a cup of tea during the adverts.

After Coronation Street I suffer The Bill, which has got to be rubbish, and then it's some fat bird who's supposed to be a comedian going on about how no one'll fuck her.

The state of it I'm not surprised.

Cynthia's sitting there watching it with her lips pursed and it must stir something up in her. When it gets to the first break she turns the sound down and says, 'That all seems very alien to me, I'm afraid. My husband Robert was a rather brutal man. He robbed me of my appetite.'

Then she looks round at me to see if I'm sorry for her.

'Must have been terrible for you, Cynthia.'

I remember now, her telling the group that Robert was 'rather too well provided for down there.'

I can't stand the suspense any longer and take a chance.

44

'It can be so lovely as well, Cynthia.'

'Can it Bomber, can it, really?' She pats my hand. 'What do you do about your needs, Bomber?'

I'm saying a little prayer but then she dashes it, looking away again.

'I mean when you're in prison.'

I lean back from her, afraid if this closeness gives me the horn she'll see it pushing out my tracksuit bottoms just as she's given me a knock back.

'Just have to get on with it, Cynthia, when you're in there.' I can't keep the zig out of my voice but after everything she's done for me, I think I'd better try to make it right. I give her the words those sort of people like. 'You break the law, Cynthia, you have to pay the price.'

'Very philosophical of you, Bomber.'

I think she's being sarky, but I've had enough anyway.

I put on a big yawn and stand up. 'I haven't done anything, but it feels like it's been a long day. Think I'll go to bed now. Thank you for that lovely meal, Cynthia.'

'Yes, of course, Bomber. Well, okay then. See you in the morning.'

I'm almost out of the room when she says, 'I did mean what I said. Convalesce here for a few more days, Bomber.'

I half-turn back.

'That's very kind of you Cynthia, but then you're a very kind woman.'

'Good night, now.'

I get into the hallway and have a big breathe out.

Chapter Five

The next morning's almost like waking up and remembering I've got to go to court. At first I'm still wrapped in the softness of sleep, then looking like a prat last night edges its way in. Even half asleep I know it's going to be a day when I'll want a drink to stop the world feeling hard and awkward.

The bedclothes are twisted so tightly around me they've made me feeble and I almost have a panic. I'm freeing myself when I realise it's Cynthia knocking on the door that's woken me.

'There's a cup of tea for you. Shall I leave it out here?'

'No it's fine, Cynthia. Please come in.'

Those blue eyes are on mine the moment she comes through the door, making sure I know she's back in charge.

I can't help seeing all the screws that ever came through my cell door.

Of course she's kind with it. 'Hope it's how you like it. So difficult to make tea for someone else.'

She smiles. 'There's a biscuit as well. Did you sleep well?'

No legs today. She's wearing sludge-coloured slacks with a baggy brown jumper.

I say what's polite. 'Slept like a top, Cynthia.'

'Glad to hear it. Sorry to wake you up but I have to go into town now on an errand or two, so I'm afraid you'll have to make your own breakfast. Hope you find

46

everything you need.'

She's out the door before I can even ask her when she'll be back. Two minutes later I hear the front door slam shut.

By the time I'm awake properly the tea's already half cold, and I can't seem to straighten out my bottom sheet where it's rucked up, but I stay in bed for a bit anyway, pondering last night and working out what to do about getting out of here.

Thinking about last night, I figure she must have decided she wanted a bit but then changed her mind.

Maybe she's one who gets the urge and then remembers later that she doesn't like it.

After an old man whose Hampton was so big she couldn't tolerate it, I'm surprised she ever thinks she's hungry.

Perhaps that's what started her drinking. She'd know he'd want it when he was pissed and she'd keep up with him hoping it would relax her so he could get in, then every time when it still hurt the drink became her painkiller.

That's the puzzle, why she came on strong, with all that in her past. Maybe she likes to know men still fancy her but she doesn't realise the way she dresses usually stops them asking.

I wonder if the looking you straight in the eyes started with the old man as well, Cynthia trying to see if he'd been on the drink when he got home and him looking back at her to see if she'd been on the sherry or the whisky she kept hidden in the garden shed.

I almost laugh to myself, her and the old man going eyeball to eyeball every night when he comes home for his tea.

But it ain't funny for long. Sitting there thinking, I get the hump this has happened. Twenty four hours ago she was my lady on a white horse and if I imagined fingering her cunt I kept it to myself, now I'm stuck under the same roof as a woman who's blown me out, without even a fiver to get on a bus.

As I get out of bed I decide I'll have to wait until she gets back, then try to touch her for a few quid when I tell her I think it's best if I leave today. With a bit of luck I'll still get a lift, but after us getting that near to riding and then nothing, I'm not counting.

In the bathroom there's a pair of tights and some knickers drying on the radiator but I ignore them even if they are a wind up, and have a long shower instead.

Once I've got dressed I try on the trainers she bought the day before. They don't look too bad, and spot on she's even managed to get the shoe size right. Outside it looks near to freezing, so I could do with a coat to keep out the cold as well as hiding the soppy-looking track suit, but if I cop for a handout I'll buy one once I'm well away. If not I'll find a Millets or something like it, wait for the next afternoon when the kids come flooding out of school into the shops, then nick something warm-looking.

Walking up and down the room listening to the trainers squeak as I try them out I half-kid myself that I feel better knowing what I'm going to do, even if it means I'll be back on the road again, potless.

A little bit more of that and I figure I'd better get a decent breakfast inside me.

When I get down to the kitchen I find she's taken the piss again. There's a place laid for me at the table and she's printed on a card so that it looks like a menu, Bomber's breakfast: grapefruit, sausages, eggs and bacon, toast and marmalade with coffee or tea.

I expect that's why she had to run out this morning, so she could have a good laugh. I feel like throwing something through the kitchen window and just pissing off but I swallow my anger and stick to the plan. At least this way I'm not going to go hungry, except because her doctor gave me a detox without me realising and because up until last night she's been looking after me I've forgotten this is only day three or four of being dry, so even little things are going to go umpty on me.

For a start I cut the grapefruit the wrong way with the bread knife, so it's double hard getting the fruit out with the spoon. In the finish I tear it into chunks and eat it as if it's an orange but I swallow as much skin as flesh and there's juice everywhere.

My fingers are still sticky as I try to remember how to cook a fry-up. The bacon comes out alright and I can stomach the eggs with the white still a bit runny but I give up on the bangers when I cut into the first one and see it's still pink, even though the outside's gone leathery.

It doesn't matter much because by then I'm too choked to be hungry anymore, but two cups of tea later and I'm wandering round the house, almost normal. As well as the front room and the kitchen there's a room that looks more like an office, with a large table covered in papers, a grey filing cabinet and piles of newspapers and magazines on the floor. I have a look through one of the piles and it's all old fishing magazines, except for a couple of nudie mags hidden away at the bottom, so I reckon either Cynthia's got some strange hobbies for a woman or they must have been left behind by Raymond with the huge chopper.

Another pile's golfing magazines and copies of The Spectator, except when I pick up one of The Spectators half a dozen prints of the same photo of this enormous prick and ball sack fall out, so maybe Cynthia's old man made a few quid out of his weapon on the side. I bet she thought that was a bastard, so big it nearly chewed up her difference and a load of geezers paid money to look at it when they were having a J Arthur.

The stuff on the table's mainly letters to Cynthia from two different lawyers and an accountant that let me know why she doesn't bother going out to work.

I soon get bored looking at figures that don't seem real. I have half a thought about whether she's got one of those little dolly wall safes somewhere in the house, but I know it wouldn't be right of me, and drift back into her living room because shooting upstairs to have a riff through her bras and stuff wouldn't be right either.

There's bookshelves the length of one of the walls, but most of her books are non-fiction, history, religion and psychology, even a couple about black magic.

I don't really fancy them or the few romances either, but next to a book about fishing there's two by Raymond

Chandler, and I remember a writing teacher in the nick talking about him, so I take them both down and settle in the armchair.

I take a look at both beginnings and I nearly start on Farewell My Lovely because I used to know a real-life version of Moose Molloy, called Arthur. He was just as ugly with about the same amount of brain, but if I saw him walk into a pub in the old days I'd do the sensible thing and walk out before he had time to start a fight, so I put that one down and start The Long Goodbye instead. I can see straight off that this bloke has spent a bit of time hanging around outside night clubs, because I've had some of that myself.

He's just put his new pal on a plane to Mexico when I hear a car, and looking up I see Cynthia give the gatepost a little clip with the wing as she comes in the drive. I make my mind up to stay in California for as long as I can.

Cynthia opens the front door as Marlowe gets home to find two detectives waiting for him.

'Don't bother saying hello – it's only the hotel keeper come back.'

It looks like Marlowe's having an easier time with the Old Bill than the one I've got coming.

I start feeling a little sick at the thought of what I'll have to swallow to get out of here, without losing control.

I put the book down and stand up to go into the kitchen where I've heard her go.

As I come into the dining part of the room she's still in her hat and coat bunging a white plastic carrier, that doesn't want to go, into a cupboard underneath the work surface.

I figure I'll try friendliness first.

'Hi Cynthia. Anything I can do?'

She shuts the cupboard door and straightens up, a bit red in the face. It's the nearest I've seen her to looking flustered.

'No, no thank you, Bomber, just a few,' Cynthia pauses, 'purchases to put away. I'll tell you what – why don't you go back into the lounge, and I'll make us both a cup of coffee.'

'You want me to make it, Cynthia?'

'No, no, very sweet of you. I'll do it, thank you.'

She's back to talking with that kind of politeness that's halfway to threatening. I figure I'd better do what the hotel keeper tells me, and coffee could be a good time to tell her I'm off.

'Go on, Bomber, won't be a tick, just need to go upstairs.'

She picks up two bulging Marks and Sparks carriers from the dining room chair and I step aside to stop her whacking me round the leg with them as she brushes past.

Cynthia charges up the stairs and I take her word for it that I haven't got to do anything, and so I go back to the living room, although I'm wondering what's up with her.

I get back into The Long Goodbye as I hear doors slam a couple of times upstairs, followed by silence.

She still hasn't come down again by the time Marlowe gets out of jail, but he's just getting a ride home from a reporter when I hear her moving around, so at least she hasn't guessed what I've decided and tried to work a flanker by going to kip.

Five minutes later I hear her come down the stairs and go into the kitchen.

When she comes in with a cup of coffee there's spilt coffee mulching up the shortbread finger in the saucer, which isn't like her at all.

'Sorry, Bomber, left yours in the kitchen.' She gives me half a smile that says she's got a lot else on her mind.

I almost get the idea, the way she sits down on the sofa, spilling more coffee. If it was anyone else I'd know before I go into the kitchen and see she hasn't made me a cup.

I open the cupboard under the work surface, and inside the white carrier there's three bottles of Finnish vodka, which explains why I haven't smelled anything.

I leave the vodka where it is and straighten up.

Half of me feels as if I might black out and the other half wants to, so I could wake up and find out this hasn't happened.

Even after last night I can't believe she's let me down like this.

I've sat down at the kitchen table when she comes in.

'Not made yershelf a cuppa yet, then?'

Now I know, I can hear the slur in her voice.

'There's three bottles of fucking vodka in the cupboard.'

'So wha', Bomber, who cares? Anyway, what's it to you what I do in my house?

She must have been trying hard before because now it's out in the open that she's pissed her voice is slipping and sliding around like a drunken old tom.

'I can't believe you've done this, Cynthia. You're my sponsor.'

'Oh, can't believe it, can't he? Lishen to him then. Well wha' do you think it's been like for me, having you here? You're hardly couth, are you?'

I don't know what that means, but I stand up, I've got to get out of there before I go into one.

She's still in the doorway, trying to fix me with those blue eyes, but she can't do it, keeps looking away.

I feel like going raving mad at her, scream at her that this is like the children's home, getting punished for things I haven't done all over again, but I know enough about myself to know there's no point arguing with a drunk. I put everything I know into keeping hold.

'I'm sorry I shouted just now, Cynthia, but I think I'd better go now.'

'Oh, up to you, is it? Don't lie to me. You'd be going anyway, after you didn't get what you wanted last night. Oh I know, alright, I could see the way you were looking at me. We women do notice, you know.'

Most of me wants to shout so loud she'll blow away like a puff of smoke and not exist anymore, but I hold back, step towards the door instead.

She moves out of the way.

'Go on then, run away.'

The state I'm in I hardly hear her. I go into the front room to pick up The Long Goodbye because that's coming with me. After that I hesitate, telling myself I'm trying to remember if I've got anything upstairs.

The truth is I'm having bottle trouble, suddenly afraid of the cold outside, afraid of it swooping down on me like it would onto a motherless child.

Panic's flapping its wings in my chest. Cynthia's standing in the doorway.

'You don't want to go, do you?' For a moment she sounds like the old wise Cynthia, my sponsor Cynthia, the one whose job it is to keep me off the booze, but the next moment she smiles. 'Have a little drink, Bomber, just a little one, keep me company. I'm lonely too, Bomber.'

This has got to be out of some movie she's seen.

She leans back against the doorframe. 'Okay, have it your way, but if you go up to the bedroom, you'll see I've bought you some underwear. You shouldn't leave without it.'

I half-believe the kindness in her voice and half-think it's a trap, but really I've caught myself by not running straight out, so I do what she says and go upstairs.

Because she's drunk she's overdone it. There's about twenty pairs of boxers and vests wrapped in cellophane, lying on the bed.

I scramble them back into the couple of carriers she's left lying on the carpet and head back downstairs.

Cynthia nips out from the front room doorway just as I'm drawing level. I have to stop and lean back not to myself crash into her.

She turns round and then stands there with her back to the front door, putting both hands behind her to press against the door, bracing herself, barricading me in.

I step forward until I'm right in front of her looking

down. I say quietly, 'Don't be silly, Cynthia.'

She doesn't say anything, just glares back up at me. She's taking deep breaths more like sighs, and I don't know if it's that or she's sweating, but I can smell the stink of her boozing.

I want to finish this, so I shout, 'Get out the fucking way.'

Cynthia just about flinches, looks down at her feet and then up again, staring me in the eyes.

She says, 'At the risk of stating the obvious, I've let you down, haven't I.'

I say, 'You aren't anything special. You sound the same as any other drunk with its mouth open. I don't listen to 'em.'

I figure if I can keep my contempt going I might get out of there before my willpower dies.

She does the deep breathing again then she says, 'Let me give you some money. I know you don't have any. You won't be able to get anywhere without some.'

I reckon she's weakening, faster than me.

I nod. 'Sure.'

'My purse is in the living room.' I stand aside to let her past.

As I wait for her I half-expect she'll work one on me, but she's back in no time.

'Here, take it.' Cynthia holds out some banknotes.

I put my hand out for the money, but I don't look at it, too embarrassed to see how much it is. I take hold of it and then look her in the face.

Cynthia smiles weakly. 'Make up for last night, eh.'

I say, 'Yeah,' gripping onto the money, still not sure

this is it, that she's letting me go.

I turn round and open the front door with my hand that's holding the money because all through this, almost without realising, my other hand's been keeping a grip on the two bags full of underwear.

As I open the door I hear what must be Cynthia going into her front room and then an 'ouf' which I reckon is the breath going out of her as she throws herself on the sofa. Then because I don't bother closing the door I hear the sobbing start but I keep going down her garden path and through the gate, not sure if I'm shivering from the raw gusts of wind or the cold and shock inside me.

I look up at the grey sky all the same, like an ex-con in his first minute outside, but then as I walk down her road taking in the tidy front gardens and run-ins, holding the sixty quid she's given me, I don't know whether I feel full of freedom or misery.

Coda

Wandering lost around the avenues and crescents, I must look bad and out of place, a cut eye on the face of suburbia, maybe somebody's picture of a nonce, because the second time I come to the school playground I've got a patrol car taking interest. Soon after that I might as well put on the handcuffs myself.

When it gets to court Cynthia does her best with a letter, and my brief ain't the worst I've had, but the judge says he's had enough of this kind of thing and I can smell it in the air he has, even before Iris has her big moment in the witness box. So I'm not surprised by another six months to do on top of the six I've already had on remand.

Chapter Six

Almost the first paper I see after I get nicked says there a crisis in the prison population, which explains my double-claustrophobia feeling.

In prison I'm like the seaman who always spews his ring the first day out. For the first three weeks I feel as if I've got asthma. After that I'm keeping my head down so hard I don't even notice I'm breathing stale air.

I stop trying to keep up with papers not long after I get my sentence. I lose the point of it. The news all happens out there, and I'm stuck where I'm stuck.

Instead I hold onto a Bible I'm given and that helps keeps me going through the darkness. The old-fashioned writing takes quite a lot of getting used to but I force myself, and after that I know I'll never run out of words to feed on. Sometimes when I let the phrases cascade through my head I feel as if I'm looking at diamonds, almost forget where I am.

Reading the Bible doesn't mean I believe in anything, but I'm an old fighter the system's got backed up against the ropes and it's my way of slipping and ducking to keep out of trouble.

Cynthia writes to me while I'm in there. Her letters are all chatter, stuff that won't hurt anybody, but I can tell she only means kindness and perhaps she knows feelings in here are bad news, so I hear all about her garden instead, and what she said to her neighbour.

59

Twice I start to tell her how I feel about what happened between us, but it just comes out rubbish, so whenever she writes I send her a description of a couple of the other cons and maybe even a disguised version of one of the screws as a reply. Cynthia always writes back how funny I am and once she says haven't I thought about writing a comedy, something like a true version of Porridge, but all I've done is try to give her a description of what it's like without swearing.

The nearest we get to saying something is when I ask her if she wants a VO and she says she can't bear it, the thought of seeing me confined.

But I wonder if she's written to prison before, because even though her life's about a million miles away her letters always come with the whiff of perfume. Sometimes the yearning that sets off is too much, and I think she's torturing me again but I write in my notebook that mostly it's like buying a ticket for a magic carpet and I feel enveloped by the smell of a woman, sometimes even imagine I'm kneeling in front of her, her hands pressing my face into her wetness. But it's a woman I don't know, because I don't remember Cynthia with perfume on her at Fellowship, and I can't imagine it on her either.

Writing to her gets me known as a letter writer and I earn a bit of blow writing for blokes who can't. Sometimes I earn a bit more letting a few smell the letters, but not until after the perfume's worn off a bit, although I don't earn as much as I could because invisible is safest.

About a year in, her handwriting starts looking

weird and then I get one that isn't anything but a scrawl without any proper words, so I figure she's got troubles of her own.

I reckon that's probably the last I'll hear of her and for the next bit it looks as if I'm right, but about a month before I get out she writes to me from her new home in Dorset, near where she grew up. She says childhood memories and the sea are helping her start again.

She also reckons she's sorting out a bit of cash for after they release me.

I've painted too many cell walls with broken dreams to let myself really believe her, but it happens all the same.

Somehow she keeps track of what nick I'm in and which one I'm going to be released from. Somehow probation doesn't fuck up. Somehow no one has a bit of the money. On the third of May I walk out of Pentonville, cross the Caledonian Road and just up a little side street to Prisoners' Welfare and collect two hundreds pounds cash from a northern bird with long dark hair and a tight lime-green jumper that I can see makes her tits look even bigger than they are, although they don't look as if they need the help. Above her left breast she's pinned a badge that says Condoms Now and considering all the junkies I've seen letting themselves get charvered for a bit of brown I make it right. Below her jumper she's wearing grey leggings which almost show her split. As she bends down to get my envelope out of the safe she explains she's a volunteer, and the sight of her arse almost makes me ask her if she fancies a steak dinner later on, but I make do taking the money and hope I still remember what she looks like for when I'm in bed tonight.

Cynthia's note says Hope this helps you make a start and Keep in touch but she doesn't invite me down to Dorset and I'm glad she doesn't.

I say thanks to the bird and go out of the door down the two steps to the street. When I walked out of the gate twenty minutes earlier I was too busy concentrating on collecting to think about anything else. But now I stand where I am and take in the weather of freedom.

This time I've bothered bringing my notebook out with me and as I look up I try to remember it in words as well as pictures so I'll have them for when I get round to writing about it. The sky's blue enough to be summer, and even if the wind's got teeth for the beginning of May the hidden sun's left promises on a ragged cloud.

The wind round the collar of my jean jacket gets enough for me to make a move and I realise since I came out of the welfare office I've been stood outside a boozer without even clocking it.

I half-want to think that's a sign. More likely it's a reminder of why I'm standing outside an overcrowded prison, holding a carrier bag with everything I own inside it. All the same I put my hands on the windowsill and stretch up to have a look over the top of the engraved half of the window. There's two pool tables, one eight foot and one standard, sitting on a polished wooden floor that's got enough of a shine on it to let you know someone still cares. Behind the bar a couple of hand pumps outshine the floor and above that there's the shorts bottles in their optics looking like Cinderella's coach before midnight.

I don't know if he's a barman or a cleaner sitting on a stool at the bar drinking a mug of tea but I must have caught his eye because he makes a sign do I want to come in. I go no with my head and turn away.

Then I shake my head again, mentally, at the top shelf looking so good after all this time.

I start off down Cally Road, having a little laugh to myself at managing Get thee behind me Satan for about the first time ever, although right then I can't tell you if I'm ever going to have a drink again and I can't tell you either how I'm feeling. I've got that high but empty sensation I get when I know I'm feeling something but I don't know what. Usually before now when I've been like that I've had a few drinks and the beer's decided for me how I feel, but today at least, I ain't doing that.

Instead I'm keeping my mind on finding a good caff, and as I chase along I make sure I don't look across the road at the shithole, because I know if I see the wing sticking up above the sprawl of the rest of it, I'll think I can smell the stink of prison coming through the brick.

Then I'm in the shade of a railway bridge that crosses the road just after the nick finishes, and I've left it behind.

Once I'm out the other end of the bridge I start looking around with my head up but liberty hasn't put on her prettiest dress and high heels for me. I'm walking past shops that look as if they're waiting to be pulled down, and on the other side I see a pub I went in once, boarded up, like the public khazi on the island in the middle of the road opposite.

There is one gaff that reckons it sells Italian coffee and I fancy it a bit, but even though everywhere around it's a dump, including the kebab house next door, I can see it thinks it's posh.

That yuppie place is about the only surprise around here except for the fact that everyone knows this used to be a place where you had to be a long way tough for people to think you were proper. Now I can't see anything worth fighting over, unless you count all the shops that wouldn't make any money if it wasn't for selling Tennent's.

I'm just shy of the canal when I see the first place that seems alright. Trouble is it's half ten, and about half the building trade workers in London must have been looking as well.

I join the end of the queue behind the second bloke standing outside the door on the pavement. Once I'm inside I can tell it's alright – you can smell today's breakfasts but you can't smell yesterday's.

At first I hardly notice the heat because I'm standing there in a bit of a dream smiling to myself. I reckon I must be the only bloke in the place who knows what it's worth. I can tell just by looking the rest of them think going for a breakfast is about the most natural thing in the world.

But after about the third geezer bumps into me and thinks I've spilled his tea, the crowd and the no ventilation begin to get to me, plus there's a Scotswoman bringing round the plates of grub who's got a voice you could use to cut open a safe.

I'm still four blokes from the counter when I decide this isn't a good idea, but by now I've got to have a cup of tea at least and I'll be climbing over people trying not to knock against them with my bag if I try to squeeze past to get out.

I don't know if there's someone ignorant at the back doing a bit of shoving, but every time the bloke behind bumps into me I have to remind myself where I am, that he's not giving me ag on purpose.

By now there's only one in front of me and I can see the man behind the counter.

He's a big fat bloke, dark-skinned with almost-black hair that points down over his forehead like a tongue. He ought to be Greek, but somehow he's not.

'Alright, Davey,' he says to the customer in front of me. He's got a foreign accent I can't place.

'You look fed up, Davey. Where you been? They keep you in the prison house up the road all night? Alright, so what you want?'

Davey gives his order and nearly spills his tea as he goes past me.

'Good morning, my friend.'

The way the heat and the crowd are bearing down on me I'm going to tell him why his joke isn't funny if he says it to me, but he must keep that for the regulars.

'What you want, my friend?'

I breathe out.

'You got any liver?'

'I've got liver. I've got kidneys as well.'

'Kidneys, egg and chips – forget the liver – cup of tea.'

I must have a big beam on my face, because he gives me a smile that's as warm as a mum cuddling her kid.

After that all I have to do is pay him, then fight me way through the North Bank when they're playing Spurs to find a seat, holding onto a mug of tea.

I find a seat halfway to the door and realise I should have asked him if he'd got a paper, but I'm kushti enough just sitting there drinking the best cuppa since Cynthia's a year previous. As it goes down my throat like a poem I realise I've forgotten one of the differences: out here a bit of tension can go away. You don't have to carry it around with all the other little bits of aggravation until there's an explosion.

Five minutes later Mary Queen of Scots brings me my food, and she's even got mustard and Worcester sauce just in case, so I forgive her for shouting.

This has to be one of my best meals ever, even tastes better than when I imagined it my cell.

I've finished it and I'm thinking about another tea but there's a voice behind me that's beginning to shatter the bliss, giving out about some bags of plaster that have gone missing.

You can hear it in the way he sounds, he's used to shouting at men who aren't going to come back at him because they need the poxy job. He's got away with it for so long he's forgotten there's another way to talk.

Listening to him reminds me how hot the café is, like he's sucking all the air out of the place.

'No more than another five minutes or I'll sack the lot of you for blackguarding.'

I sense some of the mugs behind me stir. I don't blame them – he's driving me out as well.

I don't want to look at him as I get up to leave but I have to. Underneath the sticking-up grey hair there's a fat red face full of anger and boozing, then round the eyes I can see the fear that he isn't the strong man anymore.

As I'm turning he starts up again. 'Now don't fuck about. I'm in the mood to get rid of surplus, especially you, Mulligan.'

Voice like that he should have been a screw.

I step out of the door and the sun's come out. 'Welcome to freedom,' I say to myself.

Chapter Seven

Three quarters of an hour later I've had an amble through the side streets and I'm at the bottom of Camden High Street near Mornington Crescent. I'm trying to make my mind up, use Cynthia's money for a few days bed and breakfast or save her dough and book into Barrington House down the other end of Camden Town, near the market, let the council pay the rent until I sort out what I'm doing.

I stand there for a bit, half-thinking about it and half-watching the traffic taking chances with the lights.

I still can't decide, but I move off towards Barrington anyway and five minutes later I feel like I'm properly back on the out, in amongst the throng of shoppers who walk into you every time you stop moving and don't look as if they've noticed they're on the same pavement as Down-and-Out City.

Maybe they're cold like that because put the street, the people and the traffic together, and the whole deal feels like a bad rush of paranoia off a line of coke.

I'm coming up to two phone boxes back to back on the pavement. A junkie dives into the first one while the girl who's got to be with him, stands outside the other, clutching the sleeves of her blue hood to keep out the shivers, like someone ought to tell her it's almost summer.

As I draw level with her I glance at thin hair and a white face with plenty of angry red spots and see she's bitten her bottom lip until it bleeds. Ten yards on I look back, they're half running down the High Street, in the other direction.

Just then an old girl bumps into me with her shopping, but before I take her in I think I'm being dipped and reach for my money.

'What you got in that pocket, a gun?' She's stopped alongside me to have a go. 'You ought to look where you're walking. Typical man.' Then she's away before I have time to tell her to fuck off.

I'm not in the hurry she is, so I stop outside a fruit machine arcade, leaning against the window, reminding myself I'm on my time, not anybody else's, and thinking she's probably only like that because she had an old man who turned out to be a deadbeat.

I still haven't decided what to do. Camden Town could turn out poison, especially now I'm on the dry, but it's the kind of place you can meet a friendly face, and right now I could do with one of them, as long as I stay kushti about Cynthia's money. I've even met a couple of fighters over this way before, blokes I didn't even know were down on their luck until I've run into them.

There's something else about hanging around as well. Looking at how undressed some of the women are is giving me the need. It's not just the young ones either, so maybe around here, I could get lucky.

Just then this dark-haired woman comes along and the way her breasts push past me I'm half afraid I'll really touched her arse instead of just wanting to which makes it time to start moving again.

I come up to McDonald's and nearly go in for a coffee because no one's anyone in McDonald's and if I can sit there feeling like one of the crowd maybe my brain won't blow up with trying to remember how you make decisions, but I carry on towards the Camden Town crossroads, because where I've come from I've been as short on walks as I have on coffee.

I take a left at the big traffic lights thinking the peace of Regent's Park might sort out this mood I'm in, but there's a bit more Camden Town to get through first.

A few yards up there's the centre where they do a handout. As I go past there's four or five Scotsmen outside drinking Tennent's, shouting conversation to each other in a language that almost needs translating. They look like they think they're the A-Team – maybe they are, big enough and young enough to rob off the others when they can't find the money for a drink anywhere else. I think I've seen one of them before, maybe in nick, but that doesn't seem like good enough reason on its own to go over and give him a dig, so I carry on up the road.

Twenty yards on I have to wait to cross a side road and the smell of drink coming out of the pub on the corner is stronger than you'd ever notice, unless it was a year since you'd had a drink.

Mainly I think it's the sweet smell of death, but underneath that I can feel the comfort of climbing out of the sea onto dry land.

I stand where I am, thinking any moment I'm going to turn around and walk through that pub door that someone's tied open. I almost do, but just then I see a crowd of Japanese tourists on the opposite corner, all with their cameras out, looking as if they're pointing them at me. They don't know it but they save me, because suddenly I have a science fiction experience. I travel forward in time and hear myself half-pissed at some Alcoholics Anonymous meeting, moaning the Japanese never knew what a tragedy they'd snapped as they got me walking into the boozer, getting the story mixed up on purpose so I can blame them for me having a drink.

Then I do something I've learned from AA. I decide to postpone the park and reward myself instead for making a good decision and not starting to drink.

I'm going to go back to the High Street to have a cup of Italian coffee in a place I noticed by the traffic lights, ask the guy for the strongest one they've got then follow that with a sweet shop and half a pound of Mint Creams. My mouth'll be so full of flavour my tongue won't have space to imagine the taste of a beer.

That's the plan, but as it tops up I don't get round to the mint creams, at least not then.

I'm sitting in the coffee place looking through the big open window, enjoying the sun bouncing off the cars and making up little stories about the ordinary people going by with their shopping and trying to guess which country the tourists come from. I'm managing to ignore the lowlifes, although I can't help noticing this tall skinny one with a bald dome, except for a couple of patches of fluffy blonde hair like he's got alopecia, and a sticking plaster on the back of his neck, who buzzes past twice.

Then a car edges into a parking space just the other

side of the pavement from my window.

The African driver leans out of his window looking for someone or to ask directions, just as Alopecia comes into view again.

The African looks at him about three seconds too long and the smackhead's on him as a mark. He pulls off his plaster and bends forward to show the guy the horrible yellow and black hole full of puss on the back of his neck, which looks as if he should have gone to hospital weeks ago.

The African waves him off, but as Alopecia stands up again I get another good look at his wound. The state he's let it get into finally decides me: I've got to go somewhere away from the ugliness, somewhere the people look after themselves better.

I'm out of the coffee bar and heading up Camden Road for the railway without even thinking about where, but when I get there I look at the list of the stations and reckon I can afford B and B at Acton Central better than Hampstead or Richmond, and I remember a park in Acton, as well as streets with trees in them, from being on a roofing job up there once.

Sitting on the platform holding my carrier I get another slice of loneliness, but the train turns up almost when it's supposed to and once I'm on it I'm rolling.

I'm worrying at the back of my head whether I'll find a kip, but the train doesn't take more than twenty minutes getting there, so I don't have time to really get into one. I find a place above a café less than half an hour after I get off.

The room smells a bit of the café, and the walls are all woodchip painted different colours, white, orange and purple, but the Kosovan guy who runs it, called Jo-rab, doesn't have a uniform or a big bunch of keys, and doesn't want to know anything else once he's seen my money's good. I celebrate being exhausted by freedom and get my head down for an hour.

PART TWO

Chapter Eight

My first idea is get a job on the building somewhere, keep at it all summer and see if I can still do it when the cold's freezing my nuts as I go up the ladder in the morning.

But after three days mooching around I've found out the days when you could walk onto a building site and get a start are all over, unless you want to get in the back of a van full of illegals, for a geezer who thinks eighteen quid a day is proper wages.

By now most of Cynthia's money's gone on the B and B in Acton, and the notice in the window that says no DSS is getting bigger every time I pass it, so I lower my ambitions to pearl diving.

Even that ain't a stroll down easy street, and I get five or six knock backs before I'm offered a shift at Tony's Bar and Grill, Ealing.

At the end of the first shift Yianni, the manager, says to come back the next day, and at the end of that he says, 'Hey, fuggit, Englishman, you coming back? See you tomorrow. Doan be fuggin' late.' At the end of that shift he weighs me out minus the sub I've had to pay the B and B, and says, 'Englishman, fuggit, you doan work like an Englishman. You work like a Greek, but a Greek in ancient times, one of the fuggin' slaves – ha ha. So now I'm takin' you on, but now you got to give me a name, fuggin' Jimmy or somefing and the fuggin' 'surance number.'

I tell him Jimmy Bacon, because the real Jimmy gave me his National Insurance number when I met him in Wandsworth, almost the first time I'd seen him since we were in the amateurs together. The smack they found in Jimmy's lock up, he hasn't got to worry about signing on for a long time.

I give Ealing Council my right name and the government my autograph, which sorts out the rent for Yianni's cousin's flat, over a café near the station.

So I don't exactly end up Honest John, but at five quid an hour who's got the choice?

I'm glad I'm settled, because for the first three weeks I can't believe the tiredness from scrubbing and carrying those steels. I'm amazed as well the way I keep away from the wine and the scotch that's always open in the kitchen, so sometimes the exhaustion almost feels like the holy tiredness I'd have when I was training hardest and nothing mattered but my strength.

Then I have a shift when I'm bending over with wanting a drink, maybe because Yianni screams at me once too often, 'English, lazee, gonna sack you, you take the piss, eh,' or I've had enough of the manky chicken and rice we always seem to get for the staff meal. I pass an afters place on the way home, and it feels as if there's a magnet in the window aimed especially at me. I only just stop myself going in. When I get indoors I've got a tremor.

After that I get a bit more real and slow down, make sure I have plenty of breaks, because one of the things Fellowship teaches is that tiredness and excitement are a recipe for drink.

Every time Dooley the little Scots sous chef goes out for a fag by the dustbins, I follow him. He stands there smoking and holding his fag. I'm holding a lump of wood – he doesn't seem to mind the rats, but I hate 'em. I've got the timber in case they try to run over my boots. I'm terrified they'll run up to the top of my Wellingtons, then drop down inside onto my feet.

The first time I go out there he just looks at me as if he wants to take the piss but hasn't got the bottle, then the second time he says, 'You lookin' long before yous got this start, big man?'

'About six kitchens before this one.'

He says, 'That could ha bin sixty six kitchens. You have the authorities to thank it was nae that many. You're the last white kitchen porter in captivity. Immigration came round the day before you did. That cunt Yianni lost half his staff. A KP and four waiters, Brazilians, nae papers at all. Yianni was covered in shite, case they'd find out he's Egyptian, not really Greek at all. That was your lucky day, my son. You were the answer to an Egyptian's prayers to Allah.'

That's about the only interesting thing Dooley ever says to me. Usually it's 'everyone's a cunt.' Except him.

Once he sees me with a Raymond Chandler sticking out of my pocket. 'There'll be no Farewell My Lovelies from me, big man, my ship comes in. It'll be offski for Dooley, straight up the road and fuck the lot of yous.'

I don't usually bother replying to anything he says, just make out I agree. I've been banged up with a thousand like him. No one's allowed a dream except them.

But he gives me an idea for when I have my bit of luck.

I've been there about six weeks. I've finished at five after an early, and I'm having a sit in the park with Phillip Marlowe.

When I've had enough of kissing all those Californian blondes who can't stop falling for me I decide to take the shortcut around the tennis courts, go through the hole in the fence that the kids have made.

There's one place where I have to step off the grass into the bushes, and that's when I look down because it doesn't feel like soil underfoot. I see I'm standing on one of the old-fashioned green driving licences, no photo.

There's been a dipping or a mugging by someone desperate for readies, because a foot away there's a new-looking brown leather wallet with three credit cards lying next to it.

I fancy the wallet but it's going to look too flash, and I don't want the aggravation that might go with the cards.

I bend down, bung the licence in my back pocket and stand up trying to cop anyone who might have seen me, but there's no players on the court nearest, and next to that there's a game of doubles where they're too busy having a swear-up at each other to notice, and everyone else in the park is miles off.

I carry on round the courts the way I was going and ten minutes later I'm back at the room where I can have a good look at the licence.

It belongs to James Tate, 57 Chetwynd Rd, London

NW5, doesn't expire until 2020. Turning it over I work out he was born May the fifth nineteen fifty, but the figure that interests me is how much I can get for it, because on the way back I've decided I'm taking less risk knocking it out than hanging onto it trying for a job as a driver called Jimmy Tate.

As I make a cup of tea I know holding onto it's got to be one Jimmy too many – I'm Jimmy Bacon already – and Dooley telling me about the immigration raid solves the problem of finding a customer. Yianni the Greek Egyptian's got to want to be a buyer. The only problem is how much.

I let thinking about that give me butterflies for half an hour, then I get out my directory of meetings and get ready to go out to the nearest one, in case my nerves start making me thirsty.

The next morning I do the deal. All it takes is five minutes in the store cupboard Yianni calls his office. He says four hundred, and I figure that's kushti enough. He gives it to me there and then, which tells me I've gone cheap, but it's a long time since I held four hundred quid.

I'm thinking about an advert in the travel agents I pass on the way to the restaurant: five hundred quid for a fortnight in Barbados. All I've got to do is stay off the rum and look at half-naked women on the beach.

I go back to washing up to stop myself getting the horn thinking about them. I can ask him about the time off later.

After my little bit of work with Yianni I'm keeping a closer watch on him in case I spot an opening to make a bit more to add to what I've put in the Abbey, because now instead of Barbados I'm thinking about a one-way ticket to Spain, taking my savings with me and seeing if I can find something when I'm out there.

But all I see is Yianni has plenty of visitors who go into the 'office.' There's nothing about them I latch onto, and I don't even know for certain there's anything hooky going on.

Then about ten days after I've sold him the brief I see two blokes, both flaming redheads, go into the store room with him, one morning just after twelve.

I don't take a lot of notice because it's Friday, so by then things are really beginning to buzz, coming up to lunchtime, except I've filed away the thought that if the two guys are a little team they ought to do something about their hair before they get caught.

I've just picked up a big plastic swill bin to take out to the dustbins when Yianni comes out of the office, the redhead in a blue suit beside him, the one in the casual clothes behind. The swill bin's heavy enough, so I probably only notice them because Yianni's got a confused look on his face and he's a man who usually makes out nothing surprises him. I've turned the corner of the range heading for the yard when he shouts out behind me, 'Anyone know a cogsucker, call himself An-toe-nee Jagson,' drawing out the first name, so it'll sink in.

I don't slow down and I don't hurry up. I'm telling myself get to the doorway at least. Yianni's letting me know it's on top. I've been Jimmy since I got the start, he's the only one knows my real name.

The whole world feels as if it's stopped as I try to remember how not to get caught, then I'm there, dumping the bin in the middle of the doorway, blocking the way out, going round it, up on toes.

I hear 'Oi,' behind me, wake properly up as I feel a grip on my upper arm.

I turn and pull one of the redheads with me, he almost falls onto a right hook, that sends him arse backwards into the swill bin, which blocks his mate as I turn and go up onto a dustbin and over the wall. There's shouting from the kitchen but I don't have time to work out whose side the crowd's on before I drop six foot and run down the alleyway for fifty yards, heading for a street full of shops. As I get to the end I look back and I've got thirty yards on the other redhead, who's coming after me with a club hammer in one hand – which makes it official: they're not from Housing Benefit.

I've got to choose, try to outrun him or risk there's more on the way to the alley, but I'm out of practice. He gets close enough to aim the hammer at my head, I block his hammer arm with a forearm and hit him so the back of his head bangs against the wall. He's knocked out, slipping down against the wall, as I'm tearing off the kitchen coat and hat.

I leave 'em in the alley, bit of luck this morning I couldn't find the elasticated trousers – they'd hold me up now – I just remember my black beanie hat in the coat pocket in time, reach down to get it, straighten up, turn and move.

I'm striding now but not running, passing shoppers

who haven't seen anything happen. I strain to hear if I'm being chased, only half-knowing where I'm going, feeling as if the adrenaline's going to turn to fear any moment. A patrol car goes past me, dee-dah at full volume, followed by another, too busy with themselves to notice anyone, especially now he's wearing a hat. Then another comes shooting back in my direction, and I think I'm nicked but it keeps going like a blind vulture that can't see the dead meat in front of it.

I take a look over my shoulder: nothing.

Then I come to a vacant shop. Step into the doorway and look again, still nothing that looks like a chase. I move off again. Now the shops and the people are beginning to run out, I'm an out-of-breath big lump, walking down a polite street of big quiet houses, without any cover. I feel that chill you get when you've still got to make decisions but having to choose can drown you in panic, like when you're seventeen and you half-want them to catch you so it'll be over, but I turn and cross the road back to find some more people to hide me.

Looking back at where I've come from I see white shirts and blue uniforms multiplying at the entrance to the alley, must be how they got the name bluebottle, swarming like flies round shit.

I cross the road and take a right by a pub, about fifty yards before I'd draw level with Old Bill.

I'm in a cul-de-sac, terraces both sides, no paths down the side of the houses.

I can feel my back sweating as I turn round, but no one's there, walk back to the corner, turn right, brazen it out as I pass them at the end of the alley. I'm on the other side of the road but close enough to notice one of the policewomen's a slim blonde, looks nice even in the uniform.

There's an entrance to the shopping centre, now I've got to decide: stay out on the road, risk getting spotted or risk they'll make a drag through the arcades. I can't walk properly in these Wellingtons. Someone's got to notice them, and they're uncomfortable. Every time I put them on I cunted Yianni off for being too tight to buy us proper kitchen safety shoes.

I've got about eighty notes on me. I'll take a chance on the shopping centre, buy some trainers.

Between two shops there's an Indian fellow with a stall. He clocks my hand's shaking as I give him the money for a pair of shades, and he looks me up and down before he gives me my change.

He's as blank as a good card player. I can't see anything he's thinking.

He says, 'Thanks, Boss. Be good to yourself.'

I nod and walk towards JD Sports thirty yards away.

Then a walkie-talkie crackles behind my right shoulder and another slice of cold goes through me as I think that's it, but a security guard goes past, half-walking half-running, but not as if he wants to get there first.

Two other guards come out of an arcade at right angles to where the trainer shop is and as I draw level with JD's all three are inside the doorway, standing tall over a half-grown black kid. Going by his face he can't make his mind up, play innocent or cuss 'em out.

I wish I could stay and watch, pretend I'm a real writer, taking it in, for my notebook later, but the hassle he's caused I can't chance the shop. I've got to keep going, take the risk someone notices the Wellingtons.

I head right to some fire doors I come through in the other direction sometimes, on the way to work, push the crash bar and I'm in an open-air pedestrian way. There's a high pebble-dashed wall one side, and on the other there's a shop sells Belgian chocolates, a café next to it with tables outside I've sat at for an espresso, and then just before the main road there's Belle Epoque, fancy underwear for women, where I usually have a gander through the window, but this time I say au revoir, and poke my head out round the corner onto the main road. It only takes a glance: a hundred yards down in the London direction, there's a police car and a van outside the café where my room is, so it's goodbye to the bank book as well.

I look the other way and there's a number 207 coming. I leg it across the zebra and then I'm getting one of the best getaway vehicles there is, so slow you shit yourself you're going to be seen, but all the cover in the world.

I sit downstairs by the door where you get off, and look the other way as we pass the café, still half-expecting to be noticed, but then we're crossing Ealing Common and I've got to be unlucky if I haven't left it all behind.

I have a look at everyone who gets on in case one of them looks like Old Bill, but you've got to be important for them to chase you off the manor. They always reckon you'll turn up somewhere later – even a couple of their own getting a clump doesn't make 'em want to travel, probably means too much paperwork.

I jump off the bus at Marble Arch and head down Oxford Street towards the cheap end, thinking I'll sort out a pair of trainers and hoping I can come up with a plan for what to do next. But I've hardly got past Selfridges before I've had enough, the way the crowd jostles against me I can't think, and every little collision feels as if it could have handcuffs attached.

I cut down a side street going north. Now I'm away and free, my nerves are coming out. I know I can't do this any more but I can't see a way through the grief yet.

Then I come to a little square with gardens in the middle. I cross over, walk through the gate into the quiet of the green and slump onto a bench.

It must have been raining here because the seat's still a bit wet and I perch on the edge, trying not to let too much of the damp come through my jeans.

I look down at the ground, hunched up with my hands in my pockets, my shoulders aching with what's happened, my arse glued to the bench whether it's wet or not. Down by my right foot on the tarmac pathway there's a large snail, makes me think I could do with a shell to crawl into as well.

Sitting like that gets too tiring so I lift my head up and lollop back against the back of the bench instead, still with my hands in my pockets.

Right in the centre of the garden there's a brass statue of a bloke with his hand out as if he's making a speech, but the face is covered in bird shit so he looks as if he lost before he started. If he was real I'd take him down the pub. We could both forget everything.

I let myself carry on feeling like that for a bit because it feels like therapy and I know I can pull myself out of it even if I'm exhausted.

Then I take my hands out of my pockets and make myself stretch, give myself some oxygen so I'll be able to think my way through this.

I reach into my pocket again and get my money out. I was right when I worked it out earlier: eighty quid and a bit of smash.

These boots aren't right for walking and they make me stand out, so they're going to have to go and the weather isn't warm enough just for a t-shirt on top so I'll have to buy a sweatshirt as well, which is going to leave me thirty or thirty five.

That means I've got no hope of a B and B, so it's kip out somewhere without a doss bag when it could be coming on to rain again, or find a hostel. Three hours ago I thought I was going back to jail, so a hostel only seems half bad.

Chapter Nine

Finding a hostel's worse than getting a job. First I go all the way up Baker St to one that isn't there any more, then I'm zig-zagging across the West End, Victoria first, because there's three down there, back past Buckingham Palace with all their spare rooms, over to Soho and then Covent Garden, but it's the same everywhere: none of them want to know unless I've got something called a CAT number, which I've never heard of before. One of the places explains you can't get one unless you've been found, kipping out.

After the third 'no' I'm walking out before they have time to say 'sorry.'

In between hostels I think I'll buy a pair of trainers, but none of the shops have got my size in the cheap versions they stick outside as a come-on, and once you're inside it's murder: none of the kids who work there come up to help you, while the rap music's so loud it's like a guy trying to front you down in nick with his tunes.

By the time I get a knock back in Holborn it's four o'clock and the Wellingtons are giving me blisters. I have a cup of tea in a café even though I'm trying to go along as if I haven't got any money so I can keep afloat longer.

While I'm sitting there I decide I'll have to swallow, and try Barrington House, even if it's only a month since I thought I'd left Camden Town behind.

Then going down Gray's Inn Road I see a shop selling

work clothes. The monkey boots come to just over half the price of a pair of trainers and I pick up a sweatshirt and a bomber jacket as well.

'Bomber by name, bomber by jacket,' I smile to myself as the bloke shows me where the mirror is. He's friendly enough but I don't share the joke with him – I'd have to too much to explain. He's probably going round his mum's for his tea when he finishes, but I've got to stay tough.

The sweat's a Lonsdale and I quite fancy myself in the bomber, makes me look as if I'm back in the skinhead days.

Buying them and the boots is going to leave me thirty quid and I tell him I'll have them. The place is two shops knocked into one, with camping gear in the other half and I walk through there, wondering about a sleeping bag, but I take the gamble my luck hasn't got that bad.

I tell him I'll keep the monkey boots on and ask him to put the Wellingtons in a carrier.

Outside again I'm glad I've bought extra layers. There's a chill on the edge of the breeze as if the air's getting ready to set about me because it knows I'm on the slide but there's nothing I can do about that except keep going. I head for Barrington House, through King's Cross quick enough for none of it to stick to me then up to Camden Town, keeping away from the main drag so that I don't see any of the lowlifes and put myself off.

I make up a CAT number for the fat bloke behind the jump: three, three, fifty four, my birthday a month and a day early, but he grunts that he's got to go to look me up on the computer and lowers himself off his stool.

His white t-shirt could have done with a wash about three days ago and as he walks away I can't make out whether or not that's a small shit stain on the arse of his joggers.

I don't know why I bother hanging around, especially as I've told him Jimmy Bacon.

'Sorry, it's never heard of you,' he half-laughs and half-wheezes when he comes back, out of breath as he gets back on his stool. 'Better luck with the next place you try it on.' That's so funny his stomach starts moving up and down.

I don't fancy the place much anyway. As I turn to go out through the big door I see there's a squashed turd on the lobby floor over by the lift.

'See you,' he says to my back. 'Best try Pea Street House,' he shouts.

Out on the pavement twenty yards away there's an old boy in a blue suit holding onto the railings that run along the front of the building. His body's facing the hostel but his head's twisted halfway round and up towards the sky.

'Fuuuuuck off, will yer,' he shouts at no one.

As I walk towards him I take in the strong head of still dark hair standing out above his red face, drops of rich new blood on his white shirt as well as the piss stain in the crotch of his trousers.

He's dropped his aluminium crutch and I go over to pick it up from the pavement but he aims a boot at my hand. 'Fuck off wiv yer.' He almost catches me with his spit.

'Best of luck,' I say to him, but I reckon he's got to be a messenger, and I start striding it out, getting away from everything that's happened to him, case it comes on me.

Five minutes later I realise I put the bag with the Wellingtons down when I was talking to fatty but I don't even think about going back, someone's probably traded 'em in for a couple of cans already.

Another quarter of an hour and I'm back through King's Cross. I'm taking fatty's advice and making for Pea Street House near Mount Pleasant, even though I've never fancied it before because I've never met a good hostel that used to be a spike.

It's getting late to get booked in somewhere so I'm almost jogging, wishing I'd got a sleeping bag, but ten minutes through the back doubles and I've found it.

The front of the house looks quite good, smart white rendering and a plaque that says there was a hospital on the site in1831, but a sign points to an entrance down an alley and as I turn into it I have to walk round a skeleton of a junkie gouching out on the pavement with his feet stuck straight out in front of him for everyone to tread on.

He's so still I don't even know if he's dead or not but as I'm buzzing on the door trying to look harmless for the CCTV, he comes out of it as if nothing's happened, like a dog waking up that doesn't even know it's been akip.

I pull on the big metal door when it buzzes and as I go through to an airlock I've left natural light behind.

I'm trying to look through the darkened reinforced glass pane in the top of a plywood door that never got beyond a light blue undercoat, then that opens. I'm inside a dark blue reception, two or three doors off it, and staff in a little room that opens onto it.

They're behind a built-up counter Daley Thompson couldn't jump over, then there's gap of about six foot and above that a metal shutter hanging down a foot from the top, ready to be whipped down in case someone goes for the impossible or more likely tries aiming something in at them, like a chair or a fire extinguisher.

'Welcome to Fort Apache,' I think as I walk over to the counter, although nearly all the light's on their side, so they look a bit like Jesus in the manger my Nan used to take me to see at Christmas, and for about two minutes they've got about as much life as a pair of statues.

I can tell the ginger-haired woman at the computer's seen me from the looks she's giving the blond kid who's sitting there not noticing anything while he reads a hardback with the sort of plastic cover that means it's a library book.

I don't say anything because I figure it's got to be another 'no' down to the CAT number, and when it is I'm going to be on the edge of going and finding a drink because I've had enough of being a zero the wrong side of the counter, so I spend the time going through why that would be a bad idea.

Then Ginger says, 'Daniel,' to the kid and 'Can I help you?' to me, as she gets up from the computer.

'Any chance of bookin' in, love?'

She looks at her watch then smiles at me, says, 'Let me have a look,' and disappears through a doorway at the back.

That smile of hers is enough to keep a weak man sober. I feel better even without a result, although I'm going to be a lot better if I get one.

I reckon she's got to be about thirty five.

I'm still waiting when I hear shouting outside. The blond kid puts his book down and reaches forward under the counter for what must be the buzzer for the door, because just then it opens behind me.

I look round and see a short black guy, almost a midget, wearing new-looking denims and a red headscarf.

He mouths off in an American accent, 'Goddam motherfuckin' motherfuckers, fuckin' Scottish thieves, maan.'

The blond kid looks at him without saying anything, but his face is telling me he'd rather shit than do anything about mighty mouth's attitude.

I turn to look over my other shoulder as the Septic walks behind me across to another door. 'They be back in LA they be fuckin' dead men, cross one of the Crips, thaat's my gang, the brothers look after me. Open the motherfuckin' door, man.'

The blond kid reaches under the counter and the door buzzes open. The Yank's got to be all of five foot two, probably hopes mouthing off is going to keep trouble away.

I decide if I get booked in I'll keep a lookout, see if it works for him. Ginger nob comes back, 'We can let you have a shared room with one other?'

'Sure.'

'Surprised?' she says.

'Don't need a number, then?'

'Not after half past seven, and I make it seven twenty... eight,' she says, looking at her watch.

I'm beginning to think any more of this kindness I might have to marry the bird but then she spoils it. 'Afraid we can't let you into the room yet. There's still some clearing-out to be done.'

The look she gives Daniel, she must be the guvnor, and he should have done the clearing out.

I don't let on I've noticed. 'Thanks, love.'

'You can go through for some supper if you like. The canteen's still serving. You pay for it in the service charge.'

'Yeah, thanks.'

'Straight through there.' She points to the door the Yank went through.

The blond kid still hasn't said anything, but he buzzes me through.

I come into a top corner of a rectangular room, same blue as reception, no daylight here either, longer walls down the side, shorter each end.

The servery's along most of the shorter top wall next to me and the front of the queue's facing my way.

There's a metal rail around an area with the heavy benches and tables fixed to the floor, taking up all of the middle of the room. On the lino floor there's an arrow showing you which way to walk to the back of the queue, in case you can't work it out, probably left over from when it was a spike.

There's still about forty blokes sitting there, even though most of them must have had their meal by now. I don't know if it's the dark walls or the fag smoke or the ceiling's low but I feel like I'm in a dark blue cave, and as I walk round to the end of the queue I can feel a tension binding the place tighter, like a dining hall in nick that's ready to go off, except in here I don't know who's who.

I have a glance around in case I can spot where the ag might start, but half of 'em look possible and I don't want anyone to think I'm noticing too much.

There's two big groups that stand out. About fifteen Somali-looking blacks around tables near the servery and about ten white blokes, mainly youngsters, a couple of them obvious junkies, down the other end.

Nearly everyone's got a look on their face as if they're straining to shit.

I feel eyes on me as I'm walking round and a few more glances when I join the end of the queue but I'm after some tea, not a fight, so I make sure I look as if I'm standing cool.

There's four or five in front of me alongside the counter. Looking forward at the bain maries I can see some white fish in one and crusty steak pie in another. The tall African dishing out the food puts a couple of spoonfuls of mixed vegetable from a glass serving bowl onto each plate.

I'm next but one when the Septic turns up again, behind me in the queue. 'Come on, damn, slow mother-fuckers.'

The bloke who was being served moves away to find a table and we all move forwards. 'You new in here, ain't you? Let me go first, maan.'

I just ignore him because I don't think he's serious,

95

but then he says, 'You deaf, my man?'

I'm still looking ahead of me but I can feel a few heads come up. He carries on I'll have to decide whether he's only a joke around here or the mascot of some little team, finding out whether they walk round me or over me, because sometimes you're new in a place and you get a little test like that. Either way I don't want to have a straightener with him in full view, especially as I haven't even booked in yet.

Then I'm rescued by the white-haired old grandad who's standing in front of me, one hand resting on his walking stick.

He's given his plate by the big African, a good helping of pie and veg on it.

The old boy picks it up from the counter with his free hand, holding it by the rim, a thumb on top and two fingers underneath.

He looks down at his meal. 'No fuckin spuds!'

He moves the plate back far enough to get a swing and then throws it. Luckily the African's got a duck on him and the peas bounce off the shoulder of his whites as the plate carries on to a crash-landing on the gas range at the back.

'There. Fuckyer, yer black bastard, sellin the potatoes down the market, robbin' the old men.'

The African's half-hiding behind a water machine at the end of the counter.

'Fuckin' nigger.' The old boy picks up three slices of bread from a big plastic tray and walks away.

I'm thinking at least the Yank's shut up but that's

probably it – now they're going to stop serving, only then the African comes out from behind the water machine.

'Meat pie or fish, that's all we have.' Going by the accent, Nigerian.

'Meat, mate. Don't worry about the spuds.' I wink at him but he doesn't react.

'You want pudding?'

I nod and he gives me a chunk of fruit pie, ladles custard over it.

I pick up my tray and walk over to the tea machine. Looking round, it doesn't look as if anyone's taken any notice, and the old boy's nowhere to be seen. Maybe he's well known for it and no one cares.

I see an empty table and as I sit down I see the Yank disappear through a doorway with TV Room 2 marked above it.

I start on the pie and the meat in it isn't too bad. Then I realise why the seat was empty: there's a mess of blood and tissues and could be shit where my feet are.

I can't see another free table so I move to one with a bloke who's crashed out in one of the seats and sit the other side from him.

He must be farting in his sleep because every now and then I can't smell anything except poison and I don't get more than half the fruit pie down me before I know I'm going to puke if I carry on eating.

I get up and go over to the doorway with BBC 1 written above it, but even with no light except the telly I can make out it's full up, and the stink of the bodies and the fag smoke are almost as bad as the sleeping farter, besides maybe they've cleared my room now.

I go back to reception and ginger's there. 'Still here, then,' she smiles.

'No choice, love.'

'Might as well do the paperwork then.' She smiles again.

I say 'Sure,' and realise she didn't bother asking my name before because she thought I'd do a runner after seeing the canteen, so she was going to let me have the meal for freemans, which makes her a lot better than most of the staff in these sort of places.

'We'll go over there.' She points to a little room off reception.

I wait by the door until she comes from out the back and unlocks it to let us in.

She's got a coshel of forms in one hand, so it's going to be the usual performance.

I squeeze in behind a desk and she sits opposite on the other chair.

She puts all the forms on the desk and takes one for Housing Benefit off the top.

'Bugger, sorry, just got to find a biro.'

'Don't worry, love I'll guard the paper, make sure no one nicks any of it.' That gets me half a smile as she gets up and goes out again, and I've got a bit time of time to work out how to play it with the forms, because Old Bill know they want Anthony Jackson and they might want me as Jimmy Bacon as well.

I figure I'll give her a different name altogether, with Jimmy's NI number and then if the guy I'm sharing with is half-sensible I'll ask him if Old Bill come round on fishing trips, which they do in some hostels. If he reckons they don't and I decide I can stand the place till I'm sorted then tomorrow I'll tell her the moody name was all a big mistake – I've forgotten I changed it by deed poll or something, and I'm really Jimmy Bacon. Sometimes the staff like it if they think you're a bit mental or a bit soapy so it might end up doing me a favour.

By the time she's come back and we're halfway through the second form I don't know how I'm going to work it. It sounds like the DSS are going to want more ID than Old Bill need to get you three years, but by now I've told her I'm Ray Leonard, and she's told me her name's Tess.

I ask her if she wants me to get started on the last form but she says she's got a 'system', so I sit there trying to work out what she'd look like if she wasn't covered up in a pair of Wrangler dungarees, but about all I can make out is she hasn't got much up top and I'll have to hope she's got a tasty pair of legs. All the same I've just got her bent naked over the side of the bed when she looks up and gives me a little frown before she says, 'That's the lot. You might as well wait here, while I see if Daniel's finished clearing the room.'

I think about that frown as she goes out and hope she doesn't do mind-reading on the side, but this is as close as I've got to a bird since I left Cynthia's before the last lot of nick.

The chair's being giving me arseache for about ten minutes and I stand up to stretch but I'm just putting one arm out when I notice a wet smear of blood on the wall where I'm about to put my hand, which makes me sit down in a hurry. The walls are the same dark blue as the rest of the gaff, and looking round I can see more blood.

The place must be full of bang-on junkies, but I'm too far gone with tiredness to care. All I want now is a pad mate who doesn't try too hard and a bed that won't give me the pox.

Tess opens the door and gives me her warm little smile. 'I'm very sorry. Daniel was called away to stop a fight, but he'll be up in your room very shortly. The last bloke left a lot of stuff. Would you like to sit here while you wait?'

I want to ask her what Daniel's doing for a clean pair of trousers.

'Sure, why not. Got anything I can read?'

She comes back and gives me a War Cry and a paperback. 'Didn't know which you'd prefer.'

Then she explains she's going home now but she'll see me in the morning to do my support plan.

I put a look on my face to let her know that doing my support plan is going to be better than Christmas.

'Good night, now.'

'Night, Tess.'

I think about her smile for a bit after she's gone but then I drift round to bending her over the bed again, and all that's going to do is make me worse so I have a look at the reading matter.

The book's a western and I wouldn't piss on the

Salvation Army if they were covered in flames, so I sit there riding the range around Dry Gulch, ignoring the HIV on the walls.

The way the book tells the story I wish I hadn't let the writing go since I got out because, a bit of practice, I reckon I could do better.

I give it to page forty, but the room's still not ready so I tell Daniel I'm going out for a bit.

Once I'm in the street I dig out the coins in my pocket, make sure I can make a phone call. I'm going to find out how badly the sheriff still wants me, if there's any chance I'm going to forget Daniel and the dump and get over to Ealing, for the bank book at least.

I find a phone that's working about five minutes on towards Farringdon, opposite Mount Pleasant Sorting Office. I remember a bloke telling me once that it used to be a prison, so I hope that's not a sign.

An English voice I don't know says, 'Good Evening. Tony's Bar and Grill.'

'Yianni, please.'

'Sorry, sir, there's no one of that name here.'

'Can I speak to the manager, please?

'I am the manager, sir. My name's George.'

'Yianni been nicked?'

'Very likely, sir. Who would you like me to say if I see him, sir?'

'Tony Blair, mate.'

'Very good, sir.'

As I turn to go back I'm thinking how smooth this geezer George sounds, and wondering if Dooley's told him to fuck off yet, but that doesn't make me smile for long and I walk back to Pea St feeling like my face is bumping against the pavement.

Chapter Ten

Back at reception Daniel's got a bird with him who looks like Elvis.

Her black hair's greased back into a DA and she's wearing a shiny white shirt like a copper's, with a boot-lace tie and black jeans. She's got a soft pink and white face but I reckon she's early forties. The only thing that doesn't go with the Elvis look is the old-fashioned black-framed glasses.

'You the new chap, are yer. My name's Lindsay. You sure you want a bed here, are you – it's not always very nice.'

The way she talks she's from somewhere up north, somewhere they have a lot of rain.

'Ritz was full, love.'

'Oh I see. Yer like a jest, then, yer a bit of a joker.'

Neither of us is pretending to smile.

I want to tell her she's not a screw and I don't have to put up with her misery, but it looks like I might have to as the price of getting my head down.

Maybe she can see I'm wound up, because she softens a bit. 'Okey-dokey, Raymond, just a couple of minutes. Sorry it's been such a long wait.'

She says 'long' like 'longer.'

After that she doesn't say anything else to me so I stand there feeling out of place for the second time that night while she keeps on fiddling about with something under the counter and firing off questions at Daniel about what's been happening in the hostel during his shift, except you know she knows the answers already, she's only asking because she's got the zig with him.

After four or five minutes of that she says, 'Okay, then,' and comes out from round the back, takes me through a door she unlocks by the side of reception.

We go past a couple of offices which don't look much better than the rest of the gaff, then we go through a door with a Yale on it and up a staircase, me one step behind her.

She hasn't told me my room number or what floor I'm on yet. I'm not giving her the satisfaction of asking. Instead I feel like asking her what it's like working in Heartbreak Hotel, but I'd probably have to explain the joke.

'Staff only this way,' she says. 'You'll see other stairs when we get there. You're on the fourth floor, you are.'

She says it like she's not expecting me to make it.

The route we're on I can see her point. I wish I had a map: there's more twists and turns than the Crooked House at Southend – the conversion work must have been a bodge-up.

'Room forty three,' she says. I'm hoping it's just the accent makes it sound that bad.

I can tell by the way her shoulders are turned forward she didn't fancy her shift tonight.

We keep up the stairs to the second then along a couple of dark narrow corridors. None of the rooms we pass have got their doors open, but twice when we turn a corner there's two or three blokes hanging about who do one as soon as they see us.

It's like walking along with a screw.

Then on the threes you can hear it's party time before we get there.

We go through some fire doors and down a long corridor with ten or eleven rooms on each side.

Everyone's got their doors open, most of them with different rap music blaring out.

Up here it's nearly all youngsters, standing in the doorways or moodying about between the rooms.

Everyone's pretending they're having a party, but there's the same atmosphere as the canteen, so thick in the air you can almost touch it: everything's waiting to kick off.

I just come level with this one older bloke, a skinhead about my age, tattoos all over his face, with a young blond skinhead standing next to him, when he shouts out, "'Ere, how the fook do yer fook a fookin lesbian.'

In front of me Elvis's shoulders stiffen and a blush spreads up the back of her neck but she walks on, ignoring it. I feel sorry for her. The geezer's probably having the blond kid himself, telling himself no one's noticed. She probably has more birds than he does.

Last doorway on the left there's a black kid, about six foot, scruffy-looking dreads, blue overalls and a maroon t-shirt. He's eyeballing me as I come up to him but I stare him out and he can't hold it, looks away as if I've crushed him.

He doesn't like it he can complain to his social worker.

I did my Borstal a long time ago – this lot think they're still there.

'Last stairs,' she says as we go through the other fire doors.

She starts explaining how the place has been re-habbed and it used to be dormitories. I only half-listen, thinking about who I'm going to be two'd up with instead, hoping he's not like one of the herberts we've just passed, and noticing it's a lot quieter up here, so maybe all the troublemakers are on the third. All I can hear up here is the murmur of tellies from a couple of rooms with their doors shut.

Elvis knocks on number forty three. 'Hello, Patrick. New chap's here,' she shouts at the door.

The door opens. 'New playmate for yer, Patrick,' she says to whoever's inside.

I step in front of her and walk in, see a black guy in his early thirties sitting back down on his bed along one of the side walls.

My bed's along the opposite wall.

She says, 'Ooh, nearly forgot yer keys, wardrobe and door keys.'

I half-turn back towards her, she puts the keys in the hand I'm holding out.

'Hope you're okay then,' she says.

'Yeah, thanks.'

She goes out and I turn back to the black guy.

All he's wearing are a pair of black boxers and flip flops on his feet. I can't help noticing plenty of muscle on his upper body, reminds me of a light middle I used to know.

He's looking at me the same way I'm looking at him, neither of us with any ag, just checking each other out.

He could be an ex-fighter who's kept himself in shape. I say, 'Hi.'

He leans forward, half-getting off the bed, and shoves his hand out. Either he's relaxed or he knows how to pretend.

'Fitz', he says. 'Only Buddy Holly there call me Patrick.' I shake his hand. 'Ray.'

I notice his eyes, yellow and brown, hardly any white, like a cat, must be contacts: take 'em out if you get ID'd.

I say, 'Thought she was Elvis, not Buddy Holly.'

'Yah ever see Elvis wear glasses?'

'No, mate, I haven't.'

'Ah, she alright, Lindsay, best girl in the 'ouse.'

I nod to show I've heard him.

'She like most of them staff though, only know a lick-le what goes on,

bes' keep it that way, innit.'

'Got to be, mate.'

I sit down on my bed, halfway along it. The sheets are whiter than I'm expecting and the bed's a lot softer. I feel the tiredness creep down from my arse to my feet.

He seems alright but I wish he wasn't there so I could just crash out. After all the kickings I've had today all I want to do is go to sleep, then get up in the morning, start thinking again.

He says, 'Shut de door, mon.'

As I reach forward and shut it I see a short brown

plastic stool that's been hidden behind it on Fitz's side of the room. On the seat of the stool there's a round shaving mirror, five or six lines on it chopped up and ready to go.

Fitz half-sits up again, sticks his foot out and hooks it round the stool to drag it over so it ends up between us.

He's sitting up now, almost opposite me. I'm looking at the white, thinking that could be anything, coke, angel dust, horse dope, laxative, all ready for Fitz to get me up on, fuck me up with or just have a laugh at me, but I look up at him and see how hot his face is, so I reckon better than evens it's charlie.

He almost shouts, "Ousewarming, innit.'

He can see I don't know.

He chuckles. 'You tink it's poison. Let me show you, mon.' He takes out a twenty-pound note from under his pillow, does a line up each nostril.

I'm looking at his face as he comes up from the mirror, watching for the quality of the hit, thinking I'm behind with him already even if the stuff's rubbish, then seeing on his face it's probably primo, which drops me further behind, but it's three or four years since I did some, and I used to love it a lot.

Besides, a couple of lines of charlie I can fight him all night if I have to, even if it's him who knows the dance steps right now.

He breathes out and gives me the twenty. 'Is good stuff, mon.'

I look back at him straight in those eyes that aren't their real colour, in my chest it feels like surrender as I bend down to the mirror and throw three months' AA out of the window.

I do a line and the rush is a rocker, freezing my brain until I can talk again.

'Yeah that's good, Fitz.' And then I'm going like I've never been tired. 'Yeah, lovely, and know what, I haven't even had a drink for three months. That is good. Years since I had some.'

'Knew you'd like it mate,' he says.

That's about the last word he gets in because now I'm definitely on one, telling him about the pearl diving, getting back from the job at two in the morning, having to go out for a run, three or four miles, almost like roadwork in the old days, just to tire myself out, because otherwise the walls are going to come in at me. Then I start the story at the beginning, how I used to think I was going to be middleweight champion of the world and where I ended up with that.

Fitzy chops up a few more.

I'm saying, 'You're about the first geezer I've talked to since I got out.'

Fitzy gives me a smile.

I feel like I haven't been warm for about a million years until just now and I wish I could explain it to him.

I'm trying to make my mind up whether it's a good thing to tell him about the licence and having to have it on my toes when he says, 'Yeah, knew you been a fighter soon as I sees ya, and a teef an all, innit. I sees you I reckons plenty a porridge, just like me, mon. Tell you about my last lot, I was in the Ville, seven months' remand, my brief reckons I'm on for a bender. I said only one doin' any bending is me in some other geezer's cell and I ain't like that, then I get three years' sentence, after I've been nutted off he don't say anything to me at all, can't look at me in the face.'

I say, 'Yeah, like most briefs mate, come outta cunt town.'

Fitzy chops up a few more and now we're both going.

I tell him, 'Last three I did, they give me the diesel treatment, better than grassing, especially if you think the geezer's going to come round and kill you.'

Fitzy chuckles again. 'Yeah, mate, 'bout the same here, 'cept I don't even know the man's right name they want me to give 'em.'

Then we're onto the worst screws we've ever met and I can't even say how long we're talking because I'm in the time tunnel, but I know we've talked loads before Fitzy has to go out.

He stands up, puts on a pair of black joggers and tucks a money belt down inside them.

'Help yourself, be 'appy,' he says, nodding towards some more he's cut up on the mirror. 'Bitta business,' he says as he goes.

I don't even really want any more coke, but without him the night's gone a bit cold so I do another couple of lines.

Ten minutes later he's back, with a Tesco's bag he didn't have when he went out.

A minute after that there's a knock on the door. I look at Fitz and down at the mirror to say shall I get rid of it, but he says, 'Safe, mon,' and gets up.

When he opens the door it's one of the crackheads from the canteen. The way he looks at me he thinks I've stolen his train set, sold it for smack.

'Dahn the corridor, mate,' Fitzy orders him.

Fitzy goes out after him, then comes back on his own about a minute later.

For the next half hour it's like rush hour on the tube. I even hear Fitzy outside in the corridor telling them to line up properly and keep the noise down.

That finishes and he comes back and gets a couple more wraps out of his pocket, shakes them gently onto the mirror and does the business.

I'm wondering where he's put the money, in his pocket or the Tesco's bag he's slung on the floor, then I remember the money belt.

Now he's going top speed, all about boilings he's seen in Highpoint, except he calls it 'Nighpoint', the way he's telling me about it it's almost like he doesn't think I've seen it happen.

Then he stands up again, 'Could be good, mate, you an me, make a whole heap a money,' then he looks me in the eye and for a few seconds holds his cock through his tracksuit bottoms, to let me know he's not just talking about the dough we could get hold of.

''Bout ten,' he says, but I see a shadow cross his face before he goes out of the door.

This time he hasn't left any out, and it begins to die down a bit.

I reckon he's had well over his ten minutes when I

notice an alarm clock on top of his bedside cabinet and see it's half past four.

Five o'clock and he still hasn't come back, but there aren't any knocks on the door so he must have gone out, for a meet.

I'm still hanging in space with the coke stopping me sinking as I sit there pondering what he's said, knowing I could stay here, do some work with him, have a bit of a champagne life with all the powder and money and feel those muscles as I discover his cock.

But I remember his face when he was telling me about the boilings he's seen, know he can still see the sugar going into the cup before the water's drawn off so it'll do more damage, still hears the screaming in the middle of the night and looks out the window for the ambulance, because the last time they let him out half his brain stayed behind, and if I wait for him I'll probably go the same way.

I don't move though, because I'm potless skint, way behind with him for all his charlie, still thinking about his muscles, and I've got no other place to go that feels like home.

Six o'clock and the coke's lying down but I've realised the shadow that crossed his face just before he went out was the shadow of the jailhouse. He isn't coming back.

I make myself stand up.

My wardrobe and bedside cabinet are still locked, so there aren't a lot of places to look but I get lucky straight away: there's four wraps and eighty quid in tens in a rip in the bottom of his mattress.

All I've taken off is my jacket so I bung that back on and I'm out of the room, hoping I can find the right staircase.

I crash down the stairs and this time's God's smiling. The bottom brings me out right by the canteen.

I can hear staff moving about behind the shutter that's been pulled down over the servery but the only punter on the residents' side is mighty mouth the Yank, who's sitting at a table leafing through a newspaper as if he's only looking at the photos.

As I go over to him he looks up at me as if he wants to run, but I smile at him. 'Want some Uncle Charlie? Tell me where there aren't any cameras.'

'BBC One, man.'

I turn round and he gets up and comes with me. The only people in there are two old boys who've crashed out and looking up I see he's right: all that's left of a camera is the metal plate that held it.

I show him the wraps. 'One-er, it's Christmas.'

'Yeah, man.'

'Show me.'

'Here, man.' He's complaining but he's holding out a ton for me to see. That mouth of his must be what he hides behind when he's making his money.

He looks as if he thinks I'm going to mug him. I give him the wraps. 'Be lucky.'

I walk through reception hoping I don't run into Buddy Holly, but the only staff is a black guy asleep behind the jump.

At the end of the alley I turn away from King's Cross

and trouble.

I count my money as I walk along: two hundred and thirty quid, and I need a rest at the seaside.

A black cab comes along with its light on. It's my first one for years.

'Victoria station.'

I don't know if I'm happy or my head's falling apart.

PART THREE

Chapter Eleven

It's got to be Treacle Bumstead-on-Sea, but two days after I get there I'm working for a little subbie with a nice run of work, gutting a long row of terraced houses.

The houses are only two storeys but it doesn't take long to work out it's always my turn for the barrow when we're on the second floor, taking it straight out of the window down a single scaffold board into the skip.

That's why they need the grackle – the locals haven't got the bottle for it, but I like it, like the June weather on me when the shirt comes off and finding out Yianni's pans weren't that heavy after all because once I get on that fourteen-pound hammer I can feel it bringing muscles back out of retirement that I'd forgotten about, and we're only two roads away from the beach, so by the end of the day I go back to the guest house with the smell of the sea on me and the little bit of pain keeping me real.

Most nights there's only me and a salesman in the other single room. After I get the start Dorothy the landlady says I'm going out too early for her to do me a breakfast, but another fiver a week and she'll give me a dinner instead, so I have a shower and when I go downstairs it's waiting for me.

She's early sixties, strong grey hair with a wave at the front, everything lacquered into place. Whatever she wears her bust always stands up like the outside wall of Wakefield nick. If you tried to climb up it you'd only fall off. She's got a posh, deep voice that makes her sound like an old colonel sending his men off to battle.

Every night she brings in my dinner she says something like, 'Sorry, mucked up the spuds tonight, never could get the hang of cooking,' but the collar I'm doing I'm ready to eat anything, and usually it's alright, even when the potatoes are lumpy.

I've been there about ten days when I wake up in the middle of the night and think I can hear faint sounds of a woman being fucked.

Next morning I decide I must have imagined it, put it down to a frustrated sex dream, but that evening there's a sweet stale smell of wine in the dining room.

Dorothy comes in and puts the grub down in front of me. 'Sorry, sorry, meant to warn you, had the girls over for bridge last night, drank far too much, got rather silly, behaved badly.' Then she goes out.

First Buddy Holly then Dorothy. It must be something in my horoscope. I keep running into them, and her hangover shows up in the fish pie she gives me, so runny I nearly retch swallowing it.

After that I do what I do every evening, go out with my notebook and find a bench on the jetty that juts out from the prom and runs alongside the mouth of the river almost to where it merges with the sea.

The sea's the main event around here and every evening I try to write down the difference between how it looks now to how it looked the night before. Sometimes the words come easy and other times I'm writing them and crossing them out until I know I can either settle for what I've got or else go mad. Last night I was stuck for anything at all, but tonight the sun's hidden by cloud and even though it's June the sea's grey with the menace of a shark. After I get that down I stay where I am, waiting for the light to go, and when it does I walk along the promenade and feel the darkness settle down, making the emptiness of the place bigger.

When I get back I try to keep the peaceful mood but I'm restless, wanting a beer to turn me off thinking about how I could go down the hole tomorrow before I've had the chance of sex again, and as I'm going to sleep I'm wondering what you have to do to get it around here, because the only decent women I've seen have either got a ring on their finger or about three chavvies stringing along behind.

But the next morning my head's clear again and I'm in the café by about five to seven for tea and two toasts before I get the bus to the job.

Usually I see O'Brien, the old boy, in there. He's a light duties man, doesn't do much more than sweep up. I find out later he's family to the guy who owns the firm, which is why they carry him.

I'm working with him and a young wind-up merchant, Viney, who never stops trying to dig everyone out.

It's the three of us together, doing one house at a time then moving onto the next.

There's another two blokes as well, Damon and Ginge, but Dennis, the foreman, has got them knocking over outhouses and sheds at the back.

Dennis reckons they're a demolition firm but really

they're just general labourers. Apart from Viney I'm the only one climbing more than six foot off the ground.

O'Brien marks my card early on. Viney's Dennis's nephew, and the other two are cousins to each other.

They all come to work in Dennis's van, from the estate outside of town where they all live.

When O'Brien tells me, I say, 'That Viney must be an inbreed.'

He nods his head and takes his pipe out of his mouth. 'Just so you know.'

Then the second Thursday I'm there I think it's going to be all over for me and the job. By now I've got the routine: Dennis starts us up and then goes away to another job he's running until half nine, when he comes back to drive us to the nearest café about a mile away, but this day he just sits in his van parked on the other side of the road giving us the deadly eyeball so we can't have our usual blow once he's gone.

I'm on the first floor with Viney, where we've taken out most of the front wall so Dennis has got a front row seat.

I make it look as if I think I'm on treble bonus, stacking any brick that's good, while Viney play-acts at filling the barrow with the rubbish, but I can feel Dennis looking at me the whole time, then after about fifteen minutes he shouts up, 'Oi, fuckin' come down here.'

Viney makes out he thinks Dennis means him, but we both know he doesn't.

'What have I fuckin done.' He throws his shovel down like a kid, almost hitting my leg with it, and then turns round to look down at Dennis from the edge of the drop.

'No, not you, you cunt. Tell the fuckin' Butter to come down here.' Because that's been my nickname since I nearly dropped a bucket of clips on O'Brien's head and he went, 'Yer put butter on it, to make it more slippery, so yer did?'

I walk over and start down the ladder, thinking this must be the bullet because he's got another relative to work onto the firm.

As I step off the bottom of the ladder to cross the road I make my mind up to play dumb, make him wipe his lip and come out with it, let him feel the fear I'm going to lump him.

I go up to the offside window, still standing on the road. 'Go round, you'll get fuckin' run over.'

I don't say anything but walk round onto the pavement wondering if he's going to pay me for the eight days I've done, wishing I'd subbed up last week.

He slithers across the front seat till he's leaning a strong forearm on top of the open window that side and looking out up at me, giving it plenty with his blue eyes as if he's trying to suss me out. I look back down at him catching the almost bald head with the few curly grey strands dragged across it, half-imagining a tool splitting it open and the spurt of blood.

'You done any burning with a torch?'

He's going to have to go better than that as an excuse to get rid of me.

'Yeah, done a lot of it, dismantling cranes in the docks, Isle of Dogs, if you've heard of it.'

He knows I'm being sarky because he's already told me he grew up in Custom House till he was seven, but he blanks it.

'See that at the end of the road?' He points to a warehouse at the end of the houses we're working on. 'Warehouses, two of 'em either side of that one, backin' onto a creek. Plenty of work, plenty of burnin' to be done. Can't trust the rest of them, specially Viney, the cunt, even if he is my sister's boy. You stick around, Butter.'

I say, 'Yeah, thanks, think I will,' but I don't soften much. I know the type. He could sack me tomorrow.

'Payday tomorrow. Know where the Blue Anchor is? Go down there with the others about four. Landlord's an old mate of mine. He'll cash yer cheque.'

'Yeah, sure,' I say, and walk back across the road, thinking about getting weighed out in a pub, wondering if I can stay strong.

O'Brien looks at me as I walk past him cleaning brick.

'Kushti.' I wink at him.

Back up top Viney's sitting on the barrow nearly busting it. He'd find somewhere to sit falling through outer space. 'What did he fuckin' want, the old fucker?'

'Told me you were a cunt, mate.'

Viney looks as if he doesn't know what I mean, which is where I want to keep him, helps me not have to have it with him.

Five minutes later Dennis has gone and we all have a blow, everyone slagging him off, but I take it easy on the criticism, in case someone backstabs me.

The next morning in the café we're still there half an

hour after we've had our grub. Dennis is too busy with the Sun he's got spread out on his lap to want to take us back.

The café's the only one around there, always over-crowded, the five of us crammed round one table and they still haven't cleared the plates away, so there's hardly anywhere to put your elbows or hands.

Viney starts performing about how much he's going to drink that night. 'Fuckin' bottle of vodka under the table, toppin' meself up, I'll be well blasted.'

Stuart says in his slow country boy voice, 'Few pints of Guinness, that'll do me, go 'ome, give her the house-keeping, if you know what I mean.' We all laugh. His accent makes it sounds extra funny.

'You dirty fucker,' Viney says across the table as if he means it.

I can see Stu doesn't like it but he doesn't say any-thing, must be used to Viney trying to ride him.

He says, 'Give us one of your roll-ups then, Ginger, mate.'

As he makes his fag he says, 'Having a few with us tonight then, Butter, new man on the job, like. Should do, shouldn't he, Den?

Dennis grunts from where he's sitting next to me, but doesn't look up. I glance over and see the nudie magazine lying on top of the open newspaper.

He sees me looking and holds the paper closer together before I can get much of a gander at two black birds plating each other.

Maybe it's his Friday treat and the rest of them know

about it, because as I look up Ginge winks at me. 'Think you want another cuppa, Butter.'

He half-turns in his seat towards the counter. 'Five more teas, love.'

When she brings them over, I decide I might as well get it out the way. I say, 'Can't drink any more, lads, no good for me. Every time I had a drink I put myself in bother.' I've never had to say it before. I half-expect the walls to come crashing in but all that happens is Ginge looks at Stu and Stu looks at O'Brien, who gives me half a smile.

Then Viney says, 'You a fuckin' queer boy then, who don't drink. I reckon that London's full of poufs.'

Stuart says, 'Don't' go on, Viney, about subjects you know nothing about.'

Dennis grunts again and nearly knocks the plates off the table getting up. 'Goin' to the khazi,' he says, and goes off with his rolled-up paper in his hand.

I say, 'Lucky he ain't making the sandwiches,' which gets a laugh out of everyone except Viney.

He's back three minutes later. 'Come on – fuckin' get moving.'

I think about having a shit but I don't fancy finding his spunk on the seat. Besides, he could drive off without me.

Chapter Twelve

Five hours later Viney's still trying to get me at it.

'Anyone goes in a pub doesn't have a drink, that's got to be cuntish.'

It's half three. He's standing talking to O'Brien, making sure he's loud enough for me to hear.

O'Brien's sitting on an orange box dusting off his boots with a rag. He's been taking it easy all day and Viney hasn't done more than a stroke since dinner. Now they've both packed up altogether.

I'm still walking round picking up the tools Viney's left lying about.

Just then a scraggy-looking teenage mum comes along on the pavement opposite pushing a buggy with a kid in it, shopping bags hanging off the back.

Viney spots her. 'Oi , cheer up, Lucy Lou.'

She looks over to give him half a smile and he's on it, giving it a funny walk as he crosses the road, Popeye when he's just had his spinach. He's only a shortarse, so it suits him.

He shouts, 'Oi, haven't I seen you on telly?'

I stand looking at them, the way she starts to laugh at him he's in there straight away, which makes her half-soapy, but at least she's giving me a breather.

I bend down to get a grip on the handle of the jackhammer he's left jammed in a concrete stanchion the skip lorry backed over. The stanchion's bent over, the top half under the skip pushing it up at one corner. As I get hold my back gives a twinge to remind me how stiff it is but I plant my boots into some hardcore either side of the bottom of the stanchion and give a good pull as I gun it. I pull the jack loose, bend down to get a hand under it and whack it over the other shoulder. As I stand up I feel a warning tension in the neck near the old injury. I'm tense everywhere, some of it down to Viney, most of it down to thinking about being in a pub again when I'm holding wages.

I see O'Brien looking, wonder if he's seen I'm only fifty percent.

He nods towards Viney over the road. 'Don't let him get yer down. He's only a useless bollocks.'

'Probably all bollocks and no fuckin cock,' I front back to him, but it's not O'Brien who's taking the stick. 'Seeya later, Pat.'

I turn the corner of the house we're working on and walk along the hardcore path to the back, taking the tool to the lock-up in the field behind.

When I turn the corner at the other end of the house I see Stu and Ginge standing just outside the doorway of the shed, smoking.

They don't look like cousins at all. Ginge has got the mottled redhead face under the carrot top but Stu's hair's almost black and his skin's halfway to being Italian or Greek as if there's old-fashioned Romanichal on his side of the family. They're both big lads though, hands for catching cows with and both going about six three.

'Alright, Butter,' says Stu and they both stand aside to

let me into the shed.

I step into the darkness and dump the jack. As I lean it against a plastic dustbin I'm thinking how it's nearly always Stu who speaks and Ginge hardly ever, but as I come back out Ginge says, 'Want some of this then,' and I can smell the weed in the roll-up he's offering me.

The way my back is I could do with a bit of draw to help sort it out but I've got to keep my nut together for when I'm in the pub.

'No, you're alright, mate.'

Ginge nods his head, doesn't say anything.

Stuart says, 'Sensible man, Butter, not like me and 'im. We'll do anything we can get our hands on. Take it easy now, anyway, Butter, POETS day, ain't it.'

'Piss off early, tomorrow's Saturday,' Ginge explains.

'Yeah, nice one.' I smile at him as if I've never heard it before because why should I hurt his feelings.

'You gonner suck the arse out of that all by yourself 'en,' says Stu.

I get another nose of the spliff as Ginge hands it across in front of me.

Stu takes a drag, says, 'Gone, that one is,' and drops it on the ground.

They look finished for the day so I reckon I am as well. Better stay there with them though, case I go round the front and Dennis finds me a little job before off time – besides, talking to them I don't have to think about the trip to the pub.

'So, clean livin' man then,' Stu says, half-turning his face towards me.

'Don't smoke wacky baccy, don't drink, how come then? I mean, hope you don't mind me saying, but me and Ginge was just talking about how you don't look the type, somehow ?'

I could tell him he's nosey, but I've come out with half of it in the café already.

'I'm with AA. Had to be. Every time I had a drink I kept ending up in nick. That keeps happening, you got to pack it in. I have a beer, next thing I'm on the pavement with me arse hanging out. Last time I didn't last that long, smashed up the first bar I went in.'

I half-expect them to take the piss, but Stu nods his head. 'You must go to them meetings, then. Sturgey does that, lives on the estate, next door to Ginge. You might meet him.'

I feel myself relax.

Ginge says, 'Watch out, though. He's a dirty beast, keeps trying to fuck my little niece, Gina.'

'How old is she, then?'

'Coming up to sixteen. Lovely pair of Bristols already,' says Ginge.

The way he says it Uncle Ginger fancies a bit himself, but I hold back the smile I feel coming on.

I say, 'I see him I'll give him a body swerve,' but I'm not thinking about finding a meeting at all, just let them think I am as a way of explaining things.

Stu looks at his watch. 'Quarter to, finishing time on a Friday.'

'Yep,' says Ginge.

'What about the gear in the shed?' I ask.

'Dennis's problem, I reckon,' says Stu. 'He don't trust no one with the key apart from himself.'

Judging by his tone they must have been thieving some till Dennis put the block on it.

It comes to me I feel a bit slowed down. Maybe I've taken in some of the spliff just by standing next to it.

Ginge says, 'You going to tell him then, Stu?'

'Yeah, I am. See, we like you, Butter, so please don't take this the wrong way, but last new man on the firm, he was a good bloke an all, spoilt himself over Viney, couldn't stop himself giving him a couple of slaps. Course, Dennis had to sack him.'

Ginge says, 'We know, he is an annoying little cunt, but you got to allow that. Even me and Stu can't have him, because of Dennis.'

I say, 'Yeah, thanks lads.'

They look as if they think I ought to get loved up with them but all they've done is give me a little warning there's no back-up if I have it with Viney.

Stu says, 'Okay then, wages time.'

I can't work out if he sounds disappointed or not.

We set off without saying anything else. When we get to the passage alongside the shell of the house we have to go in single file, Stuart in front. Behind me Ginge starts singing an Oasis song, I don't know what it's called – I never liked 'em. Maybe he's warming up for when he's had a few lagers or perhaps he's giving Stuart a secret message that I'm an ungrateful bastard but if he has taken the hump I'll be out the pub by the time the drink reminds him.

Round at the front Dennis isn't back yet but the effect of smelling that joint must have worn off and I'm too keyed up to hang about.

'Going to the shop, lads, back in a minute.'

It's fifty yards down the road, a paper shop that sells groceries as well as seaside stuff, like toy buckets and spades and sun block.

As I choose sweeties I can't help my eyes skittering over the shiny cans of Tennent's piled up almost as tall as me, but seeing it in shops doesn't seem to bother me anymore. Since I've been at Dorothy's I get my paper and a bottle of R White's every night from a proper off licence because it's nearest, and besides, I never used to drink the mad stuff except when I didn't have a choice.

I pick up a big bar of Cadbury's fruit and nut and a bag of wine gums as ammo, in case the beer starts calling in the Blue Lion. As I pay the wine and spirit bottles behind the counter look dead, as if no one ever buys them, afraid of putting a dent in the display.

When I get back the van's already there with O'Brien in the back and Viney in the front passenger seat. Stu and Ginge are still on the pavement sharing a smoke again. Dennis must be locking up the shed.

As I get in I wonder if Viney's got a date with the passer-by but he's only going to say yes if I ask him, probably make up something about how he's going to rump her.

Ginge and Stu climb in one after the other and Dennis jumps in the front, turns the ignition. The van does a bunny hop as it stalls and throws everyone in the back forward.

'What fucking wages, not in a fucking hurry are you?'

The way the blokes ignore him it must be his Friday joke.

Then he starts off properly.

As we get going O'Brien says, 'Pride of the Princess, did you do him, Ginge?'

Ginge says something back about another race, but I tune out, making myself try to remember all the pubs I've got nicked from after I've started a row but it's like counting sheep: I still haven't remembered them all when we get there.

I've made sure to come out to work with a few quid in my pocket this morning so I can get the first round and be away quick once I get weighed out, but Ginge and Stu are in front of me as we walk in and Stu gets to the bar with his money out first.

'What do you want then, Butter? I already knows what all the rest likes.'

'Coke, mate.' Then I remember sometimes you only get a small glass. 'No, make it a pint of orange juice and lemonade.'

'Fair enough, Butter.'

I go over to where the rest of them are sitting at a long table.

Dennis is writing cheques.

He finishes one, gives it to O'Brien and then looks at me, trying to make his mind up about something before he starts on the next one.

O'Brien gets up, goes over to the bar and gives the kite to a big lump of a bloke standing behind it.

I look back as Dennis gives me mine, made out to Tony Adams, but I don't mind playing for Arsenal because there's nearly two hundred more than I expected, working it out from the hourly rate that he told me when I started.

Dennis must see the question because he says, 'That's with bonus. Only told you the hourly in case you were a pisstaker.'

'Alright, then, thanks very much.' As I stand up I feel as if the smell of all the booze could be getting me pissed. I pop the last bit of chocolate in as I walk to the bar.

O'Brien's still standing there. 'He'll be back right now, just had to change a barrel. How yer doing?'

'Yeah, not bad. Wages better than I thought.'

'Should be and all. Even Dennis the bollocks knows you're valuable.'

I look down at a pint of bitter on the bar that belongs to a young geezer the other side of me from O'Brien but I look away feeling a bit dizzy, afraid I'll go weird and float away, end up watching myself swimming in the beer.

The big bloke comes back. Close to, his face is scrunched up as if someone got hold of his nose and twisted it pushing his eyes further back into his head, but the way he carries himself it isn't just his size lets you know he could still enjoy making one.

'You another one of Dennis's, are you?' He holds his hand out and I give him the cheque.

'Tony Adams, then. I charge a flat fee of fifteen, Tony. Sign it on the back. Any fucking name you like, long as it ain't readable.'

O'Brien gives me a Ladbrokes pen and I scribble on the back of the cheque.

I give it back to him. He reaches into a pocket and peels my money off the lump he takes out.

'Count it,' he says, but I already am: it's what it should be minus his take.

'Thanks,' I say, even though his fifteen's a liberty and I'm about to give him some more of it back. 'One for my mate here, and what the rest of them have?'

'I'm Lenny,' he says, 'by the way. I don't know what the others are drinking.'

The way him and his pub are winding me up I feel like a fight with Lenny sober, but just then Stu comes over with his cheque. 'Do us a favour, Stu.' I give him a twenty. 'Don't want to ask for beer, mate.'

'Okay then, Butter. You take it easy, mate. Same again for you, is it?'

'Yeah, might as well.'

I do a couple of the old deep breaths then I go over to sit down with the rest of them again.

Dennis is telling a story about some scaffolding collapsing. I half-listen as I look around. It's a typical Courage's house: small windows with brass window rods and lots of dark wood so there's not much light and Lenny can save on the cleaning.

Viney gets up. 'Fucking piss.' he says. I'm thinking apart from him I don't mind these blokes.

Just then Stu and O'Brien come back with the round.

Guinnesses for O'Brien, Stu and Ginge, lager for Dennis and a short for Viney that looks like vodka.

I look at each drink, tasting the flavour, pretending I'm trying to choose, the sour creamy Guinness, the harsh cold of the lager or the little poison shot of the short.

I reach into my pocket, bring three wine gums out from the packet and sneak them into my mouth, then another three. Dennis looks at me like he thinks I'm not the full quid, but no one else seems to notice.

'What's that, pork scratchings?'

'Wine gums, Den. Better than the real thing.'

He doesn't seem interested. 'Thought they was scratchings. I fuckin' love them, but I can't eat them with my false teeth.'

I glance down at his lager right next to me on the table, lovely and wicked at the same time.

The lads are talking around me but I've got too much going on in my head.

I'm doing alright, but trouble's still there as if I'm only keeping it away with the jab and any time it could slip me and get inside. Then I see Viney edging his way through a crowd at the bar and I get a tremor of panic, know what I've got to do to save meself.

I stand up. 'Alright, lads, see you Monday.'

Dennis says, 'Oi, not so fast.' He puts his hand on my arm and looks up at me, perhaps he can see he hasn't got long. 'I'm short on another job. I want you to come in tomorrow and Sunday. Ginge and Stu are coming in. The other two don't want it, lazy bastards.'

I say, 'Yeah.'

'Pick you up where you usually get the bus with

O'Brien. Seven thirty – don't be fucking late, cos I'll fuck off.'

'See you tomorrow.'

I get outside and cram in a few more wine gums before I set off. Going down the road I think of Cynthia, the first time for a couple of months, wonder about calling her, telling her I managed it, went in a boozer and came out with my wages, but I remember her voice when she was pissed the day I left her house, couldn't bear it if I rung her now, heard her drunk.

Chapter Thirteen

Another three weeks working weekends and I've got enough for a deposit on a caravan. Dennis puts me onto a bloke he knows, called Colin, who lets them out.

On the phone Colin says, 'It's a bit of a wreck,' even before I've seen it, but he doesn't want a lot of rent.

Dennis must have told him I'm alright because when I meet him to go over there he drops a big hint he could do with me as handyman at weekends if I fancy it, looking after the rest of the vans on the site, which I wouldn't mind because Dennis hasn't heard Saturday and Sunday are supposed to be early finishes.

There's another sixty or seventy vans on the park but Colin reckons they're all holidaymakers, so all my neighbours are going to be happy people and when they're not they'll be going home soon.

I can tell it's going to need a scrub by the pikey smell as he opens the door, and looking round there's nothing there except a bed and a calor gas stove, not even pillows and sheets, but he says he doesn't want any rent for another fortnight if I give him the deposit there and then.

That's alright with me because I love where it is, across the estuary from most of the town, and I'm there at just the right time of day to look out of one window and see the sun set behind the curve of the shore at the end of the long bay. If Colin wasn't there I'd sit down and swim in the warmth of the idea of settling down, right there, but I stay normal so he doesn't think he's got a nutcase on his hands.

The week before I move I'm in Asda's three nights running buying gear for the van.

Then on the Saturday morning I'm blocking up Dorothy's hallway arranging it all for when the cab comes, trying to sort out what to take first, having to hold back tears of frustration because it shouldn't be this hard to work out. The carrier bags are almost climbing all over me when Dorothy comes out of her living room to have a look, rescuing me without knowing it.

She says, 'Got a bit more than you arrived with – well done.'

I almost feel like I'm back at junior school and the posh old girl's come for prizegiving, except I don't mind because Dorothy's alright.

I say, 'Yeah, not bad is it.'

What she doesn't know is I've never had this much stuff, even a couple of times. Years ago when I've been living with a woman, it was always her things we were using.

Dorothy comes out of her room again to give me a hand when the cab turns up.

The driver's a proper porky, he might have had muscle once but now it's all fat, probably afraid of getting out in case he gets stuck.

We're both putting stuff in the boot when she says, 'Had a look about you said life had been pretty bloody to you for a long time when you first turned up. Good to see you doing better.'

I wink at her. 'Must be that home cooking of yours, Dorothy, sorted me out,' although we both know that ain't really the story.

The driver gets the hump with it but there's so much gear it takes two trips. I'm just about to get in the car the second time when Dorothy comes up to me on the pavement. 'Look, almost forgot,' she says, holding out a piece of paper. 'Expect you've got needs, want to do something about it now you've got a place of your own, only natural.' She gives me the piece of paper. 'She'll do you a session. Local girl, supposed to be good.'

I say, 'Yeah, thanks.'

'Yeah, bye.'

I've been meaning to shake her hand and go thanks and all that but instead I get in the car so fast I bump my head. I put the scrap of paper in a pocket and Fatso drives off as I'm fastening my belt. Then I take the piece of paper out again to have a look. It's in Dorothy's handwriting, and all it says is Maria and then a phone number. I look across at the driver, wonder if he's been there: the state of him I reckon he's got to have to pay for it. He's already told me about his wife running off. I might ask him but he's still letting me know he's got the zig over the job taking so long. I don't know what's wrong with him. All he's got to do is charge me extra. He must be upset all the time, at letting himself go like that.

I decide to hang onto the number just in case. Like Dorothy says, 'A man's got needs.'

I almost forget about it during the week. I'm coming back every night but even with all that gear I've bought the caravan doesn't feel like home. I'm having to go out on runs along the beach to wear myself out until I'm tired enough to flop because otherwise I'm going to go in to a pub and drown myself.

Then Friday morning someone says something and I get over it. I'm in the café before I get the bus, about five to seven as usual. I'm feeling in my pocket looking for change but all I come up with is three twenty pound notes.

'Sorry mate, no change.' I give him one of the twenties.

'That's okay. You're doin' well, money like that on a Friday morning. As long as it isn't a sub,' he laughs.

'No, mate, it's all been earned.'

As I take my tea over to a table I'm thinking he's well out of touch because these days nearly everyone gets paid Thursday, but waiting for my tea to cool down, I think about it a bit more, compare now with when the booze has left me so skint it's felt like a bad kicking. My first time in a Rowton, one of the worst, down in the big house at the Elephant, nothing to wear except shorts in December because I'd shit myself the night before and nothing but pennies for another twelve days, so far down I was thinking about rolling one of the old boys who'd got a few quid.

Pondering that I know the bloke's right: I'm doing okay.

Just then O'Brien turns up and tells me he's late and we've missed the bus.

'Want to be there today, boy, to pick up the geld.'

'Yeah, right an' all mate,' I say as I stand up, but not that bothered because we'll just make it anyway if we get the next one, and the money in my pocket's making me mellow even with a heavy day's graft to come.

I've already told Dennis I'm having the weekend out so I don't have to worry about that, and now I'm beginning to feel a bit more like it.

During the morning I think about how much I'll have once I've been weighed off and wonder about a train into Brighton on Saturday morning, but the only pictures of the place I can come up with are being in a boozer or club after the races, when I've been down there giving it large after a fight when I was still on the way up, letting Brighton help me pretend I was almost a film star, suited up, mohair probably, dark glasses for the cuts, that lucky pork pie hat and getting rid of money like I was afraid it was going to poison me.

I'm in such a dream I almost lose my footing when I'm up on top and I have to tell myself to get back to reality. I'm still thinking about the weekend though, even if I have pushed it into the background, and I almost ask Ginge or Stu if they know this Maria, because I figure in a small place like this everyone's going to know a good ride, but I decide to stay schtum in case I do try her out. I joke to myself that if she's any good I'll come onto the job Monday and sing I've just met a brass named Maria but all day I keep thinking yes I will give the number a call and then thinking no, because no one wants to pay out. If it tops up you would have felt better having one off the wrist, which is an experience I've had before.

Maybe Viney can see I'm buzzing a bit because he's more blatant than usual at trying to get me at it as we're all waiting around for Dennis and the van at the end of the day.

He's only three feet away looking me straight in the face. 'Be a man tonight, Butter. 'Ave a fuckin' drink.'

I look straight in his eyes till he has to blink, then I shove myself forwards off the back foot, making sure I stop before I touch him. He stumbles back in surprise, almost falls over. 'Don't fuck with Batman, Robin.'

The sound of the rest of them laughing is too loud for him to think of a comeback, and then Dennis arrives.

I could say to him, 'Saved by the van, cunt,' but I don't because then it would be right-handers and I'd be down the road, no job.

We get to The Blue Lion and I'm into the pub and up to the bar like a greyhound out of the trap.

I get one in and then get my kite off Dennis in double-quick time. Three or four vodkas and Viney's going to be boiling over that I've taken the piss out of him, so I want to be gone.

'See yer, lads.'

'Yeah, see yah, Butter.'

'Take it easy there.'

There's always a couple of cabs ranked up there on a Friday and ten minutes later one of them's dropping me at the camp. I could have him take me inside all the way to my caravan but I want the walk. I get out and there's a strong smell of the sea on the evening breeze. I can feel it blowing thoughts of Viney away, telling me I don't have to bother about him till Monday.

Just as I get inside the gate there's a board with a

poster on it advertising 'Friday Night's Variety Night in The Clubhouse with comedian and singer Eddie Mars.' Walking over towards the van I get a jolt of feeling sorry for myself that I can't go to the show because I'd only end up having a beer, but then I think the bloke can't be all that to be playing a place like this and I wonder if he's a could-be-bigger or a never-could-have-been.

It's isn't half five yet and there's still little chavvies running around all over the place. I pass one little crowd of them messing about in a plastic pool. They're scream-ing so loud with pleasure it hurts yer ears. I've been so down on myself I haven't even clocked how many kids there are here.

I turn the corner of one row of caravans into a shady part and there's a couple, mid-thirties, kissing, he's standing one step below her outside the caravan, both of them in jogging bottoms and vests, I can see a bit of her white bra strap hanging down onto the top her arm just above a tattoo. I'm about six feet away but they don't look as if they notice, both of them with their eyes shut kiss-ing away, their heads going round like a couple of little cement mixers.

I'm just going past when she slips her hand down the waistband of his joggers.

I'm glad I'm wearing jeans so the hard-on that gives me doesn't show. I'm like that all the way back to the van and when I get there I'm looking for that piece of paper Dorothy gave me even before I start trying to warm up the shower.

In the shower I have a J Arthur. Seeing that couple is

plenty enough to get me started.

Once I'm dry and dressed in clean clothes I'm relaxed enough not to go straight out to find a phone box and see if I can get hold of this Maria for tonight. Instead I decide to treat myself to a Ruby and phone her after that, see if she's okay for tomorrow.

Chapter Fourteen

On the phone I haven't even asked her what the score is and how long I get. It was just a 'Yes, this is Maria,' in a bit of a countrified accent.

'Someone gave me the number. What about tomorrow night?'

'About eight, if you like.' I've told her my name and where I am on the caravan park.

I know it's not a proper date but I can't remember what one of those feels like so all morning I'm giving the caravan a sweep and a mop-up going into the shower every now and then to have a look in the mirror, because I've got it running through my head that when she sees me I want her to think, 'Yeah, not bad, wouldn't mind doing him even if I didn't need the bread.'

When I've finished cleaning I lay out the new jeans and a short-sleeved white button-down from Asda's.

After that I go to the shop and have dinner in the café then come back, pick up my notebook and biro and take them and the rug and the plastic camping chair I've bought around to the shady side of the caravan, because it's a cracking summer day and I've decided to have a go at a short story instead of my usual nature writing.

I'm going to base it on a night I was in a drinker off Old Street when three brothers came in and thought they were going to kill everyone in there. I'm trying to remember who was in the club and describe the interesting ones, but my head's not really in the story because all I'm doing is waiting for tonight, half-wanting it and half-nervous, like before a fight.

I give up on the writing for a bit and lie down on the rug, try closing my eyes, but then I remember one of the blokes who was in the club and his missus, Annie, a couple of years later after he'd gone down and I can't help thinking about the way she pressed into me as I was looking for her front door key, me thinking I was just doing her a favour helping her home because she was pissed on a Sunday afternoon and her telling me, 'Come on, he's still away for another four.' But even when I copped on I didn't follow through, thought I'd end up getting shot.

Lying there with the sun and the breeze kissing my senses I could fancy playing with myself trying to imagine what she'd have been like, but even right up the far end of the site I'm afraid of someone walking past so I make the stalk go down thinking about how it's nearly always ended with bitterness whenever I've been with a bird who was more than a mystery.

I do manage a little kip in the end and then it's time for another shower and the new clothes.

By quarter to eight I'm sitting back out of view from outside keeping watch through the little window from behind the lace curtain because I don't know for certain this isn't going to be a clip and roll job, so I've got to be sure my cock doesn't take over the thinking until I know everything's kushti.

It's the same cab that brought me over from Dorothy's.

Porky in the front and a single passenger in the back. All I see is a glimpse of a head of dark hair, then I hear him stop just past where I can see them.

I get up, check I can't see anyone out of the window at the back or the one on the other side, then there's a knock on the door as I go to open it.

She ain't a beauty but she'll do, a little bit dumpy, around five foot six, dark hair almost black, shaped round her face, white face except for the cheeks, which are a bit red.

'You must be Anthony.'

'Yeah, come in.'

I make her about thirty five.

I notice a good pair of tits as she comes up the step and legs that aren't bad in see-through black. Above that it's a blue skirt above her knees and a sea-green blouse with a pattern. She ain't dressed like a jam tart.

I move back to give her space. I'm feeling shy and having trouble keeping my eyes off her tits, all at the same time

'Now, before I sit down I've got something to tell you.' When she says that I'm thinking just my luck: she's on the blob and all I'm going to get is a hand job. But she says, 'I want to make it clear, I'm not a prostitute, I'm a lady who likes to enjoy herself and gets paid for it. You don't have to wine me or dine me, but you give me eighty quid, I'm yours for the rest of the night, or shorter if you prefer.'

She hesitates and I'm watching her, a quick slyness at having talked for so long crosses her face but then it's back to brave features again. 'But you give me eighty Mr. Anthony, I'll blow your mind and if you don't mind me putting it like this, anything else you'd like blown,' she puts her head slightly to one side for a second and smiles at me with her eyes.

I've got a ton in my back pocket, because any more than that and I was going to blow it out.

I don't mind her seeing me get the ton out while I peel off the eighty, because I've hidden the rest of my dough.

I hand her the money and she gives a little hop. 'Thank you,' she says, and takes her handbag off her shoulder, unzips it, puts her wages inside, zips it up again and puts it on the table at the side in front of my telly.

She must be an expert at weighing blokes up. She looks me in the eyes and knows I'm stuck, don't know how to start, a featherweight in with a heavy, 'Maybe you'd like to sit there for a minute.'

She holds my eyes with hers as I sit down on the cushioned bench and then she reaches up under her skirt, pulls her tights off, steps out of them and her shoes and slings them, still looking me in the eyes.

My old boy doesn't know what to with itself, it's straining already.

She looks down at her bare feet then says, 'Floor's clean, isn't it,' and crosses the four foot between us.

I still don't know what to do but that doesn't matter because she puts her hand on my chest to push me back and sits down on my thighs, facing me, her legs either side of mine. Then she kisses me, the kind of kiss you're terrified you'll never get again when you're in your twenties and at it, pulling strokes that could get you put away forever.

I don't know if it's because she can feel my heart melting or my prick about to go off all on it's own but we stop kissing and she whispers, 'Has it been a long time?'

I grunt, 'Yeah.'

'Let's take it slowly then, eh.'

She reaches forward and kisses me on the side of my neck.

I'm shaking, worked it out this afternoon: haven't had a bird of any sort for nine years.

After all that time it doesn't matter how slow we take it and I shoot off five minutes later before I've even got her bra off while she's still rubbing me through my jeans. I'm thinking that eighty quid wasted and she's going to go but it tops up she wasn't having me over when she made her little speech.

She says, 'Let's see how you feel after a rest then, shall we,' although she gets the hump a bit there's only tea and coffee when she asks me if I've got any vodka. But she makes do with the lemonade she finds in the fridge, and even makes me a cheese roll.

Then we do it take a bit slowly the second time and before long I'm thinking this is more like making love than having a brass and either my memory's going or it feels more like love than most of the birds I've ever been out with.

Then all that goes out of my mind because I sense she wants it a bit fierce and then I'm having her properly whether I've paid her or not and if that's all acting she's in the wrong job and it's lucky she hasn't got a meter running because we even go a third time slow and luxurious that time, and I can hear birds starting to sing before we both fall asleep.

I'm still half-asleep when I hear her moving about.

I watch her getting dressed with my eyes half–shut, knowing if I wake up properly I'll be wanting it again but not wanting to bargain, knowing I can't odds it if she tells me my time was up when we finished last night.

She puts her handbag over her shoulder and comes over to the bed, rubs my cheek with the back of her hand. 'It's eleven o'clock, sleepy head. I'd better be going. Maybe hear from you again, then?'

I say, 'I'll ring you,' and watch as she walks over to the door, close my eyes as she shuts it behind her, half-wondering if she's got a meet but still sleepy enough to push the thought down. Instead I fall asleep picturing a probation officer I had once, only one I ever fancied, Miss Priestman, haven't thought about her legs in black tights for years.

The next time I look at the alarm clock it's one o'clock. As usual my prick's the first thing up but it's not the same without her there and I settle for five minutes of remembering last night before I get up and into the shower.

After a bit of breakfast I climb through the fence onto the dunes.

The beach is wilder this side of the estuary, more stones and seaweed than sand and the seaweed stinks a bit. The holidaymakers with kids keep mainly to the beach on the other side.

I sit down with the notebook and try to get myself back into that club I want to write about but every time I look up it feels like I've never seen so many couples over here, loving each other.

At first I'm wishing I had a mate, the kind of regular guy I could go down the pub with, tell him about this bird I've just met, but then I think any regular joe's going to think I'm a wally for liking a brass. Although I can't help imagining the taste of a beer and how it would make everything feel softer, I'm still okay because even a woman who can turn me inside out with a fuck isn't going to make me risk it.

Chapter Fifteen

I get to work the next morning and find out Christmas has moved to the beginning of July.

Viney got himself locked up at the weekend and for the moment he's staying there, remanded for a week for possession of a firearm.

Dennis is so full of it we're down the café by half eight.

'A right idiot he is,' Dennis says, 'revolver in a shoebox under his bed, hasn't even got any bullets.'

'Thought he was supposed to have given up all that silliness,' says Stu.

'Course he has,' Dennis says. 'Three years since he was hanging about with those idiots, but he's a cunt for never dumping the gun.'

Ginge says, 'He shoulda thought about that before he went round and threatened that Stevie Moon. Everyone knows he loves runnin' to Old Bill.'

'You telling me the fucking obvious, Ginge?'

'No, Dennis, just saying, like.'

When the grub comes it all goes quiet and I'm thinking it tastes extra good without having to listen to Viney give out, but sitting here talking about him is better than working, and the other three lads must think the same, because as soon as we've finished eating we're all chipping in with remarks to keep Dennis going, and it's half ten before he looks at his watch, tells us to make a move.

By now the job's moved along to the row of ware-houses alongside the Creek.

Up until now Dennis has had Viney and me on jack-hammers chopping out concrete, exposing the reinforc-ing on the loading platforms that hang out over the wa-ter all the way up the building. In the morning I carry on doing the same.

In the afternoon Dennis comes up the ladder to me.

He walks over, waving for me to stop the jack. I step back off the platform into the building and put the jack down.

'Alright, Butter?'

'Yeah, okay, Den.'

He looks as if he's trying to decide whether I'm going to rear up on him.

He takes twenty Bensons out of the pocket of the old suit jacket he always wears, flips open the top with his thumb, grey with dust against the gold packet. He's only half-facing me.

'Want one of these?'

Only the second time he's ever offered me a fag.

'No, course not. Used to be a boxer, didn't yer? Must've been a hard game, that?'

He turns closer to me.

He's after something but I ain't going to let on that I know.

'Too fond of the beer, weren't I – let meself down.'

'We all do that, son, one way or another.'

He puts a fag in his mouth, lights it and takes a drag, he breathes out then comes out with it in a rush: 'Look, sorry 'bout this, mate. Little cunt, he weren't family I'd finish him. Lucky I've got you to pull me out of it. See if you can knock it out double-quick. Worry about who's going to do the burning later, okay?'

I make it look as if I'm weighing it up, deciding whether I can go twice as fast, do Viney's work as well, because that's what he's getting at. He waits for me to say something.

I hang it out as long as I can then he's got to get it back under control. He goes to say something but I shrug, bend down for the jack, lift it over the toe board onto the platform, step over the toe board and start the jack again.

He's only a foot behind me but I can't hear him even if he shouts.

I don't look at him but I know he's looking at me trying to find a winner. I don't give him the opening, looking so hard at what I'm breaking up you'd think it was personal between me and the concrete.

He has to give up, starts walking away to go back down the ladder. I half-turn, smiling at his back. He's only trying it on – either that or it's a wind-up, but I don't think so, because with no Viney he's going to have to try twice as hard to keep me sweet. Things can only get better.

I don't stop putting my back into it after that but somehow I don't feel it as much, and suddenly the job starts to seem a lot more velvet.

Then Wednesday morning I nearly have an accident. Without bigmouth around I haven't got to keep looking over my shoulder but with no one to talk to I've got too much time to think: instead of looking where my boots are I'm thinking about whether to ring Maria. I've got one foot over the edge before I realise I'm stepping forward off the platform instead of back into the building.

Dinner time I ask Dennis if I can have someone with me, and he sends O'Brien up. He doesn't have to do much except a bit of tidying up after me but every time I stop to have a blow we talk about racing, and even though I never have a bet that's better than wondering why I'm letting last Saturday night make my gut feel liquid.

I give in anyway and ring her Wednesday night, nervous on the way to the telephone box, which almost makes me turn back and forget it because why am I feeling like this when my eighty quid's got to be as good as any other punter's.

'Yes, this is Maria. Yes, I remember you. Same time, eight o'clock this Saturday. Okay, see you.' Then she giggles. 'See you then, Mr Anthony.'

I walk back to the caravan wondering why she said, 'I remember you,' whether it's because she's had so many there's a chance she could've forgotten or maybe she thought it was a bit special too. I like the way she says 'Anthony' as well but I'm glad I've got work the next two days to stop me going mad thinking about her.

Friday evening we get our money in the Anchor as usual. I get the first one in then I cash my cheque and go over to the table where Dennis is sitting with O'Brien and Stu. Ginge is at the bar still waiting to get weighed out.

I've only gone over to say 'see you Monday,' but Dennis says, 'You alright, for the morning?'

I've forgotten to say anything during the week, so I say, 'Yeah, sure,' because even though we had that little straightener about Viney's work there's still a limit to how much I want to give him the hump.

'Sunday as well, if you want?'

'No, sorry mate. I'm on a promise, ain't I.'

'Thought you was too old for all that, dirty bastard,' he says, but he's smiling as he takes a mouthful of his lager and I'm not getting into any fights anyway.

'Making up for lost time,' I say, winking at him. 'Weren't no pleasure in Her Majesty's Pleasure, know what I mean?'

O'Brien says, 'Never know when it'll be yer last. Give her one for me.'

I'm thinking what a mellow evening I could have with the other lads without Viney about, but the drink would only end up giving me the poison about something, and I'd want to smash the place up, so I say 'See you later.'

On the way home I stop off for a curry. As I'm crunching the poppadums I'm telling myself the ping of the bubbles from the fizzy water is just as good as lager but knowing it ain't.

Saturday drags the whole day, but I get back to the caravan about half four and after that I'm busy turning into Mr Saturday Night, giving the caravan a good mopping then putting on some more new clobber from Asda and topping it off with a couple of splashes of the Old Spice I picked up on the way home from the job this morning.

My stomach gives a little kick as I open the door to her but she doesn't feel as if she minds that we stand kissing in the middle of the floor pressing against each other even before I've let her have the dough.

We say hello like that then I give her the money.

'Eighty again?'

'Girl's got to eat.' She smiles, but I'm not smiling back.

'Was looking forward to seeing you again though,' she says, and undoes the buttons on her blouse. 'These are looking forward to seeing you as well,' she says.

Not long after neither of us has got clothes on, but even after pulling myself this afternoon as a precaution I still shoot off too early.

'Let's lie here and be gentle,' she says, and puts her head on my chest.

After a couple of minutes she says, 'Want to tell me what you was doing all that time you was missing out on sex, then?'

I don't know why, but I say, 'Prison, weren't I.'

She lifts her head up a little. 'You didn't murder no one, did you, not your wife or some other girl?'

But I don't want to tell her it was mainly on account of being a drunk and a bum, so I tell her about a five I did years ago for sticking up an off licence, but making it sound as if that was my most recent sentence, and how it still feels as if I only just got out even if it was nearly three months ago.

'You ain't doin' nothing to get put away again, are you?'

'Not now. I'm working, and the wages aren't bad.'

She says, 'You workin' with Stu and Ginge, ain't you?'

She must feel me tense because she moves away, twisting round to face me. 'They don't know I come here. I'm very what that word is, you know, when you doan talk about other people.'

'Yeah, discreet.'

'Discreet, that's what I am,' she says. 'Lucky you're clever with words.'

She says, 'I'll make a cup of tea, then,' and gets out of bed, which means I enjoy seeing her naked from behind for the first time, which is enough to make me forget to worry whether Stu or Ginge might be having it as well.

The fear of it's back a bit by the time she's made us both a cup of tea and a sandwich, but as soon as we finish that she wants my prick standing up again and what she's doing to it means I can't think about anything else even if I want to, and after that it's another long night of feeling like her body and mine are all there is in the world.

I wake up about nine o'clock, afraid she's gone, but she's still next to me soundo, her dark hair fanned out on the pillow.

I look at her for a bit then try to get back to sleep, not wanting the moment to come when she's going to wake up and go. That works till about eleven, when she stops pretending she's still asleep and kisses me on the cheek.

'My turn to make the tea,' I say.

I'm just coming back towards the bed with the two mugs when she walks towards me naked.

'Got to pee. Wait for me here,' she says, which I think means she's going to tell me no more bed or eighty nicker.

I stand there like a lemon having to hear her piss and making sure I put the mugs down on the table as gently as a pair of hand grenades because otherwise I might sling one the length of the caravan in temper at having her here but not knowing how things run, then when she comes out of the khazi she gives me a cheeky smile and jumps up so I have to catch her. 'Can't get enough of you,' she says.

Afterwards I want to go back to sleep but I know I've got to ask her about Stuart and Ginge because otherwise I'll be forgetting again where my feet are when I'm over the drop too busy wondering if the two cousins are laughing at me behind my back.

'Stu's mum looked after me when I was little, she was a better mum than my mum. My mum was always pissed. Stu and Ginge was telling me about someone called Butter, used to be a boxer, great lad they think he is for a Londoner. I worked out must be you. Ginge had a feel of me when I was about thirteen. That's the only sex I've had with either of them. What do you think I am?'

She tells me that and I don't think she understands why I squeeze her so hard she can hardly breathe, and I'm not sure either but as she gets dressed she says, 'Middle of the week, you know, I'm never busy.'

I think my heart just turned over but I don't let any of that show because we're still boxing and you don't let the other guy see how you're feeling.

'Yeah, Wednesday. See you then. Be good.'

The next day Dennis drops us back at the job after the breakfast and then goes off to take his sister, Viney's Mum, to the magistrate's court.

He comes back about three. Viney's remanded over for a month.

Everyone stands around quiet for a bit when Den tells us. I guess we're all thinking about Viney and I even start feeling a bit sorry for the little nuisance because that's all he is but then Dennis mentions he doesn't look so good and he's got a black eye and I have to smile to myself that he's getting educated at last.

After that I keep on with the collar and wait for Wednesday evening.

When it comes she surprises me, sitting on the steps to my caravan when I get back from work, hour and a half earlier than I thought she'd be. I feel myself getting the arsehole with her for being early as I walk towards her but I'm trying to keep it under the surface.

She stands up and I notice how smart she is, in a red skirt with a white top and a black jacket, high heels and a new-looking handbag. She looks as if she's expecting me to kiss her but I can't get rid of the zig, don't really I want her here, all dolled up while I'm still in dirty clothes, shitted up from work.

'You're a bit early, ain't yer.' I don't mean it to come out so unfriendly but I see her wince.

'Don't matter, do it?' She tries to put on her brave look but I think she's going to cry.

She's got me all over the place. I don't want to kiss her out here in case someone sees us and wonders what the coup is but I don't want her crying either. I walk past her to the step, find the key in my jeans pocket, unlock the door. 'Better come in.'

I put the key in the bowl on the low table and turn to face her. The two of us stand there, neither looking as if we belong. She hasn't got the bottle to sit down and I'm not asking her.

Inside my chest it's the same misery as waking up, remembering I lost last night: the only difference is my face and ribs aren't mashed up. I nearly smile, thinking at least I'm not pissing blood, and the thought must play across my lips because while it lasts she looks hopeful as if things are going back to normal but I've got too much to sort out with her and I don't know where to start.

I say, 'I can't believe it's gone bad so quick.'

She looks as if she's going to fly across the space between us, but I give her a look and she rocks back on her heels.

'Shall I go, then?'

'Yeah, you better had,' I say, turning away because I can't look her in the face while I say it.

She hasn't even put her handbag down. I'm still turned away, looking at her past my shoulder. As she goes out I get a hot flash of anger that I haven't explained anything and all I want is to get rid of this feeling in my head. I step forward, turn right, then hit the bulkhead with a right hook, only I can't even get that right and I shout out because I think I've smashed my wrist.

She must have heard the bang of the punch, because she's back through the door while my gob's still open.

She looks at me as if I've gone mad. My hand hurts so much it's almost like I'm back in a fight, trying not to let the other guy see how bad it is, then the pain begins to ease off, and I realise it's only my thumb I banged.

'Hit my thumb,' I say, hoping my eyes won't water.

'Bit silly,' she says, looks me straight in the face, trying to suss me, not moving towards me.

I don't move either, because I don't know how to sort it out, don't know how to tell her I haven't got that kind of money or how to tell her I drive myself mad thinking about her with her other punters.

I take a chance, jump off the cliff. I step forward. 'Come here, put your arms round me.' But she says, 'Not while you're in those clothes. You have a shower. Go on then,' she says. 'I ain't going nowhere.' I move towards her to go to the shower, cold and dead, all the feeling gone out of me.

'Don't be too long,' she says. She puts a hand out to touch my arm as I'm level with her and then neither of us can help it, holding and kissing each other. Her hot tears start washing my cheeks and then it feels like a wall's crashed over inside me. I can't stop crying as well, first time I've cried when I've been sober in about five hundred years.

Five minutes later in between the 'there there's' and the 'we must be stoopids', we both decide we've got to sit down but even after more holding each other I still don't know what to say to her, although perhaps she realises she's got to leave me alone to have a think, because she says, 'Look at the state of us. Let me make a cup tea and you have that shower.'

Once I'm stripped off under the hot water I start to feel there's a chance I can explain things to her. I come out of the shower, dry myself off and sit down, wrapped in a towel.

She comes over with the two teas and as she sits down she says, 'Haven't you got a dressing gown?' Like this is the first time it's mattered even though up until now we've spent more time naked than dressed.

'Only had one pair of jeans for a long time, love, then I give in, started buying secondhand. After that it got really bad and I was going to the Sally Ally.' I feel stupid the moment I've said it because it's admitting I used to be a down and out, but she doesn't seem to mind.

'Both of us been through I hard times, I reckon,' she says.

I want to just enjoy sitting there feeling I'm with someone who understands me but I know there's thoughts I've got to get out.

I look her in the face. 'Look, I haven't got the kind of money you want, love. I can do eighty once a week but that's it, otherwise I won't have any left.'

'Oh' she says, 'is that it? Is that the problem you've got yourself upset about?' She carries on, 'And there I was, thinking you was going to make me my first million,' but her sarcasm doesn't make me smile.

'Look,' she says, 'I don't want you to pay every time. Why don't you just pay me eighty on a Saturday? I'll get you a few things as well. If we was married you'd be giving me that as housekeeping.'

I don't tell her I've got bills to pay as well because that would be just nasty and what she's saying is a deal, but I know I've got to tell her the rest even if I'm sitting here wanting to get hold of her and give her one till she only belongs to me.

I look down at the table as I say it. 'How many other geezers have you got that you see? I hate thinking about it – can't stop myself sometimes, wondering if some geezer's fucking you as I lie here trying to go to sleep, whether you're loving it the same way you love it with me.'

I'm still staring at the low table.

'Surprised you never asked before. Didn't know you was going to get fond of me, did you, Mr Anthony? Don't suppose it mattered long as I was a tart gave you what wanted.'

I don't say anything because I don't know if she's giving me the elbow or she's going to explain something.

'Pity you never asked before, though. I could have explained, I just do a bit of cleaning mostly, shops and that. I was between customers you could say, first time you called me, my last one finished about three months ago. His wife come home unexpected, and that was that.'

I sit back and look at her. 'You telling me the truth, about what you do for money?'

'There's one I haven't mentioned, an old boy. I clean his house, he don't touch me but he likes looking up my skirt when I'm dusting his bookshelves, gives me seventy pounds every week, right posh he is. "Get yourself some nice knickers, my girl," he says to me.'

She's smiling at me with her eyes as she tells me about him but then it's her turn to look down. I follow her eyes, see she's tearing a tissue into little bits without realising.

'I'm a good girl now,' she says. 'I done all the rough stuff when I was young, only sixteen when I had my first pimp, in Bognor Regis that was, as soon as I got away from the council. At first he used to call me his darling little spunk bucket, then it was you fucking spunk hole and then he started beating me up. Afterwards he'd be excited, make me do things.'

Her shoulders start to go and I'm along the bench with my arm round as she starts to sob.

I'm whispering, 'It's going to be okay, Maria.'

I keep my arm round her, wishing I could make her memories go away. As her shakes start to subside I unclench her hands from that tissue with my other hand and grab a new Kleenex out of the box to wipe her tears away.

When she's quiet I kiss the top of her head. As I do I cross my fingers mentally for both of us.

Chapter Sixteen

We don't have it that night and neither of us sleeps properly, even though the tears and the feelings should knock us out.

She's got an office to do at half seven the next morning, so we walk through the site together.

There's never many around that early but all the same I feel like I'm on parade. I'm glad her bus goes one way and mine goes the other, because I can't see the two of us sitting in the café having tea and toast with O'Brien.

I wave at her as she gets on the bus. By the time mine comes along two minutes later I'm missing what we could've done last night.

I grab hold of Dennis as soon as I get to the job and tell him I've got to have Saturday out.

He says, 'What, on the nest again? You cuntstruck or something?' But he only says it because he enjoys moaning.

Then it's just Thursday and Friday to get through before I spend Saturday morning wondering what we're going to do when she gets there, because the last time I was waiting for a woman to turn up at my drum on a Saturday afternoon I was about sixteen and I figured the coast would be clear because the old man would be busy doing the two-step between the pub and the bookies.

Then I stop worrying, because she turns up with two carrier bags, one of them with a dressing gown in it for me and the other with a bottle of vodka and three small lemonades.

I give the vodka bad looks but either she doesn't notice or she's pretending she doesn't because she wants me to try on the dressing gown.

I put it on but she says, 'Can't tell if fits proper when you've got your clothes on,' and after that I remember some of the things you can do together on a Saturday afternoon when you take your clothes off.

She doesn't mention the vodka and I put it in the fridge with the lemonades, hoping it won't start talking to me if she leaves it here.

In the evening she asks me if we can go for a Chinese, and it feels natural walking through the caravan site holding her hand.

The waiter brings us a pot of the green tea with the menu and she says, 'Vodka and coke, please', then looks at me. I say, 'Tea's alright with me.'

We carry on talking and then the bloke brings it over to her. I can't keep my eyes off it. 'That won't get me drunk,' she says, smiling at me as she picks it up.

'Might get me drunk watching you drink it,' I say.

'Lucky you're not driving, then,' she says and I can't help smiling because it's her.

She has three more with the grub and I go on to pineapple juices, because otherwise the Chinese tea's going to make me piss all night. I'm watching her but I can't see the vodka making a difference.

When we get outside she puts an arm around my waist and snuggles into me. 'My lover man,' she says, but I figure she'd say that anyway.

We get back to the caravan and we're both still standing up, her looking up at me holding my hands.

'Maybe it's the drink, Anthony', she says, 'but you do seem more handsome than ever.'

'Must be the pineapple juice talking, but I feel mad about yer.'

Later when I go down on her, I can taste the sweet poison of alcohol in with her natural juices and as she's coming with my tongue the way she's showed me the weekend before I'm wondering if the taste's going to turn me into a lunatic again, but AA must have got it wrong because I wake up the next morning and I'm still a normal human being.

She doesn't touch the bottle of vodka that weekend and after she's gone I put it in a stowaway space under the bench that I don't use for anything else but I get it out and put it back in the fridge for when she comes on the Wednesday.

She gets there and we kiss hello but she's not concentrating.

We break off and I tell myself to play it cool even though it's the main thing I've been thinking about for three days.

She sits down on the bench with the squashy red plastic-covered seat.

'I could do with a drink,' she says. 'You haven't drunk that vodka, have you?'

I say, 'You forgotten who I am?'

'Oh,' she says, 'I'm sorry.'

'That's alright.'

'Lost one of my jobs,' she says. 'Office is moving to Portsmouth. That's three mornings' work I had with them, all gone down the pan. Can I have that drink, Anthony?'

I get the bottle out and take the top off. 'How much you want?'

'Lots, no ice,' she says.

I pour a big one into a tumbler, add a bit of lemonade and put the glass and the bottle on the low table in front of her.

'Cheers,' she says, does it in two gulps.

She makes herself another one about the same size, and that goes in two swallows as well.

I get up to put the grill on for the steaks because I don't want to watch, and I can see it won't be her cooking tonight even though she said she would if I did the shopping.

I put the steaks under then muck about with frozen peas and test the spuds I put on before she arrived.

When I turn round half the bottle's gone already and she's got another big glassful in her hand.

'Don't like ice,' she says, and I can hear the booze in the way she says it.

I'm wondering if I throw her out whether she'll come back when she's sober.

I turn back to the grill, flip the steaks over with a fork, and give the other side a quick blast. I stand there looking at the grill but hardly seeing it.

Through the window by the back of the cooker it's still a summer evening, the sort of evening you know is out there sometimes when you're banged up, messing with you because you can't touch it.

I'm thinking about the cooking on automatic pilot, notice the steaks are getting close.

I take three times longer than I need to finding the condiments and the knives and forks and getting the plates out

'Wassa matter?'

I turn round and she's lying back on the bench, hasn't even taken her shoes off, her legs apart so I can see almost all the way up her skirt.

There's about two fingers left in the bottle.

'Wassa matter? I'm jus an ol' scrubber, Mr Anthony – you know that.'

She thinks she's giving me a smile but it looks like an illness.

I look at her, trying to keep the anger cold.

'Don't you wan' a fuck me then? Men always wan' a fuck Maria. You're nothin' special anyway.'

I can smell the steak's burning as I turn round. I flick the grill off, pull the grill pan out, both of them burnt.

I turn back to her, she looks as if she knows what's coming. I sling one of the steaks. Her position's too awkward for her to move, she catches it full in the face.

'Have some fuckin' dinner.'

I feel like throwing the pan as well, but I bung it back under the grill, turn off the flame.

She's still half-sitting half-lying, looking as if she doesn't know what's happened, the steak sitting on her bare chest just above the top of her blouse.

Through the open windows I can hear a radio playing ska. If this had been the evening it was supposed to be I might be telling her how I got into Two-Tone in prison, fell out with the other skins, all down to an anti-Nazi cell mate, Clovis, then went back to country music but didn't tell anyone because by then I'd realised they were a bunch of morons.

My temper's gone now. In the stillness I know what's going to happen before she does. I'm grabbing her by the hair with one hand and by the back of her top with the other as I hear her burp, dragging her into the khazi, shoving her head over the bowl before she spews.

When she vomits it sounds like her whole life's coming up. Three times it happens. I try not to look so she won't be embarrassed later, then she must be empty, her head still down there when she starts crying.

When the sobbing stops I bend down, kiss her on the back of her head. 'Come on, let's get you cleaned up.'

I wipe her face with a flannel to get rid of the sick but there's yellow dabs of it stuck in her dark hair and as I stick out the hand holding the flannel she can see I don't want to touch it.

'I'll wash my hair in the shower if that's alright, if you don't mind.' She says that last bit like she's full of love for me.

'Yeah, course.'

I mooch around cleaning the grill as she gets in the shower then dig out the dressing gown she bought me for when she comes out.

After that I've run out of things to do instead of

thinking, so I sit down, start trying to work it out because this could still be the end of it all.

I lean forward, elbows on my knees, feeling my shoulders ache with it, thinking I've got the shit touch with women: first Cynthia, now Maria, but that doesn't help because I want this one to stick around.

I look at the vodka bottle still sitting on the low table, about an inch and a half left in it and I'm thinking what a nice little start that would be to making me warm and relaxed instead of dry and worried, which is how a bit of me always feels even when I'm happy and how it would stop me feeling hungry for that meal that's just gone in the bin.

I reach over and pick up the vodka with one hand, remembering the pleasure of how a shorts bottle feels. I take off the screw cap with the other hand as I stand up thinking about sniffing it, playing with the idea of having a drink, but I hold the bottle away from me at arms length and out of the open window, empty it onto the grass outside.

I haven't heard her coming out of the shower but when I turn back she's stood there, her wet hair clinging to her face, the dressing gown so big on her she looks like a chrysalis turning into a butterfly.

I put the empty bottle back on the table. I nod towards the window. 'Thought I'd let the worms have a livener.'

She doesn't know whether she's allowed to smile or not so I give her a big laugh with my eyes and she comes towards me and I give her a big hug, which is enough to get me going but she steps back a couple of feet. 'Think I'll sit over there,' she says, nodding towards a fold-up chair. 'Reckon you must have things you wanna tell me.'

'Yeah, that's right.' But I still don't how to make it sound right, how to tell her she's going to have to stay away from it because either I'll end up hating her or else I'll be racing her down the shop.

I sit back down on the bench the other side of the low table from her, but I still don't know how to start.

I smile at her. 'This is worse than a meeting where no one wants to share.'

'What meetings are you talking about, then?' When she says that it helps me because realise all the stuff I've never told her but now I'm going to.

'Perhaps you haven't wondered why I don't drink.'

'I have,' she says, 'but I thought you'd tell me when you was ready.'

'Well, I'm ready now.'

I don't know how long I'm talking for but by the time I've stopped I've told her nearly everything: people calling me a prospect when I was still only twenty, what it felt like blokes wanting to buy me a beer just so they could tell people they knew me and how it started going wrong, my old man turning Judas, telling the East London Advertiser I was a deadbeat before I fought Terry Cooke, then not earning enough from boxing so I was out doing Joe 90s when I was supposed to be training and then how I really went down, Christmas in jail and Christmas outside when I wasn't any better off and all the times I thought I'd given up the booze then what happened with Iris and Sidney, only I don't tell her much about Cynthia because she doesn't have to be part of the story, and I don't know how Maria would take it.

When I finish, I look across at her. 'Babe, I've never opened up like this to anyone.' But when I say that it doesn't sound true, I don't even know how it sounds.

'That's alright – you're safe with old Maria, Anthony.' And I want to believe her but I don't know if I can or not, and she looks frightened behind that front of hers. There's such an atmosphere I keep thinking how much I want a drink to help put these feelings away.

Perhaps she knows I'm confused because she gets up and half-steps and half-slides across the width of the van towards me, then she's sitting on my lap, facing me the way she was our first time. She kisses my left temple. 'Have me now, Anthony, then you can talk some more later if you want to.'

Later we do say more but I don't tell her she can't drink because truth is I'm the one with the problem, besides I don't want it so she has a drink behind my back.

When we go quiet again I tell her how I was going up the ladder with a bucket of mortar the other day when I started singing that Johnny Cash song I Walk the Line because I was thinking of her and wanting her to be the person I earn my dough for.

Maria laughs. 'Oh, you and your country music.' But I can tell she likes the story and just before we fall asleep she says quietly, 'I'm very sorry what I done. I won't get drunk again, Anthony.'

Chapter Seventeen

I hope that's going to be the last trouble between us, but next Sunday morning we're sitting in bed while I read her the first half of the story I've started about the three brothers who wanted a shoot-up in the club.

I get to the end and she's says, 'You gotta finish that, Anthony. That's really good, that is. I wanna hear you read the end of that.'

I'm made up she likes it but to tease her I say, 'Pity you never done Borstal. You been there and learned to read and write better you could write stories yourself.'

I'm halfway through saying it when I see her looking like I've punched her in the mouth, which is when I remember her brother hung himself in Borstal, and that was when her first pimp started really stronging it to her.

Maria lets out a noise like she's been kicked in the guts, hits me in the face by accident as she throws her arms back, pushing herself off the bed, and shoots into the toilet. By the time I get her to open the door, she's cut herself, once on the arm, once on the face.

She stands there shaking, looking down at the blood starting to run across her forearm as if she doesn't know how it happened.

I grab a coshel of toilet paper, put it under the cold tap then bring her out of the toilet over to a chair.

The blood doesn't worry me even though I'm wondering about HIV but I feel like sitting down and closing my eyes till all this goes away because I don't know how to sort it out, although in the end it's alright because I get the arm to stop bleeding and it's only a nick on her moosh so she doesn't have to go to hospital.

She doesn't want any breakfast and I feel a bit too sick to eat so I dose her up with a couple of sweet teas and once her shock's worn off she says do I mind if she rings a cab and goes home early. I don't tell her I'm glad but when she goes I lie back down on the bed, go to sleep for two hours, worn out with it.

After that I'm more careful about keeping an eye on her.

It's only a small caravan so there's nowhere for her to hide, but there's a corner up one end where she sits when she's down and when I see her there I know she's going to have a face like a plateful of misery and I feel myself shrink inside because I don't know how to make it right for her. Sometimes I have to keep my anger down and one Saturday morning I don't manage, shouting at her, 'What the fuck do you want me to do,' and she runs off.

She's back twenty minutes later and I feel so bad about having a go at her I wish she'd make me pay for it, whack me on the nut with the saucepan or something, but she says, 'Don't like it when you shout at me, Anthony. It upsets me, but these things happen, you know, when you're having a relationship.' Only I don't like her calling it that because I reckon it's still a big love affair, and 'relationship' is what people call it when things start going wrong, and most of the time we're good as gold.

She comes over on a Wednesday so we've got something to look forward to midweek, and then comes back Saturday afternoon, which is when the weekend starts, because I've cut Dennis back to Saturday mornings.

Dennis doesn't mind. The firm hasn't got much lined up after the warehouses so he's been told to hang it out as long as he can.

It doesn't leave either of us skint. I'm okay with what I take for five and a half days, and Maria starts making her money up once she persuades the old boy that he'd like to watch her go up the stepladder twice a week instead of once. I don't like it but I keep my trap shut except for saying, 'You'd better stick with proper knickers. He sees those g-strings you wear round here the golden goose could have a heart attack.'

She doesn't stop having her black fits, but the way it is between us most of the time when she isn't in one of her moods I'm half-expecting her to start dropping hints about moving into the caravan and I reckon I'd say yes, but the only time it comes up she looks sad and says, 'Doan know what I'd do without my little room, thank you very much. No one ever comes there, and that's how I like it.'

I could get the hump when she says that but she's already told me it's only two years since she was living with her last pimp, a geezer called Johnny. 'Used to beat me up every Tuesday whether I done anything or not, said it was what every scrubber needed.'

She tells me that I think I wouldn't mind him turning up when he gets out so we can have a little straightener, but I don't say anything. I give her a cuddle instead, let

175

her feel my arms holding her safe.

The only worry I've got is that Viney's been remanded so long he could be out straight after the trial whether he gets a result or not, and with the contract running down Dennis might make space for him by giving me the elbow.

He still visits him once a week but he's stopped saying much about it, so I haven't got a lot to go on when it comes to trying to work out whether I've got the tin tack coming.

The one time his name comes up is when we're hanging around in the café one afternoon because it's been pouring down since about eleven, but Dennis can't make his mind up we're rained off for the day.

Dennis is on one about a screw who's been picking on Viney.

'Don't say nothing to his mum.' Dennis points his finger at Stu and Ginger. 'But the way this Grainger is persecuting him he's nearly ended up on the block twice. Can you imagine that little cunt with no one to rabbit to? He'd be straight on suicide watch.'

The way Dennis says it is funny, but I don't start to laugh till everyone else does, still the new man on the job.

'Anyway, he's sorted,' Dennis carries on. 'Guess who he's teamed up with?'

'Who's that, then?' says Stu.

'Moxy, ain't it, been moved down here to finish his sentence. He's been in Nottingham for eighteen months over that stabbing, gets out in about six weeks.'

Stu says, 'What, he's helped Viney? You tell him to be careful, Den. That Moxy never helped no one for free.'

'Yeah, I know, but he's got this Grainger off his back, straightened him out. Viney reckons it's Grainger brings in the Bob Hope Moxy's selling in there.'

Stu says, 'Still, a bad bastard, he is.'

Ginge hasn't said anything, but since Dennis mentioned this Moxy he's been looking at me. I don't think about it much – I'm busy waiting for an opening to find out what Dennis is thinking about Viney coming back on the job.

Then Stu looks at me as well. 'Got to be careful who gets close, haven't you, Butter?'

I say, 'Yeah. Favours can get you in a lot of trouble.'

'Glad you think that', Stu says. 'That Moxy's a right evil little cunt.' But instead of looking at Dennis to make his point he's still staring at me.

Dennis says, 'Course, he's back to being Jack the lad again now he's got backup. Can't stop himself being double-flash, trying to make up for shitting himself every day he was in there till Moxy turned up. First time he hasn't hung onto his mother like he wants to stop her goin' at the end of the visit.'

Ginge says, 'He better not bring Moxy down here with him when he comes out. It's a bit personal between him and us, ain't it Stu?'

Stuart says, 'Yes, it is. Me and Ginge got cause to remember him, fucking bad whoreson he is.'

Stu and Ginge are both looking at me now but I'm making out I don't notice. They've both been a bit edgy last few days. Stu told me they'd run out of grass: their usual woman just got caught, and everyone else they know is keeping their head down.

Dennis must have had enough of 'em, because he gets up and says, 'Alright, fuck it. Don't be late tomorrow.'

I don't think he mentions Viney again until the trial about a month later. That only lasts three days. Dennis isn't the best explainer in the world, but it sounds like the CPS have made a fuck-up of the case. Viney walks out on a year's suspended, but I'm keeping my job anyway, because the firm's got another contract, knocking down a college and sports centre.

Dennis says, 'Plenty for everyone, including metal money. I've had a look at it.'

'I need you there, Butter,' he says, to me. 'It's going to be out of town but he's giving me a people carrier. You get to that café you go to first thing, I'll give you and O'Brien a lift from there, start in about a fortnight when we finish up here.'

Viney comes back three days after he gets out when the moonshine they make on the estate where they all live has run out and his coming-out party finishes.

Stu and Ginge've asked me if I wanted to go. 'One of us now, Butter. You come if you like.' But I told 'em I didn't want it, said I was afraid of having a drink. I left it at that. They both know he ain't exactly Nelson Mandela.

I'm even glad when he finally turns up. The thought of him coming back has been winding me up worse than he did when he was here, because by now I really feel at home on the job, and even Dennis seems alright.

Viney gets out of the van and walks onto the job like he's just won a fight. 'Yes, I'm fuckin back, you dozy cuuunts.'

The other three are still getting out of the motor, so it's me and O'Brien he's calling a cunt, but he gets close and I put my hand out to shake his. 'Yeah, alright,' he says as he walks past ignoring my hand.

Two more days and I'm thinking about bringing sandwiches, so I don't have to listen to Al Capone down the café.

On the Friday he announces, 'Big drinks tonight. Moxy's getting out. Now we're going to show some cunts.' He's looking at me.

I make out I haven't seen the threat. It's him or the job and the way my savings are going I'm thinking about a fortnight's holiday in Spain end of September, he can think I've swallowed or he can think what he wants. My wages are building a future for Maria and me.

I say, 'I'm still off it, Viney,' as if I think he's inviting me to the drink-up, only he's too thick to know I'm playing him.

I know in advance he'll put that look on his face telling me I'm a sad cunt, but it's him who's the loser because bang-up hasn't taught him cunning or manners, and in there it's like out here except fiercer: you've got to have both.

He doesn't say anything else and I leave it as well, aggravated with myself I've let him draw me in that far, besides it's nearly the weekend and I hang onto that, although it doesn't turn out to be a classic.

When Maria turns up she's got greasy hair and I've

never seen her like that before, not even since I've stopped paying her. Her face doesn't look too good either: usually she's got a bit of a glow but now she's nearer to a deathly worn-out white instead of her normal shine.

I don't ask her what's up, though. Asking her questions when she's got troubles can make her go a bit garrity.

I figure it'll come out over the weekend, but it just gets worse instead.

By the time I make her a cup of tea she's watching the telly I bought for her. I hardly ever put it on. I like my radio and my music, comes of all the porridge I've done.

She glues herself to that for a couple of hours, not saying anything unless I say something first, then she says, 'S'pose you want to go out tonight?'

I say, 'Thought we'd decided on Wednesday we're going to the Chinese?'

She says, 'Not against the law to change our minds though, is it?'

I say, 'Yeah, sure,' although usually she loves the Chinese. One of the waiters, Mr Lee, always plays up to her: 'Ah, here comes beautiful,' as he opens the door, gives her a big bowl of prawn crackers, a large vodka on the house.

She looks me straight in the eyes and I can see she's trying to look excited, like she's really keen. 'Why doan we try the club on the site, s'posed to be good, the grub down there, and there might be an act on,' except she isn't much good at pretending, and instead of her sounding enthusiastic I can see there's something she hasn't told me, but I say, 'Yeah, okay then,' because I definitely won't be able to work anything out if we have a barney, although the way she's performing I reckon I'd be entitled to have a pop.

Sometimes I iron her clothes for going out if she brings them over in a bag but she says she's going in what she came in, which looks more like shopping down LIDL than Saturday night out, but I don't say anything about that either.

We get down there and I'm still trying to do something about the atmosphere, so I make out the fish and chips is the best I've ever had, even though the cod is breaded instead of being in a proper batter, so it's the sort of thing you can do for yourself midweek, and she leaves half her steak pie. After that I give up: it's like trying to melt an iceberg with a warm piss.

I say, 'Bit like the food down Walthamstow Dogs,' which is me being snide, because she won't know the restaurant there is rubbish.

They're still taking the plates away when the act comes on, which is some geezer telling queer jokes.

I don't know why he doesn't try some clean stuff, unless he doesn't know any, but there's loads of people with their kids there and you can feel the embarrassment.

In the end the silence gets to him and he gives up. No one claps him as he goes off.

After that it's the disco, but she says she doesn't want to dance so we walk back to the van. We're holding hands but it feels like she's five hundred miles away.

When she strips off she's wearing a pair of old knickers a bit on the grey side, so I know I'm definitely not on a promise.

I wake up in the morning remembering the day before, wishing I was still asleep.

Then I must fall back asleep for a bit and when I wake up again I know it's got to be Plan B.

I wake her up with a cup of tea. 'Got a surprise for you.'

At first she's still sleepy, and thinks I mean the cup of tea, but then she gives me a look as if to say she doesn't like surprises, but I say, 'You're goner like this one. It's a bit different.'

'Oh, alright then, Anthony.'

She isn't drowning me with encouragement but now I've got to do it anyway.

'Stay there a minute.' I lift up the top of the blanket drawer, dig about in it then bring out the coffee jar full of savings I've hidden in there.

She's sitting up by now, and I lay the jar on the duvet where it covers her lap.

She says, 'Is that real money?'

'Yeah, five hundred quid, for us to go on holiday. I'm going to take the chance my name won't come up and send off for my passport, use Dorothy's address and you got yours already. Another month or six weeks, we'll have enough to go to Spain.'

She's holding the jar in one hand, looking at it, first time her eyes have smiled all weekend.

She says, 'Did you steal that for me, Anthony, just for me?'

'No, I grafted for it. I don't go thieving anymore – told you that, haven't I.' I go, 'I told you you're the one

I do my work for.'

But she doesn't get it.

'Don't matter where it come from, does it?'

I don't know how much longer I can hold myself in. 'Look, I got a few things to do. See you Wednesday, alright.'

She's getting out of bed before I finish. 'Alright then, Anthony, seeing as you're in a bad mood.'

I go through and put the kettle on. 'Want another cup of tea?'

'No thank you. One's enough for me. I'll see you Wednesday, Anthony.'

The kettle's boiling as she goes.

Chapter Eighteen

After she goes I try to settle down to write but I keep looking at the words and thinking about her instead.

A few times I get up and walk about but that makes it worse, the fear she's slammed the door on me.

I tell myself it can't be, because something this good doesn't just finish: she's upset about something and now it's got worse because I haven't sussed out what it is, but the fear keeps coming back.

It gets to five and I give up on the story. I've hardly written anything anyway.

I bung Bruce Springsteen on the CD player, one of his later ones, not one of the big rockers. The creative writing teacher in one of the holiday camps used to rave about him, 'the poet of white working-class America.'

I didn't used to like him, didn't like the way he sings like he can't get his mouth open, then I bought a couple of his CDs and the CD player my first pay day after I moved into the caravan, started listening to the words properly, reading them off the CD cover. These days I'm really into him because even if he's a Yank he's writing about blokes like me, blokes with twisted-up lives who haven't got anything – perhaps that's the trouble tonight, he's reminding me, without her and the caravan I wouldn't have anything.

I turn him off, watch her telly instead, let the moving wallpaper take over.

I still can't think about anything else when I get to the job Monday morning.

Viney's still got his mouth open but I tune him out.

I feel the way I used to after I'd had a drink and didn't have the money for a livener: all I can think about is feeling sick.

When I feel the same way Tuesday I'm thinking I should've tried to get hold of her Monday night, seen if I could sort it out.

Walking back through the caravans after I finish, I decide I'll have my shower and then go and find her.

Once I decide that I'm in a little dream, wondering if I can find a shop with some flowers, make it right with her, love her up a bit.

I'm still half away with it when I turn the corner by the last caravan before I get to mine.

I see Colin the site owner first, realise he's standing by my caravan and my door's open. The first thing I think is what's going on, because I've never been behind with his money, then I notice the side window nearest me smashed then the further one broken as well.

I come up to where he's standing, see the door's come away from the top hinge.

'Evening, Tony.' His voice is calm but his face is pulled tight with anger.

I say, 'Kids?' But I half-know the right answer already.

'Kids, you fucking idiot?' he half-shouts, bits of spit flying out. 'That fucking ride of yours. Family down there saw it all, her and some bloke who threatened 'em, said he'd pour petrol over their kids.'

I go to step up into the caravan. 'I want you off this site. Get your things. You've got ten minutes before I call the law.'

I think I nod at him, in too much shock to say anything, then I turn my back on him, go into the caravan.

They must have wanted it to look like kids. There's my CD player and the telly both lying smashed up on the ground and beyond them there's some of my shirts someone's cut up.

The top of the blanket drawer is hanging off. I know the story before I find the empty coffee jar.

The bed's half-pulled out and wrecked. When I walk up to the other end there's smashed crockery, bits off the cooker and sugar on the floor which the ants have found already. The power shower's pulled off the wall and just outside it on the floor someone's had a shit I nearly step in.

I look out of the door. Colin's not there for me to explain this isn't down to me, don't think I could convince him anyway.

I pick up the extra-size carrier I bought the other day, one of those with a zip in the top, red-and-white pattern on the outside.

The duvet's wet so I just pick up jeans, t-shirts, pants and socks.

Half-hidden by some wreckage under the bed I see my notebook, and flicking through it none of the pages are missing, like that's the one thing she's letting me keep, because they've even scratched the CDs and thrown my personals about so they're not worth bothering with.

I put the notebook in the bag and then I walk out of

the broken dream.

I don't know if Colin's gone for the law or not, but I climb out through the fence like a thief, take a low profile round the site till I get to the road, cross the bridge over the river into town.

I don't even know where I'm going, but I need to move away, go somewhere I can think, because I know I'm not right, cold instead of raging, needing a cure.

The nearest busy looking one is a Wetherspoon's, lots of after-work punters, for me to disappear amongst. The first pint warms me up a bit. I don't rush it, enjoy the feeling of things starting to work again, starting to feel the anger, feeling it but controlling it. It's got to be Johnny: he must be out and come back on the scene.

I take a gamble the second pint won't slow me down too much. I'm thinking about Viney's gob and the looks I've been getting from Stu and Ginge like they've all been expecting something to happen. It's got to be the same bloke: Viney's mate Moxy and her pimp Johnny, both back on the out – too much of a coincidence not to be. She told me Johnny was local, explained that's what upset her, letting herself get tied up with someone she knew was a nutter.

She's going to be upset now. I have a little scotch to sharpen up, should have gone on that instead of the beer in case I feel bloated.

I have a piss, really strain to get it all out so it doesn't distract me when I'm in action.

I've only been to her place once, but a town this size you can't get lost if you try.

I get to the street before Maria's and leave my bag just inside someone's gate by their dustbin.

I walk along thinking I should have a plan, but sometimes you've just got to hope.

There's three shops and then her row of houses. I'm looking in the window of the shop that sells tellies. Channel Four News comes on on two of them. Her flat's in the first house. I can see the front gate and the four steps up to the front door from where I'm standing.

I can't remember if she's first or second floor. I'll have to take a chance on the bell. If I stand there ringing long enough her or Johnny are going to come out. What else they going to do, call the Old Bill?

If they're not there I'll wait. It looks like there could be an alley halfway down the other side of the road beside a prefab garage. I might have to have a piss down there soon anyway, but another two minutes and I get lucky.

Looks like a number one skinhead haircut, goes about six foot, red Harrington jacket.

He pulls the street door, gives it another hard one to make sure its closed, tries it twice to make sure it's shut.

I walk towards the house, still don't know if it's him. I time it so I can go after him if he goes the other way along the street but he comes down the steps and turns towards me, ambling along still celebrating being out, looking up at the sky.

Almost level with me, I say, 'Alright, Moxy,' and he notices me for the first time, looks like he's trying to remember me when I hit him on the cheek bone with a right cross.

'What the…' But he's still half in the land of the free, left his instincts in gaol, doesn't come at me right. I get in a jab and a right, then another left. Everything leaves his face except hatred but he's still no good, rushes in trying to headbutt me, only catches my right shoulder. I go left and my right catches him off-balance, puts him on the pavement.

He kicks out, catches an ankle and a knee, the little bit of pain sets me off trying to kick him to death while he tries to crawl back to the steps, but he's got his arms over his head, I'm only catching his arse and ribs.

I haven't got him clean yet when I hear something: there's two middle-aged blokes have come down their front paths on the other side of the road, shouting at me from behind their gates.

I lean down and grab the collar of his jacket with one hand, turn him over so he's facing me, kick him in the crotch in case he's got anything left, smile at him to let him know I see he's pissed himself.

'Where's my fuckin' money?'

He shakes his head and I punch his mouth three times.

'Bookie's,' he chokes.

'The police are on their way,' one of the neighbours is shouting. I look up, see Maria at the top of the steps. I jump over Moxy and up two stairs, her two black eyes look like rainclouds as she starts crying.

I say, 'Got my money?'

She shakes her head, nods down at him.

I say, 'Bookie's?'

She nods again, looks like a little girl in trouble with teacher.

He's standing holding onto the railings. I get almost past him, give him an elbow in the side of the neck and he goes down again, but I'm finished, jogging away in case one of the old boys have called the police.

I go into the next street and pick up my bag, keep moving.

It's the sort of place you're through it in ten minutes. By the time I stop to work out what next, I'm almost where the job is. I head towards the beach, striding along the path that runs behind it, too lively to sit down.

I'm pumped, like I've been heavy sparring. There's one more pub before the path finishes and the beach and old railway land take over.

I have three before I notice I'm getting looks, realise I'm still in working clothes, and one hand's a bit bloody, must be where I caught Moxy's teeth.

I think I've seen two of the geezers in the café.

I put my hand in my pocket: lucky I put my money in there when I went out this morning instead of leaving it in the caravan, otherwise she'd have had that as well.

He charges me fifteen for a bottle of scotch and another two quid for three packets of crisps.

There's a half-built breezeblock hut, four walls but no roof, sits on the scrubby grass between the back of the beach and where the disused railway lines run out. I've passed it when I've been down here on a run.

I'm going to drink the Scotch in there, think about the morning, how to do Viney without getting the others involved.

Chapter Nineteen

I wake up just after six, the same time I usually do in the caravan, and at first I think I'm still there, starting a normal day, then pieces of yesterday start coming back to give me a kicking.

I sit up thinking I might have pissed myself, because sometimes that's happened when I can't remember going to sleep and I put a hand down to feel my jeans. I haven't but I can feel the damp from the sea creeping into my clothes and I know I've got to move before it does me serious harm.

I catch one of my feet in a hoop of reinforcing metal pulling myself up but I manage to stand and pick up the bag. As I straighten up I cough and feel a pain on my right side. Moxy must've caught me without me realising.

The empty scotch bottle's on the ground with no stopper in it. Maybe I finished it or maybe it fell over and ran out. I'm not going to miss it, thinking about it I catch the taste of whisky in my stomach, feel like puking.

I go out through the hole the builders left for the doorway and turn away from the sea, the way I'm nearly falling over walking through the sand and the grass I could still be drunk.

I get to the main road. It's six forty five. It's a bit of luck my watch is still working.

If I go left and right I'm at the job in about ten

minutes. I don't even know if I can do it but if I don't go there I'm walking away from something.

I think about a cup of tea but I'm sick. I could get a can out of the shop for a livener but that might make me pissed again.

My stomach feels bad as I walk, like I might get caught short.

I'm about five minutes away from the job when Dennis comes past in the van, pulls over to my side of the road and parks thirty yards in front.

I'm alongside a tennis court. The plastic mesh of the fence isn't much to hang onto if there's a crowd of them trying to jump me, but Dennis gets out of the van by himself, starts walking towards me. I'm watching him and the back door of the van expecting to see Viney shoot out, backed up by Stu and Ginge, all locals together, but it looks like it's Dennis on his own.

I stop and let him come to me, both of us eyeballing the other as he gets close. I'm looking for that tiny move, wondering if he can see the drink's bashed me up already.

He fronts up three foot away, letting me know he's not scared if it comes to it although he can't hide the bit of nerves in his voice. 'Told the others to get the bus. They're coming in later. Viney's not coming in today. Ginge and Stu gave him a slap last night on account of what his mate did to the bird. She's like family to the two of 'em – expect you knew that already. I've said I'll let it go.'

His eyes are still on mine. 'Wouldn't be able to let it go if you done him though, Butter. That would be different, know what I mean?

I nod. I don't know if he wants to persuade or threaten me but he doesn't need to. Viney's got his bit of pain even if it didn't come from me. I'm finished.

Dennis puts his hand in his back pocket. I try not to let him see I'm ready if he's got a tool, but he says, 'All the wages you got coming,' as he hands me a pay packet.

'Thanks.'

Dennis says, 'That's it, mate. Want a lift out of town?'

'Yeah, alright. Think I'll stay on the coast. Drop us up towards Brighton? I'll see how I get on somewhere bigger like that.'

PART FOUR

Chapter Twenty

A week later I'm down to sixty quid. A half-decent B and B in Hove, the posh bit of Brighton, does about half my wages and the rest goes on a little holiday routine I work out for myself, a few pints lunchtime then a kip and a bit of tasty grub somewhere, after that a few more pints, finishing off on the top shelf.

Some nights it almost works and I don't miss Maria so much I want to scream her name.

The last morning I'm there I wait for the old boy who runs the place to go out for his baccy and newspaper, then I'm away in the other direction. I don't exactly hang about as I head up the hill towards Brighton itself, but I'm only knocking him for one night so I don't feel the cold breath either.

I reckon the cheaper places are going to be well away from the sea although even then a lot of them want more than I've got, but up a slope from Brighton railway station I get in at Annie's Coffee House and Pension.

She doesn't tell me whether she's Annie or it's her gaff but all she wants is twenty five a night. She's a short Irishwoman, probably in her early sixties, dyed blonde hair and too thin. As she stands talking she keeps pressing her elbows into her sides as if she's trying to stop herself feeling the cold even though it's a sunny day.

I've had a can of Stella as I've walked along and she gives me a look that lets me know she can smell it when

I ask her if she's got a room, but she doesn't say anything.

Her thin hands look as if they should have chilblains. I see she's wearing a wedding ring, so maybe her old man's a boozer and she's used to it.

I've been in cells bigger than the room she shows me but I'm glad to be in somewhere and I manage to smile to myself. I've never had flowery wallpaper in the other place.

On the way up to the room she's told me she's a widow, sounding as if she's still got the hump he got away so quick.

I have a kip as soon as she leaves me alone then I go out to find the cheapest tea I can.

I have pie and chips in a kebab shop. My stomach feels heavy as soon as I get outside but I'm glad it's weighing me down because otherwise I could fall over and roll on the pavement pulled down by gravity and blown about like a paper bag, no strength or balance to keep me fighting.

There isn't even a telly in the room so I make do with a couple of Readers Digests that are lying around. They ain't really worth reading but I try the old doing your time trick of trying to memorise the articles and that keeps me going till it's late enough to hope the two Stellas I bought when I went out for tea are going to do the trick and I'll sleep.

I wake up the next morning and my brain starts to feel alive again even if I haven't got a drink to muffle the heartache.

The place must be bigger than I thought. The dining

room's full of holidaymakers wondering why I don't give 'em a nice seaside smile back.

After she's brought me my breakfast she comes back, makes me an offer I can't refuse.

'I'm needin' help in the kitchen and around the place. I don't pay much but yer room'll be free.'

I don't even think about it. 'Yeah, okay.'

'Well, it'll suit us both,' she says. 'Yer didn't look as if you had anything when you got here and yer only gave me one night's rent. That's a man who's skint, I said to myself. You might as well start as soon as you've eaten, get the washing up done.'

I finish the breakfast, which isn't all that, then I find the narrow kitchen.

The dishes and plates are piled up waiting, must be her dog-end squashed in a yellow smear of egg, can't be anyone else's: there's three no-smoking signs in the dining room.

I'm just finishing loading the washing up machine when she comes back. 'It's not working – a good reason for having you in here. You can do it by hand.'

I go, 'Yeah, okay,' start wondering how hard it's going to be earning my wages.

She has a fag watching me get started in the sink. She doesn't say anything but there are lots of noises as if I'm doing things wrong.

There were fourteen covers at breakfast so that takes me a while by hand and I'm thinking that could be it till she comes back as I'm finishing. 'You can get started with the hoover, then the windows need cleaning.'

She goes away again till I'm just finishing putting the plates away, then it's a bollocking for putting them in the wrong place. I begin to think this is what she does instead of sex.

After the hoovering and the ground floor windows she says there'll be a few other things tomorrow but that's it for the day.

I go back up to my room and realise I haven't asked her when she'll weigh me out.

I lie down on the bed hoping it could be daily, because I don't know how long it's going to take her nagging to pick all the meat off me, leave me like a skeleton.

I think about going to look for something else straight away, but I can see that'll mean finding a lay down somewhere else, so I'm better swallowing till I've got some money.

The last thing I think before I drift off for a little kip is I can't believe it's only ten days since I was doing a man's job, swinging a fourteen-pound hammer and holding a Kango against a wall.

I go out for a tea again that night, only this time I don't bring any Stellas back.

I count my money as I get undressed: thirty quid and a bit of smash.

The next morning she bangs on the door about half five and she's got me starting breakfasts half an hour later.

After that it's about the same as yesterday only with a bit more cleaning thrown in and a few more of her tricks, telling me stuff goes in the green box then telling me to unpack it, I should've put it in the blue one.

She tells me I'm finished about three fifteen. I can start on the garden tomorrow. She must have seen me turn up and thought it was Bob-a-Job week.

She hasn't said anything about wages, either.

This time I don't bother with a sleep because her firing into me all day has changed my mind and I'm not going to hang about, only first of all I've got to work out what National Insurance number I'm going to give to anywhere new. Somewhere as big and organised as Brighton I won't find anything decent that's cash in hand, but the number I used in Ealing has been blown since I lumped the copper, and even my real number might come up three cherries on a computer somewhere.

I think about it for a bit but when I can't come up with a way out I decide I'll have to risk it anyway because if I don't go while I've still got money for a night's kip somewhere else I'll be stuck with her on the slave galley for a lot longer.

I still don't fancy making the move though, the few days drinking has left me a bit para, and even with the sun coming through the window I know I'm going to get outside and feel the chill of capture.

I let myself have another ten minutes self pity, then I have to roll off the bed because otherwise I'll lie there the rest of the day about as happy as a lump of fat in a prison stew and at least outside there'll be a bit of heat in the air even if I feel like I've got to keep looking over my shoulder.

I've decided trying to sign on is definitely too iffy,

but I think I remember the job centre's on the main drag from the station to the sea front, and I figure I'll go that way anyway, see if I come to any employment agencies on the way.

I'm just past the station when I come to Alfie's Jobs with a poster in the window: 'Labourers and fork lift drivers immediate start in factory, from £11 per hr.'

It's probably only a con and all they've got is khazi cleaner on minimum wage, but I have a look through the other window anyway.

There's one punter in there with his back to me who looks like a biker, with greasy black hair, dirty denims and a pair of welders boots.

The guy facing him from behind the counter has got a mouth too full of shiny white teeth, like God give him some spares, but he thinks they look terrific with the tan he's picked up on his holidays.

His face decides me to play it a bit cagey. I can tell by looking he thinks the world's a great place and I'm about two slip-ups away from turning into an old dosser, so I write the number down from the poster and walk back fifty yards to the station to find a phone.

His voice is about as cheerful as I thought it would be.

'Hi there. This is Alfie's Job. How may I help you?'

'Yeah, I'm ringing about the labourers wanted, saw the poster in your window.'

'Oh yeah. It's towards Shoreham, can be an early start. Okay with you?'

I say, 'Yeah, sure.'

'Want you to go out there today. Can you get there

by six?'

I say yes again and he gives me the address of an industrial estate between Fishwick and Shoreham, tells me what bus I need.

He says, 'Let us know how you get on. See you,' and puts the phone down.

I'm walking away before I realise he hasn't even asked me my name but maybe they only take people through Alfie's, and he'll collect his bit anyway.

The bus stop isn't far and on the ride out I'm wondering how soon they want people to start, and hoping it isn't nights starting tonight, because of the complications that'll make with her.

He's warned me the nearest bus stop's about half a mile away. I get off and walk along a service road without a pavement through an open gate.

I'm nearly looking for cover as an Old Bill car goes by on a bluey, but not even Alfie's Jobs knows who I am, so the hurry up isn't for me, even when a van full of 'em comes past a minute later.

I go on another three or four hundred yards and see a sign with an arrow pointing to Tuttles, which is where I'm looking for.

Another right turn and I get an idea of what it's all about: both sides of the road are fenced off, with razor wire on top, warehouses behind the fence and three rows of coppers either side of the road fifty yards ahead in front of a gate. Then by the gate there's a guy holding a placard. As I get nearer I see he's wearing a red armband. I can't read the writing on the armband but I get the picture: it's a strike.

I'm near enough for one of the Old Bill to wave me through as if he's on traffic duty, but I don't fancy walking past him and all of his mates, even if I can't hear what the guy with the placard's shouting.

I turn round and almost bump into a scruffy geezer with a long grey beard and hair that needs cutting, with a rucksack on his back.

He's so close I just miss treading on his feet as I look at his face, trying to work out if he's plainclothes but he looks away, which tells me he ain't, because they hardly ever do that, too easy to give the hard stare when you've got an army backing you up.

He says, 'Sorry mate – too deep in my thoughts.'

'That's alright, mate. You on strike?'

'Just here to support them.'

He slides his rucksack off, puts it on the ground, bends down and starts to undo it.

'I'm a Christian, see. Bert there, he's the last left on the picket line. Calls himself a Marxist, doesn't like me coming up here because I'm a Christian but I said to him you're like Christ left on the cross, Bert – where's your other mates? Most of them have pissed off, bottle trouble. Still won't have one of my sandwiches but I come up anyway, make sure they don't give him too much of a whack if they nick him.'

He says, 'What you doing up here mate? Going in, are you?'

I don't give him my life story, but I tell him about the bed and breakfast and ringing the agency.

He says, 'But you're not going in.'

I tell him what he wants to hear. 'Can't, mate, my uncles were in the docks, transport and general,' although the truth is I just don't want any ag.

'Good lad,' he says. 'The likes of Bert there won't admit it, perhaps he doesn't even know it, but I reckon he's doing God's work. It's Keith, by the way.'

'Anthony.'

He gets a thermos out of his rucksack and a silver foil parcel then straightens up. 'Cheese and pickle,' he says. 'Want one? Sorry it's not five loaves and three fishes, but He's the only one does miracles.'

He's standing beside me now and I look across at him. There's a ghost of a smile around his eyes. I figure the first time he said that about the loaves it was a joke and now it's just something he says, but I'm thinking fair play, because none of the Christians I've met ever had a laugh at themselves like that.

Most of the ones inside were nonces, looking for an early ticket, and before that it was the priest who used to come into the children's home: he was a nonce who hadn't been caught.

All the same I'm half expecting him to try to get his teeth into the back of my neck the way a lot of 'em do and then won't let go till you almost have to give 'em one so they get the message to shove off.

So maybe I'm showing out to him or maybe I'm testing him to see how he shapes up when I go, 'The first shall be last and the last shall be first. You really believe that's going to happen?'

Now it's his turn to look surprised. 'You used to believe, did you, son?'

I say, 'No, nowhere near. Only thing I could find to read doing my last porridge, all those words helped the old nut keep going instead of turning into prison mush.'

He says, 'Maybe you were looking for God though, just didn't clock it yerself.'

I say, 'Well I never found Him,' getting the hump with myself because any moment now those teeth are going to be in me, but he surprises me again.

'You wouldn't have found Him anyway, mate. He knows when you've got Him in your heart even if you're blind to it. You don't find the saviour – He finds you. All those Yanks.' I can see by his face he's enjoying himself: he sticks his hands up in the air and waves himself backwards and forwards, puts on a Yank accent: 'I have found Jesus, oh yeah, and yee-ha,' he shouts, then goes back into his English voice. 'Nothing but bigheads, mate, that's who they are. Jesus decides who's special, not us.'

He's blowing my mind and I'm wondering what he'll come out with next.

'Anyway, I'd best go and talk to Bert. Here, have this leaflet. There's twelve of us altogether, live in two different houses but we share our grub three evenings a week with anyone who wants to come along. It's all on that, tells you where the community centre is. Come along. Only rules are be sober and no praying unless you want to. See you, son.'

His rucksack's on his back again and he sets off for the picket.

Once he's gone there's nothing keeping me so I go back the way I came, take the bus into town.

I'm still trying to work out if he's mad when I get off, a bit of me wishing I had him for company as I walk through crowds of people all dressed like students, even the ones who are too old. If I told 'em I was a forty four year old has-been, pearl diving for a living, they wouldn't know what I was on about.

I've just turned into a pedestrian precinct full of trendy cafes when I hear someone shouting, 'Oi,' behind me.

Chapter Twenty One

I don't take any notice till the third or fourth time. 'Oi, Jacko – fucking you.'

I turn around and recognise him straight away: Vic Mawson, used to be Commonwealth cruiserweight champion, could've been European champ but the promoters used his Aussie passport as an excuse, stopped him getting the right fights or maybe he just crossed the wrong geezer.

He's parked on the corner where a road crosses the top of the pedestrian precinct. He must've just got out of the car, as he's standing on the road by the open driver's door.

Half of me wants to do one, pretend it's not me, but I raise a hand in the air, walk towards him, feeling a bit sick thinking he's going to ask me where I've been.

'How goes it, champ?' he shouts when I'm about fifteen yards away, sounding like I used to be his best mate, except I haven't forgotten him in the old days always looking for an opening so he'd come out the top guy.

Getting closer I see we've both filled out but his beer gut's a lot worse, especially after the labouring I've been doing down the road, so to someone else he might look rougher than me but only if they didn't notice his clothes and the motor, gunmetal grey hard top two-seater with a black roof: the only thing missing is the kind of blonde who gives everyone the horn.

I come right up to him and his smile lights up his face, which was another trick he was always pulling.

'Here, fucking hell, come here.' He puts his arms out and we give each other a hug, his gut pressing mine. I'm wondering if mine feels as soft.

As we move back from the hug I can feel his arms have still got their strength and the jacket's feels like five hundred quid's worth.

'Fuckin' good to see ya,' he says.

We stand there as if we're trying to see what's happened in the last twenty years, only I'm trying to look open and shut everything down at the same time.

I glance at the car.

'Porsche,' he says, 'only thing gets my old woman excited these days. 'Come on, get in. I'll take you for a drink.'

He's still got three inches on me so I'm looking up at him. 'I don't drink no more, Vic, had to pack it in.' I'm feeling like a kid as I say it.

He comes straight back. ''Bout fuckin' time. Only thing that fucked you up. Could've ended up something special otherwise. Still got to come down the pub mate, drink an orange juice, a lot of the lads live down here these days. Come on – yer old pals'll want to see you, 'stead of wondering what happened. I thought you must've emigrated. Would've heard if you was doing a long one.'

I say, 'Yeah, okay,' because the other choice is sitting in, looking at the flowery wallpaper and feeling sorry for myself for being skint, wondering what it would have been like after all these years.

'Jump in round the other side, mate.'

I don't even bother trying to work out last time I was in a good motor but sitting in the leather seat the excitement's still there, everything looking and feeling like money and the promise of frightening yourself with how fast it goes.

After we set off he doesn't say anything for about five minutes but I know he's got to ask, so I say, 'Yeah, just got here. Staying in bed and breakfast. Ain't too bad, thought I might find something down this way,' hoping it sounds like I could be a bit of a wheel, but probably sounding like I'm about eighteen again.

He says, 'Plenty of money around, but they like to hang onto it, especially the four-be-twos. Still I've turned over a few of the long noses. No reason you shouldn't either, mate.'

That's it for a bit and I don't say anything either, letting myself enjoy the ride even if I don't know how long I can fake it with no money, knowing I'll feel sicker and sicker the closer it gets to me having to buy everyone a beer.

About ten minutes later he says, 'Not far now, just down the road here. One bar's full of poufs, but the boys use the other bar, somewhere to get away from listening to her old bollocks, know what I mean?'

We stop outside a double-fronted pub, blue and white wash on the rendering. with The Dunrobin Arms, in a crescent of gold lettering on its blacked-out windows.

I get out and look up at the boozer.

He comes round onto the pavement. 'This side's the woofers. We're down the alley, back bar.'

I go to step towards the alley, but he puts his hand on my arm and leans over so his mouth's by my ear. 'Si Booth, remember him – used to play for West Ham?'

I nod without looking at him. He's standing too close: if I turned towards him we'd be kissing.

I catch another smell of his aftershave, glance at his face. It looks like a piece of expensive meat on a restaurant plate.

'Yeah – left back, weren't he.'

'It's mine,' he says. 'Si's the straight man, keeps it respectable, got another one he fronts as well, full of snobs, out in the countryside.'

He's gripping my forearm too tight, like talking about his money is making him excited.

'I'm doing well, mate,' he says, and reaches inside a trouser pocket with his other hand, brings it out and presses two or three notes against my hand so I have to grasp them.

'Don't like buying in my own pub – encourages the ponces. You get 'em in for me.'

As he lets go of my forearm, he's half-behind me. 'Let's go and have a drink, son,' he says, and pats my arse.

We walk down the side passage to the pub and I look down at the three twenties he's given me before I slip them in my pocket.

We go through an ordinary pub door but then we're in darkness and I think he's taken me in the wrong bar for a laugh: I'm half-expecting to have my arse felt,

I only realise we're in an air lock when he bangs on the side wall. 'It's alright – it's Vic.' A door opens in front of us and there's a muscle guy with a dyed black crew cut, showing out in a white t-shirt and black trousers. He nods at me and says, 'Hello, Vic.'

Vic puts his arm round my shoulders. 'This is an old friend of mine, Darren, Anthony Jacko, useful fighter in his time. Shake hands.'

We both put a hand out. Darren says, 'Mm, pleasure to meet you,' as if he's half-camp.

Vic says, 'Darren keeps us safe. If they don't want to fight him he threatens to fuck 'em. Always gets rid of trouble, don't it.'

Darren says, 'Never known it to fail, Vic.' I can't tell if he thinks it's funny or not.

Vic moves me forward then takes his arm off my shoulder. Something makes me look sideways. I see Vic's other hand feel Darren's crotch. I don't know if it's for sex or a threat.

The first drinkers I see are three big young lads standing at the short end of the counter where it joins the end of the bar.

I look at them and then back at Vic, raising my eyebrows, asking him if I should know them. 'Tearaways,' he says, and leans closer. 'Talented boys, steal anything or hurt anyone you ask 'em to, long as you got the mooli. They're celebrating – just nicked a Ferrari for an Arab.'

'Over here,' he says, and I see a bunch of four middle-aged geezers down the other end of the bar, three white, one black.

The first one I recognise is little Timmy Wolf, all five foot three of him, a lot bigger than he used to be, wouldn't make flyweight anymore but healthy-looking. Then I realise the guy in a dark suit and collar and tie looking like he's come from a funeral must be Frankie Weston, almost how I remember him, that sallow face and juicy lips. By now they've noticed me and Vic. They look up and I realise the black guy is Andy Strathdee, with Donny Campbell standing next to him, except someone's put tramlines down both sides of Donny's face since I saw him last and his hair's completely white.

They don't look as if they remember me at all but then Andy goes, 'What – my days – Jacko!'

Then I'm in amongst 'em shaking hands and there's hands on shoulders and hands pulling me and squeezing me. 'Fuckin' unbelievable.' 'What happened.' 'Heard you was dead.' But I notice Timmy's looking straight ahead in the other direction like he's concentrating on a telly, except I've already seen the telly's on a shelf at the back of the bar, not where Timmy's looking.

Then Frankie shouts, 'Oi. Timmy.' and stretches out a hand onto his shoulder to turn him round so he joins the group of us. 'Jesus, Timmy,' Frank says, and I notice Frank's got a gap where he used to have two sticking out bottom teeth. 'It's Jacko.'

Frank's got a laugh in his voice. 'You remember Bomber Jackson, doncha?'

Timmy looks up at me and says, 'Just kidding yer, kid,' and he laughs as we shake hands, but he doesn't look as if he remembers at all, then he says, 'You want a photograph?'

I say, 'No photos, please,' joking like I'm a film star but I see the disappointment on that baby face of his. 'Do it later, Timmy alright?'

Timmy nods his head and starts to smile again.

'Leave that man alone,' Donny says, laughing at him. 'Come over here, Timmy, let's all sit down,' and reaches out for Timmy's hand, brings him over to a chair.

I'm still standing, thinking about getting a round in, but Vic goes to the young guy behind the bar, 'Same as usual for them,' then 'What do you want?' to me.

I ask for a pint of lemonade and lime, but no one else seems to notice I want a soft drink even when Vic has to shout it to the barman above the noise of the excitement at me coming back from the dead.

I sit down with the rest of them, glad I can put off telling 'em I don't drink.

Vic brings the drinks over but doesn't sit down. 'See ya bit later, you boys. Look after Jacko.'

The rest of us lift our glasses. 'Good luck.'

Frankie asks straight off, 'Ever watch the fights, Jacko?'

I say, 'Only on telly sometimes, Frank. What about you?'

Frankie says, 'Yeah I do, still go sometimes and all, but it makes yer itchy, don't it.'

Donny says, 'You want any videos, I knock 'em out cheap. Don't tell that cunt Frank Warren though. He's worse than Old Bill, fuck 'im and 'is copyright.' We all laugh, but Donny and Frank give each other a look like something's gone down.

Frankie says, 'Yeah, but it's upsetting, cos you're

always going to think…'

Andy says, 'He's going to tell yer all about Charlie Magri now, ain't you, mate. Charlie done a big interview, reckon he never slept for six years after he give it up. I've heard this too many times now, mate. You don't like watchin', then leave it alone.'

Andy turns to me. 'You remember my boy Wayne, me an 'im got a butchers shop now. Only hooks I see are metal hangin' up the meat.'

Frankie says, 'Jacko don't want to hear about your shop. He wants to talk about boxing. That's what brought us together. Seen that kid from Manchester? He's going to be good, he is.'

Andy says, 'Going to be good, then he be past it, just like the rest of us.'

Donny says, 'Haven't seen him yet, but I hear the Mancs all like him, could make a few quid for himself, build up a bit of a following.'

Andy says, 'Anyway, I doan trust your judgement, Frankie. You go to me he's a knockout merchant so I had a little bet, but it goes the whole way.'

Frankie says, 'Proves my point. You do still follow it. What else you going to do, read up on pork chops?'

Andy says, 'Should do, mate. Lucky I got Wayne to mind the shop when I fancy a little drink.'

Frankie says, 'Yeah, like every day you fancy a little drink, yer drunken cunt.'

'Yeah but we're all drunken cunts, mate.'

Frankie says, 'You keep proving my point, don't yer.' Here's to boxing – that's why we're here.'

We all lift our glasses except for Timmy, who's looking down at his empty short glass as if he thinks it'll fill up by itself if he keeps looking.

Donny says, 'My round. Timmy's empty. He's more of a drunken little cunt than the rest of us, aren't you, Timmy?'

Timmy smiles at him. 'You want a photo?' Then he looks down. 'I haven't forgotten.'

Frankie says, 'Quick, alright then. I'll take yer,' and gets up with a hand on Timmy's forearm, helping him out of his seat.

Frankie looks over to me. 'That's what he says when he needs a piss.'

'Come on – quick,' Frankie says, almost pushing Timmy over as he stumbles against his chair.

'Take it fuckin' easy, my son.' Timmy beams at us as Frankie pushes him past the table. 'We'll get there quick enough.'

Andy says, 'You want that for yourself, every time you need a piss? Almost enough for me to go to church, say a little prayer I ain't focked up like that.'

Donny's standing. 'What is it, Jacko?'

'Pint of lemonade, dash of lime.'

'Good for you, son.'

He goes to the bar. 'Same again.'

Andy says, 'You watch him good, a magician. Don't pay for nothing in here, got a long slate he has.'

I say, 'What, Vic don't mind?'

Andy says, 'Showin his gratitude, innit. Donnie took the cuttin', should've been Vic with the messed-up face.

Frankie the same, took a three sentence for Vic, done eighteen months, happened about five years ago. You been gone a long time, mate, was all over the same thing gone bad, that's what I heard.'

I say, 'Two of them always were a little team, remember them from juniors, Frankie looking after his cousin just moved down from Scotland, till Donnie lost his accent and started talking like the rest of us. But never known 'em lie down for no one.'

'Times change, mate, an' money change people quicker than that.'

Donnie brings over Andy's and mine then goes back for the rest.

Andy says, 'Don't tell no one I open my fockin mouth, mate. It's all heavy business.'

'Course not.'

I still want to know more about it, but then Donnie comes back so it'll have to wait.

Donnie says, 'You always on the dry, son?'

'Yeah, usually. Best as I can,' I say.

'Might be something for you if you keep it together, mate, know what I mean?'

I say, 'Yeah, I could do with that, Don.'

We see Frankie and Timmy coming back. Donnie says, 'Don't want to end up like him, do you, too much scotching it, that is, nothing to do with boxing. Headaches, that's all you get from boxing. Everything else is not looking after yourself.'

They get back to the table and I see Timmy's got a little stain at the crotch of his trousers. As Frankie helps him sit down, Timmy beams up at him. 'Didn't forget, did I.'

'No, you did not, mate,' Frankie says, winking at me. 'Just don't take a photo, know what I mean Timmy?' But Timmy's already got his drink halfway to his mouth.

Donnie says, 'What happened to your boy, the one you fancy?'

Andy says, 'He's still good, breaking all the rules, mate, could be sign of greatness.'

'Yeah, what about the rule of keeping his balance?' Frankie says, 'You look at the way he throws his left.'

'Anyone for videos, get 'em all here, study the fights,' says Donny, as if he's knocking them out on a market stall, and we all laugh, although the two cousins have that look again.

After that the Somali kid stays as the topic and I start to realise he's a regular subject and they're like actors in a play coming out with the same lines every show so it doesn't matter I don't know enough about him to say anything.

I don't even mind being sober when they're drunk and trying to talk over each other all the time because it's more than twenty years since I was with a bunch of fighters and I've taken a lot of kickings since.

Vic keeps coming over buying drinks, enjoying being the big man, but tonight I don't even mind that and when the conversation gets a bit boring and goes on to racing I have a few quick looks around taking in who's here and trying to see if there's anyone else familiar without looking as if I'm having a nose.

Over by the Ferrari boys I notice a little shortarse in a nice-looking black leather bomber jacket. He's looking at the bar not talking to anyone. His bony white face is stretched tight and the way he's chewing gum he looks like a hungry kid looking through a butcher's window. He's got a tree trunk on either side, minding him. Gangsters must be getting smaller.

There's a few faces that could be people I used to know but none of them definite enough for me to get up and say hello.

By nine o'clock the place is packed, still nearly all blokes, but there's a dark-haired woman sitting at the bar on a stool, about thirty five or six I reckon, bit young for me, but the longer I'm there the harder it is to stop looking at her legs, even if she's definitely with the guy who hasn't moved from beside her all night.

Then I have to shut all that down because suddenly I'm thinking about that first time with Maria, and the pain hits like the first few seconds when you realise you've been plunged but still can't believe it.

I look back at the chaps, concentrating a hundred percent on what they're saying, hoping nothing shows as I listen to the talk, which has moved on to some rough old bird who reckons she's a professional boxer, wants to take the Board to court.

Once the pain's died down I can't help myself, I go back to looking at the mystery. I even start having thoughts about her noticing me and me taking her off the other geezer, because a woman with a bit of class could be just what I need to start getting over Maria.

I still haven't bought a drink, but after all the pints of lemonade I've got to have a piss so I've got to go to the khazi first, only the place is so crowded I can't help bumping against a few bodies on the way. I catch Darren, the boy on the door, looking.

When I get there it's cramped, and I have trouble aiming.

By the time I get back, Donny's getting another one on the magic slate.

I pass right by the bird and the bloke's looking the other way talking, so I slow down, let her see me enjoy her legs although the look she gives me doesn't mean anything.

I'm still thinking about her when I nearly fall over trying to sit down. The way my arse hits the seat of the chair and my arm knocks over an empty glass, tells me for definite, someone's done the dirty and slipped me drinks, most likely vodkas, because I wouldn't taste 'em in the pints of lemonade and lime.

I'm trying to work out who but all I can remember is Donnie got one early, then I think Vic's done the rest but it doesn't have to be him, could've been Andy sitting next to me, pouring in glasses of short while I've been looking up talking to Vic or busy rabbiting to the others.

I look across the table at Frankie and Timmy, but it's like they're in a film and they can't see me.

Inside I feel like crying but there's anger underneath at being Judas'd. I look sideways at Andy next to me: he's reading a Sporting Life on the table, not saying anything but maybe he knows I need bringing back to the real world. He pushes his paper away, looks up at me and puts a strong arm round my shoulders, holding me, squeezing the breath out of me, leaning his face close to mine. 'What happened, mate? Shoulda been you, bruv, the old European champion, for definite.'

I breathe in when his arm relaxes and look at him, feeling my head flop about a bit as I try to see in his eyes whether it was him. I don't mean to but I say, 'Tell me it wasn't you, mate.'

'You want me to say it weren't me, it definitely wasn't me, Jacko. You're the boss, mate, the return of the prodigal.'

I want to kiss him but I ain't drunk enough so I half-turn away.

Then Donnie comes back with mine and Andy's, gives me a lemonade – or that's what it looks like – and a scotch for Andy.

I look at my drink and back to Donnie but there's nothing happening on his face. Across the table Frankie looks like he's trying to explain something to Timmy, which I could've told him is a waste of time unless it's about drink.

Donnie turns back for the other drinks on the bar, everything's slowed down, I could be swimming in glue with no thoughts coming except just then Andy stands up so quick I think he's going to rear up on me but he swallows the scotch in one and leans down. 'Time for me to make a move. Few people in here I don't like at all.'

I look up into his face. 'Don't go, mate – fuck 'em. Where are they?' But Andy says, 'You come, see me an the boy in the shop sometime. Here, take this. Buy yourself a nice Porterhouse steak, give me back my money.' He laughs and puts a note in my hand.

I look down at a fifty pound sheet.

'Doan argue – put it in your pocket.'

I say, 'I'm too gone to argue.'

He says, 'Yeah I know, mate. That was Vic, thinking he was having a laugh – big joke, I tell him, but he thinks he's the number one gangster now, innit.'

I half-stand up and we hug each other, then Andy turns and I sit down, watching him go.

I'm looking at his back as he moves through the crowd. First time I've noticed the patch of white in the hair on the back of his head. I see him nod to a couple of people, including another black guy I haven't noticed before, then suddenly it's like all the noise of the place has stopped, and everyone hears the word 'nigger.' Andy looks like he's jumping and aiming a head butt at the same time but instead of landing he's falling through the bodies.

I'm off my chair and pulling two blokes out of the way before the noise of the club starts again and I hear Vic shouting, 'Fuckin' leave it, Jacko – you don't know...' then someone tries grabbing the top of my head from the right but my hand's free that side, and I uppercut him before I realise it's Vic, but I'm going forward again, pulling more out of the way trying to get to Andy, who I can see through legs and feet kicking him on the ground.

I'm getting caught by a few, top of the head, back of the neck, shoulders, back, think one was a glass on the nut but I keep going, pull the last one in front of me out of the way, go to pull Andy up, but he's up himself, the chewing gum boy goes hard into his side, but Andy's moving so I end up level with the white-faced kid, and I hit him as smoothly as a good hard punch should feel. I even have time to see the badge pinned to his leather: I've seen it before, screws wearing it in nick, like the sign for electric, Cunt 18 or something, they call themselves, then I knock him back with a short right, carry on towards him as his hand goes into his jacket but he hasn't got the room or the time before I give him the same punch again, feeling like I've done his nose this time. He falls back, where one of his minders catches him. I can't see the other gorilla but I'm turning left to the door, see Andy go through it with the other black guy – don't know where he came from – catch a big one in the ribs on the right but manage not to stop. Someone aims a chair leg at me but he misses as I go left, then it's punches, kicks and weapons bouncing off my back, arse and legs till I'm through the first door into the air lock, then the second and I'm in the alley. Darren's standing there, looking like he's trying to make his mind up about the cosh he's holding. He's still deciding when I nut his face, push him out of the way. I pull over a dustbin, grabbing the lid, can't see Andy, he must be away. I'm at the end of the alley before there's any noise behind. Someone shouts, 'Get the fuckin' niggers and their mate,' but nobody's following through and coming towards me.

Then a security light comes on and I see Vic come out. 'Cunt – Jackson, you're a dead man walking.' But he knows he's too far. I take a swing with the dustbin lid, hit a side mirror on the Porsche full force and smash the glass then I'm on my toes, away from Kemptown heading for the centre.

I keep going till I'm the other side of the main drag that goes down to the pier, on the way I'm zig-zagging, up one hill, down the next, trying not to get caught in a cul-de-sac, looking back to where I've come but no one's following.

I look at my watch and think it must have stopped because it's only got ten o'clock but I look through the door of a pub, see a clock saying the same.

I check myself in a shop window but I can only feel where I got caught, can't see blood or bruises yet so I go back to the pub which is one little bar, bit like Bethnal Green in the old days except down here you don't have to be family.

Stella on draught, two pints of that and the excitement of the fight dies down. I remember I haven't eaten so I head on, trying not to feel sick, realise I'm not walking straight but don't think I've done anything for the punters in the boozer to remember me, case anyone's searching.

I find a chip shop ten minutes later, get most of the hot pie in my gob, dropping chips as I go along, not bothering.

I'm struggling with the street door when I suddenly have to stop because I've remembered what it was I'd forgotten about Donnie and Frank, a time when I was down nearly all the way, fighting a Gypsy in a field for eighty quid, hearing afterwards the two of them had backed the other guy.

The door lets me in and I crash about through the dining room and up the stairs. I'm too gone to do the alarm clock but it doesn't matter: the old bitch always wakes me up.

Last thing I remember is realising I don't know where Andy's shop is.

Chapter Twenty Two

The first thing I feel is the sting of cold wetness, half-think I've pissed the bed then I realise it was on my face. 'Get out, yer dirty bastard, fecking out.' I get my eyes open at the next splash, see her holding a saucepan then I catch another lot of water and realise I'm still in my clothes, the same time as I try to start thinking.

As she moves forward I'm caught in the bedclothes, can't get out the way if she's goes to whack me with the saucepan but she stops, staring down at me like the wicked witch. 'Five minutes before I call the police. Yer pissed over me furniture in the dining room. I can't feed people in there, yer dirty bastard.'

I see her thinking about the saucepan and my face again but she turns to the door instead. I'm out of bed before she's gone though it. I don't even know what's happened but I've got to go. I'm throwing things into my carrier bag and then running down the stairs, hoping I ain't going to meet Old Bill coming up.

I run through the dining room which is a mess, see a wet looking corn flakes packet on one table, so I could've pissed there.

She's in the hallway on the phone. 'Fuckin' 'ell,' I think and then I'm through the door, starting to run one way, then remember the club last night, realise I've got to double back.

I'm running for five minutes then I have to slow down

because I think I might puke, then I have to stop moving because I feel it lower down and have to clench my arse.

I stand there taking deep breaths to relax my stomach but still holding onto the muscles in my arse in case.

I'm in a street of houses with no passages between them, nowhere to drop my strides if I can't help having a shit, but the breathing starts to work and a couple of minutes later it feels safe to get going again.

I'm walking down the hill and across towards Hove, but not like I've got a plan or anything: all I know is my nerves are getting worse every minute and I must be a cunt for having had a drink. There's a lot I can't remember before the tear-up in the club and I can't come up with anything for after the fight except for having it away and being in the little boozer, but everything feels like I'm bang in trouble.

I can see the sea by the time I start thinking about going back up the hill to the station and, with what I'm holding, catching a train away from all this ag, but I've got the horrors like a load of snakes closing in on me, and the only cure for that is a livener and a kip, which I've got to have before I do anything else.

I stay on a long road with shops in it, looking for somewhere that'll sell me a couple of beers before my head explodes, tensing up the twice an Old Bill car goes past.

It turns into a long walk, nearly seven o'clock before I find a Stella merchant.

I put the beers in my bag and make it down to the seafront as quick as I can without setting my guts off although they seem to have settled down: perhaps it'll be tomorrow I have to go a lot.

I reckon I'm safest on the beach, hidden from any police driving by, and I sit on the sand and pebbles with my back to the sea wall next to where there's some catamarans parked on the beach, then I open a can and get the first of that bubbly metallic-tasting medicine down my gob.

I feel better after the first can and I've got a bit of a buzz on so I don't mess about with leaving the second one for later. By the time I've drunk that it's all over and I've got to kip so I crawl along a few yards, feeling the wetness of the beach through my jeans like a kid enjoying a new sensation, then I slide under the middle of the nearest catamaran, feeling clever for realising it'll be a shelter in case it rains.

Just before I close my eyes I feel in my pocket for how much I've got left and then I remember Andy's fifty pound note which I must have got done for in the little pub or the chip shop, given change for a ten or a twenty instead.

I wake up afraid of the boat six inches above my face, have to keep the claustrophobia down as I wriggle out on my back, don't lose the panic until I'm sitting back where I was, leaning against the prom wall.

My watch says one o'clock, dinnertime, but I'm not hungry, just thirsty. I haven't got the horrors back but as I sit there, my tongue trying to lick the dryness out of my mouth, I can feel the old depression getting ready to come down the track and run me over, only this time

I haven't got the strength for a plan to beat it, so I do the other thing instead.

I get up and walk to a shop for some more beers, then go back to the beach because it's past the end of the summer holidays by now, so even this time of day things look quiet enough for me to be left alone as long as I don't flash the cans.

As I sit there I don't know if the warmth is the weather or the beer but there's enough of it for me not to worry about anything. The only thing is where to piss. I don't know where the toilets are, and I don't want to walk around with a bag full of beer.

I can't stand up to do it because I'll be seen from the promenade so I kneel up trying to aim under the nearest catamaran, only hit my jeans a couple of times.

Mainly I look at the sea, not thinking about anything, enjoying the drink but then I remember an idea I had, for something to write.

I reach down into my bag to get my notebook, thinking about making notes for the story which is going to be about Billy Wells, imagining he never got the job for Rank Films swinging the hammer at the gong, but worked on the demo like me instead, dreaming he was in the movies every time he swung a fourteen pound hammer.

I've got the idea clear in my head but I look at the notebook and I'm too far gone to write.

I've just slung the book back in the bag when I hear 'Oi' from above me. I look up and see this blonde bird with her hair in dreadlocks leaning over the railings.

'You got any beer?'

I look round but I can't see any little team waiting to jump me. 'Yeah, come down, but you got to leave me some.'

I watch her as she goes along the ten yards to the steps down to the beach. In that combat jacket and blue jeans she looks like some sort of punk rocker.

As she comes towards me I see the sides of her head are shaved but it doesn't stop me catching those blue eyes and I'm already in love with her arse.

As she sits down I clock the safety boots every tough girl should have and notice where the toecaps have worn through the black so you can see the steels underneath.

She's got ear rings through one of her eyebrows and a piercing on her cheek with a scab where it goes into the skin.

There's three blobs of blue on her neck, like she's started off on a homemade tattoo but never got it going properly.

'On yer jack?'

'Yeah,' she says, 'the others have gone into Brighton. Give us one, then,' she says.

'Help yourself.'

I'm too drunk to hide that I'm looking at her, trying to work out what she's got inside that combat jacket, but with a beer on the go she doesn't seem bothered.

She gets a baccy tin out of a jacket pocket, starts making a roll-up from the dog ends inside.

Once she lights up she starts talking out of the side of her mouth like it's something kushti, only for me, but she's looking straight ahead out to sea and the wind takes her words away.

I'm thinking: tasty bird, but hard to talk to.

I'm getting some of it and it sounds like there's a tribe of 'em. She says they were travelling round in a bus but they kept getting stopped by the Old Bill so her and some of them came down this way, and now there's about twenty five of them and they've squatted a big house with allotments out the back. Some of them sleep in the house, some in the allotment huts.

'When we've got some money me and Spider are going to get a flat.'

I don't tell her around here it's a dream, because Brighton's such a pound-note job, she'll find out for herself and I don't want her to get the hump. I'm enjoying the company even if it's a let-down hearing her mention a bloke.

She says, 'You sleeping down here?'

'Just got slung out of my bed and breakfast.'

'Why?'

'Pissed on the cornflakes in the dining room.'

'Yeah, right piss-taker you are.' But she's smiling.

I go, 'No, it's true.'

'Fuckin' 'ell, wait till I tell Spider,' which I don't like, but then she says, 'You dirty cunt,' and I can't help laughing as well.

When we stop I say, 'How many beers left?'

'Five,' she says.

'Fuckin 'ell – I'm not drinking enough.'

We both think that's funny as well, and I say, 'Have

another one.'

We both open a new one and she says, 'My name's Dove. Love doves, used to be my favourites.'

'Yeah, I've heard of them.'

'Didn't say you hadn't,' she says, a bit snide.

I want to keep in the game so I say, 'Still do 'em?'

'Give 'em up. Couldn't do the comedowns, kept hearing a voice, even when no one was there, telling me I'm a piece of shit.' The way she says it she could be talking about someone she hardly knows, like something got punched out of her.

'Just do a bit of speed now, keeps me going.'

I say, 'How old are you?'

'Got to tell me your name first,' she says.

I say, 'Bomber.'

'What you done, a lot of...' and I think she's going to say speed so I say, 'Used to be a boxer, only did bombers to help make the weight. Bent doctor used to give my trainer the scrip. Wasn't why they called me Bomber, though – that was because of my big right.'

I think she'll be impressed but her face doesn't move. Maybe I'm too drunk, haven't explained it properly.

She's looking out to sea again.

'Thirty one.'

I don't bother lying because I figure Spider'll turn up and that'll be it, so there's no point showing out.

'Forty four.'

'What's it like when you get knocked out?'

'Always feel stupid you let it happen. Worse thing is the headaches afterwards, sometimes you can get them without being knocked out.'

She turns to me and smiles, almost like she's had the headaches herself. 'Drink your beer,' she says.

I say, 'Help yourself,' nodding at the bag, but I can't help leaning back to rest on my elbows to let her know I mean me as well if she wants to forget about Spider.

I see her give my crotch a quick look but I can't think of a follow-up.

I decide to find out the chances anyway, except I try not let it sound in my voice.

I say 'Spider your bloke, then?'

She looks at me with a laugh on her face like she knows the score, the sort of bird who always does, just doesn't know it about herself, a bit like Cynthia except in a different way.

'Best mate, met him when we was both in the adolescent unit. Been mates ever since, see him every day unless one of us is locked up. Last time it was me, bottled some geezer at a gig, tried to have a go at Spider.'

She's through her can already, crushes it in the middle with her hand. I'm only halfway through mine.

I say, 'Have another one.' I'm too drunk to worry about running out, besides I've still got money, but I haven't told her that yet.

She opens another can. 'Love drinking,' she says. 'Spider'll bring some back with him, long as he doesn't get caught. Bit stupid as a shoplifter.' She says, 'You got a bird in Brighton?'

I say, 'No, it's been a long time,' because I don't want to tell her about Maria, and all this beer's helping me believe she's dead history.

She says, 'Come up the allotments if you want.'

'Yeah, I'd like that.'

She puts her hand in the pocket of her jacket, brings out a wrap, leans close to me so we're hiding it from view as she undoes it.

'Pink champagne,' she says. 'Poor man's coke.'

I say, 'Well, I'm a poor man,' flirting with her because the money I've got left isn't going to last anyway, so I might as well have a bit of an adventure, instead of worrying.

The way she's leaning forward, her head's touching mine and there's no smell of perfume but I can feel her softness.

We're both looking down at the powder.

'Bit rough for your nose,' she says. 'Dab it on your finger, put it on yer gums.'

We do what's in the wrap and she says, 'Won't be long. Let's wait.'

I don't feel the rush, to be honest, and I'm beginning to think the stuff's no good, but I do notice I start telling her about some of my porridge, starting with Borstal, and I'm just coming up to a bit of bird I did in nineteen ninety three when she says something about me 'going like a good 'un, and she must have said, 'Let's go,' because she stands up and I do too.

'Bit out of control,' I think, except then I don't know if I've said it or just thought it or whether I'm talking about her or about me but either it doesn't matter or she never heard me, although once we get away from the beach out of the wind I can hear her a lot better, only I still can't really follow because she's on one about all these bands she goes to see that I've never heard of, but there always seems to be a fight at the end, and quite often she reckons she's had to bottle someone to keep 'em off her or off Spider.

I'm listening to her but trying to get my head together at the same time, trying to work out if it's never with her and Spider or maybe sometimes when they're both well out of it. I ought to ask her but instead I stop by the shelter on the seafront and say, 'Yeah, but what about the opposite of violence,' and she says, 'What?'

I say, 'What about softness and sex?'

Then we're standing there kissing, and I feel the tight crotch of her jeans pushing up against mine.

We're stuck to each other for about five minutes, then we both have to have a breather and I say, 'How far is it?'

'Only ten minutes.'

We cross the main road along the seafront and try running but I start to feel sick and have to stop.

'Not too far now,' she says.

I say 'Want a beer? I got some money.'

'Yeah, lovely.'

I go into an off licence and I want to tell him about nearly having sex in the street but he's giving me weird looks and shouting out the price of the twelve cans I've picked up, and she's giving it 'Fuck him, don't pay him,' but I do pay him and about ten minutes later we've got to the house where they hang out.

We go in through a front window and I fancy the

mattress on the floor but she says. 'Leave half the beer here. This Spider's space.'

Then she leads me through the side into the garage and pulls me onto a manky old back seat of a car that's got stuffing sticking out of it.

As she's pulling my jeans open I'm thinking too late to hide the money I've got left.

Chapter Twenty Three

I've never done sulph before and no one tells me I won't come for about fifteen hours. I do get tired and start wishing I could manage a kip but until that happens I've never had anything like it. The way it makes both of us talk dirty is something I've never known a bird like, not even Maria, but this one loves it.

We do break off sometimes. We have to stop every now and then when one of the tribe wants to walk through to get to the huts at the back, and once Spider comes in and starts rabbiting to her, pretending he hasn't seen me, even after she's told him it was me who bought the beer that was waiting when he arrived back empty-handed because a security guard grabbed hold of him in Sainsbury's.

It's during one of the rests when it's just me and her talking that she tells me about some aggravation: the property company who own the house have sent two guys round to tell 'em its the easy way or the hard way.

She says, 'Bastards they were. One of them was Australian, I could tell by his accent – he should fucking go back where he comes from. He stood by his flash car most of the time, let his little mate do the talking. The little cunt was the real frightening one, nasty with it, kept saying, "Bet you sleep with niggers, don't yer, filth like you love a nigger's cock," kept on about it, and I don't even like black men. I don't want to fight him though.'

I don't tell her I think I already have and once I start touching her again she wants it in double-quick time so I don't have to think about it either.

Ten o'clock the next morning the powder finally lets me have half a sleep and she must have had enough as well. 'Stay here if you want. I'm going to see Spider.'

I say, 'Yeah, I will.'

I wouldn't call it a proper kip though, and I keep waking up till about three o'clock when I give up, tell myself I've got to call it a new day.

She's in with Spider, the two of them sitting on the mattress with their backs to the wall and a sleeping bag on top of them.

They look a bit like two kids except they're both holding a can. 'Want a drink?' she says.

I shake my head and say, 'Feel sick,' which I do, although I can still feel the stuff running around and if it was just me and her I'd want it again.

I say, 'Going for a walk,' because she's going to come out with more gear if she's got any and the way I feel, any more and my heart could blow up.

She pushes the sleeping bag down and feels in her jeans pocket till she comes out with a bottle of pills. 'Here, Valium.'

She holds out the bottle. 'Four or five, make you feel better,' she says.

I hold one hand out and she shakes five into my palm. 'Come back later,' she says. 'Have a party.'

'Yeah, thanks.' I don't reckon either of us thinks I will. Spider's busy picking his nose. I don't know what he thinks.

I go to the window without any glass that we came in through and pull myself up till I can get one leg over. I'm doing the splits over the sill with my carrier in one hand when I see a white van cruise past at about fifteen miles an hour, slow enough to see the driver look at the house then straight at me: it's Vic's little mate, the one I clumped in the club.

I go to duck back into the house but there's no point. I don't know my way around in there so I get the other leg through and drop down.

I walk along the overgrown path to where there used to be a gate, grabbing a loose brick from the top of the garden wall as a weapon, but when I get to the street he's gone and I chuck it back into the weeds.

I sort of work out where I am and walk towards the sea, because at least it's a free lie–down, and the way my nerves are jumping out of my head I've got to have a proper rest before I can save myself.

I've got a raving thirst so I go into a shop for a big bottle of tonic water, which is when I realise I've only got a tenner, so either I misreckoned last night or Dove helped herself to some of my dough, except I can't work out when she had the chance.

Five minutes later I'm back next to the catamarans where I met her.

I swallow a mouthful of tonic with two of her Valium, then it's another twenty minutes of paranoia before they kick in enough for me to crawl under a catamaran again and turn my mind off when I shut my eyes.

I don't even know what strength they are but I wake up two hours later feeling a lot more velvet and wanting something to eat which isn't something I've thought about for twenty four hours, only I know revenge could come down on me any moment if I get caught in the open on my own so I've got to find shelter, with a bit of luck somewhere I can keep my head down until I've got enough for the fare out of town.

I look in my bag and it's still there in the pages of the notebook, the leaflet from Keith, the Christian bloke, and tonight's one of the nights they do the handout.

I've got a rough idea looking at the map on the back of the leaflet and I reckon I can do it in about half an hour, which'll be alright if I get going straight away, because other wise I'll miss them.

Even with the Valium I'm still jumpy, noticing Brighton's full of white vans, but I keep going through the tiredness and even come up with a bit more of a plan, which is to get hold of enough money to get out of Brighton and keep going till I fetch up somewhere small and peaceful where I can pick up work, on the other coast maybe, Yarmouth or Cromer, although soon it's going to be the wrong time of the year for the seaside.

When I find the community centre it's like an old church hall, black corrugated sheets for the walls with a pitch and tar roof.

Keith's standing on the pavement outside.

'Hello there,' he says as I get close.

I say, 'You give me leaflet when I met you where that bloke was on strike.'

We're close to and the way he looks at my face I'm thinking I made a mistake, and all I'm going to get is pity but he sniffs and says, 'How long since you had a drink Anthony?' remembering my name.

'Last night. Haven't had a chance to brush my teeth.'

'You'd better come in, then.'

I walk past him and he goes, 'Hey, how's the Bible reading?' but he must see how bad I am. 'Don't worry – get some grub down you.'

There's a red-headed bloke standing just inside the door. 'Evening,' he says, 'I'm Michael. Sit down and someone will bring you your meal,' which nearly knocks me over because you always have to queue up in home-less places.

There's only fifteen or so eating their dinner, and enough room for me to sit on my own at a green baize card table.

There's a woman and a teenage girl could be mother and daughter, behind the counter. The girl brings over a jug of water and a glass, 'Would you like some bread with it?

I don't make her more than sixteen, and she doesn't sound like she's loved up with us dossers, but she isn't frightened either.

'Yeah, please, love.'

She's wearing a jumper and her jeans are tucked into a pair of Wellingtons. With her hair tied back she looks like she should be riding a pony.

She comes back with two slices of big thick bread and a bowl.

'Ta, love.'

'Enjoy,' she says.

The soup's got a rich brown colour, which is how it tastes, and there's plenty of carrots and celery in it with a few bits of pasta and butter beans.

Most of the blokes look like ordinary geezers, just a bit down on their luck like me, but there's two real old-fashioned paraffins, look like they've come straight out of Itchy Park, Aldgate East, big beards and both of them with raincoats bulging over the rest of their clothes.

One of them goes up to the counter to get seconds and I wait till I think his smell must have died down then I do the same.

The middle-aged woman serves me. I say, 'Yeah, lovely grub.'

She smiles as she gives me my bowl back. 'We're all blessed in Jesus,' she says.

I nod at her, say 'Thanks,' and go back to my table, wondering how much they strong it to you, but mostly if they'll sort me out with a bed.

I'm finishing my soup when Keith comes into the hall and closes the door, which makes me think this could be like the Sally Ann in the old days: no one leaves till you've said a few prayers and heard about God.

Keith gets himself a bowl and comes over to me. 'Alright if I sit with you?'

'Yeah, sure.'

He nods down at his grub. 'The proprietor eats on the premises,' he smiles.

'Always a good sign,' I say. 'Lovely drop of soup.'

'Always good but always different, that's what we aim for. We make it from whatever the local wholesale market can spare us. My brother's got connections there. He's not a Christian, Tommy, but he's a good man.'

I nod to let him know I've heard him. Something about the way he says it makes me wonder what you have to do before he thinks you're a good man.

He starts his soup and I carry on with my seconds, but I keep looking up at him trying to work out an opening.

His face is an old man's, the neck beginning to go slack, overgrown eyebrows and hairs coming out of the top of his nose and ears that he hasn't bothered to trim, but when he looks up at me there's plenty of power in the eyes.

'Something up?'

I haven't got a fanny to give him so I take a chance on the truth. 'I'm in shit street, Keith. Haven't got nowhere to sleep and could have a lot of ag.'

The way I say it I sound like a cunt with no defences.

He looks down at the rest of his soup like he's in love with it but puts his spoon back in the bowl and pushes it aside.

He says, 'St Luke, do you know it? "For I was hungry and you gave me meat. I was in prison and ye came unto me."'

I shake my head, too tired to play. The soup lifted me up for a bit but now I'm sinking again.

'Okay, I'll explain. Those chaps on that table over there,' pointing to where Michael the redhead is sitting with four others, 'they live in one of our houses. We're a charity, a Christian charity. We describe it by saying we're living in Jesus. Mabel and Sally behind the counter, they live separately from us but they're part of the community too. There's another house, but they're away on a Christian holiday at the moment.'

He carries on, 'No one turns up, and we just let them in. Sorry, mate.'

He says that and I think I'm blown out, but he nods towards me. 'Sometimes though, Anthony, we have people turn up desperate, and later they decide to join us and live in Jesus too.'

I sit there looking at him, thinking he's blackmailing me into to saying I love Jesus, but I must've got that wrong because then he says, 'My brother, Tommy, his farm's up near the Downs, he's got an outhouse, puts people up sometimes, want me to ring him?'

I feel so much of a ghost I can't help croaking like a schnorrer, 'Yeah, please.'

He stands up, taking a mobile out of his pocket.

'Won't be a minute,' he says.

I sit there trying to make myself strong enough to walk out proud if it's a knockback, but three minutes later I haven't got to. 'That bag all you got? I'll drive you up there.'

I'm expecting more Bible stuff on the way to his brother's and knowing I've got a lie-down has got me feeling a bit more up to it, but instead he asks me what's been occurring, and I tell him most if it, explaining I used to be a fighter, then about Vic and the tear-up in the club and even a bit about Maria breaking my heart, but I just say I spent a night in a squat. I don't say anything about the sulph or fucking Dove because I don't know how that would lie with him and now the drink and drugs have left me I don't know how it lies with me, either.

He doesn't say much, just nods or says, 'Yes,' or 'Carry on.'

After about three quarters of an hour we turn off the road onto a track heading up towards the Downs.

The track takes us into a farmyard and we stop outside the farmhouse. I'm looking round but the only lights I can see are from inside the house so after dark it looks like it could be a safe house.

A door opens as we're getting out of the van and Keith says, 'Alright, Tom,' to the guy standing in the doorway with the light behind him.

Put them together and you can see the likeness. Tommy's the younger, bigger version: strong labourer's shoulders, plenty of dark hair streaked grey, both of them with that pointy jaw sticking out, except Tommy's isn't covered with a beard.

'You Keith's mate, are you?' And he puts out a hand that's rough from hard work like mine, only his is about twice the size, and I hope he isn't going to break any bones in that grip.

'I'll show you the outhouse.'

He looks back into the doorway, shouts, 'Here, Sheba,' and a German Shepherd shoots out from the darkness behind him and sticks her head forward, sniffing my crotch. I'm standing very still – never met a farm dog that liked strangers.

'Alright, Sheba,' he says. She barks once, then runs ahead.

I'm expecting something like a hut but we walk over to a one-storey stone building across the yard from the house.

'Converted it myself', Tommy says. 'Watch it don't fall down on yer', he laughs as he opens the door, guiding me inside with his hand on my shoulder, reaching for the electric light with his other hand.

Most of the space is taken up by the bed but there's WC and a hand basin squashed in one corner.

'You can use the shower in the house if I decide I like you,' Tommy says with a laugh in his voice.

Keith's hardly said anything since we arrived.

I nod at both of them. 'Lot better than what I thought. I really appreciate it, both of yer.'

Keith says, 'Have a lie-in. I'll be over about eleven tomorrow, talk about things then.'

I say, 'Yeah, lovely,' and shake hands with both of them, hoping 'talking about things' doesn't mean I've got to move on straight away.

Sheba's the last out, gives me another sniff.

I'm in bed three minutes later. The last thing I think about is wondering how Maria is.

Chapter Twenty Four

The way I wake up with hammering on the door and a dog barking and growling, I'm half panicking it's a raid, till I recognise Tommy's voice. 'Come over the house – there's breakfast.'

I go over to the farmhouse and go in through the door Tommy came out of last night, which leads straight into a big kitchen.

I'm expecting Tommy to have a missus but as I go in he's standing at the range getting two fried eggs out of a frying pan onto a plate to go with the rest of a breakfast.

'Sit down,' he says, nodding at the big wooden table.

He bungs the eggs on a plate and puts it in front of me, so much grub on it some of it's hanging over the edges.

'Had mine,' he says as he gives me a half-pint mug of tea.

'Get stuck in, mate.' He leans back against the range watching me start to eat.

'Look like you need that.'

I say, 'First proper sleep for two nights, feels like waking up in a different country.'

'Yeah, Keith said you've had it rough,' he says. 'You know, sometimes Keith brings his waifs and strays up here and one of them tries to take the piss.' As he says that Sheba gets up into a sitting position from where she's been lying, and now there's four eyes looking at me, man and dog, both checking whether I'm a piss-taker.

He looks as if he thinks I might rear up on him, but I slide away from it instead. 'Not me, Tommy. I ain't that stupid.'

He carries on looking, trying to see if there's anything that says I'm a liar. His tone of voice has made the dog stiffen as well but they must both decide I smell honest.

'Paper there,' he says, pointing to a Mirror on the table. 'Keith rung. He'll be over in about an hour. I've got to be somewhere.'

He picks up a waterproof jacket that's over the back of a chair and puts it on. 'Come on, Sheba.'

'See you later,' he says.

As I finish eating I'm wondering whether Tommy's made his mind up about me or if there's going to be other little tests, but mainly it feels good, hidden away like this.

I get up to do the washing up, but suddenly I'm bending in half wanting a beer, not a lager either, but a light and bitter. The memory's so strong I can taste it even if it's twenty years since I had one. I went on lagers when I left the East End.

I go over to the window and look out at the yard and fields beyond, remind myself there's no pub, look at some cows on the side of a hill till the need dies down, glad I'm out here because I've had this wanting before, broken out of a detox twice, same place both times, down in Kennington, walked out the door straight into the boozer you could see from the room where they did groups.

I think about it as I wash up, how feeling fitter can

trip you up.

After that I try Tommy's Mirror but it doesn't hold me so I get a cookbook down from a shelf, concentrate on the photos, trying to imagine how the different meals would taste.

I recognise the sound of Keith's diesel van coming up the hill about an hour later. He parks in the yard again and comes into the kitchen.

'Morning there. Fancy a walk?'

He doesn't say much for the first ten minutes. We're going uphill with him in front, barbed wire on either side of us as we walk between two fields, then we come onto a broad ridge where we're walking alongside each other, and he starts to lay out what I've got to do if I want to stay.

He says I can have another night for freemans, but after that I've got to choose to move on or get involved: that means helping out with the community meal twice a week and Bible study with the community two other nights.

He says, 'Some of us go to a church service on a Sunday, but our work and our study is the major part of how we worship.'

As we're walking the sun's soft on my face and I'm looking up at the freedom of a clear blue sky, wishing I could keep going like this without having to decide anything.

Keith says, 'The other thing is if you stay with Tommy he likes it if you give him a hand, do some work round the place, then he makes us a donation instead of paying wages.'

I say, 'Difficult to decide, Keith,' but truth is, now I've stopped and had some rest I can feel how tired I am. I know I need to be somewhere I can rebuild my strength.

Keith says, 'Well, you're safe up here, mate, and no one's going to have a go at you in Brighton because you'll always be with the crowd of us.'

I nod, letting him know I've heard him, trying to decide how bad the Bible study's going to be but figuring if he keeps me busy with the community it should help me stay off the booze. Also if I'm a bit useful on the farm Tommy might bung me a few quid and then I can be off.

Keith must guess some of what I'm thinking. 'After all, Anthony, Jesus might find you, but if He doesn't you can treat it as a rehab and detox, then go on your way when you're ready.'

I can't odds that unless I want to stand by the side of the road trying to hitchhike with about three quid in my pocket, so I turn towards him, stick my hand out.

'Good decision,' he says, shaking my hand.

Not long after he says he's got to get back and we go back down to the farmhouse. Before he shoots away he gives me a Bible and says he'll call Tommy on the mobile, tell him I'm staying.

He says, 'Bible study tonight. Tommy'll give you a lift down. You'll enjoy it.'

I watch him drive off and then go back into the outhouse.

The Bible's the only thing I've got to read but I decide I'll lie on the bed and have a go with my notebook first, instead.

I want to write something about the night with Dove

while I still remember how some of it felt, but I give up after quarter of an hour, haven't got the words for the way the drug felt, and everything I try about the sex comes out crude, so I put it away and pick up the Bible.

I look through it till I get to the Psalms, because I remember liking them, but suddenly I'm full of the feelings I used to get when I was in porridge, and now they're trying to strangle me, as if instead of getting weaker the memories have been waiting for me to be somewhere dark before they jump me.

I sling the Bible on the top of the bedside drawers and swing my feet onto the floor, sit there almost doubled-up for a minute then I get on the floor and do forty press-ups following up with crunches until the only thing I'm thinking about is how the exercise feels.

After that I do some stretches then I get on top of the bed and put my head under a pillow, tell myself it'll pass and I'm still drying out, keep my eyes closed till I'm asleep.

I'm spark out till about half four, when Tommy wakes me up banging on the door again, tells me he's brought back a Chinese for both of us.

After we've eaten he says, to help myself to the shower.

He shouts up the stairs as I'm drying myself, says he's bought three pairs of vests and underpants Keith told him to get me in case I need them.

Chapter Twenty Five

Keith's just inside the door as I walk into the community centre. 'You're looking a lot better already,' he says.

'I'll introduce you when we start,' he carries on. 'The other house is back – that's the blokes you haven't seen before.' He nods towards the dozen blokes standing around outside a circle of chairs.

The tables from last night have been pushed against one of the side walls, stacked on top of each other.

The two women are up near the stage. The older one's sitting behind a keyboard, and the younger one's facing her standing up, tuning her electric guitar.

Keith says, 'I've just got to collect my thoughts, Anthony.' He calls over the redhead bloke from last night. 'Look after Anthony, will you – he's probably feeling a bit nervous.'

Michael shakes my hand. 'Glad you're still around, Anthony.' He takes me over to where the other blokes are standing and starts introducing me.

I shake hands and try to remember the names. A couple of them say welcome in the love of Jesus, but others just say hello and pleased to meet you. If they say something else as well I try to give them a reply but mainly I'm working on not letting it show I'm making buttons.

Michael's still introducing me to people when Keith gets up on the stage.

'Welcome everybody,' he says as the chatter dies

down to silence. 'Welcome in Jesus,' he says, opening his arms to us all, the palms of his hands facing upwards.

Everyone except me says, 'Welcome in Jesus.' I'm looking around but no one looks weird as they say it.

Keith says, 'An especial welcome to those of you who've been away. We hope you found your retreat spiritually fulfilling and deepened your faith in Jesus as well as relaxing of course, sun, sea and…' He smiles as he hesitates, and I'm thinking he can't say 'sex.' He carries on, 'Ice cream,' which gets a laugh from most of them.

'Laughter and the love of Jesus. Not incompatible, brothers.'

I start to think it's going to be a lot of long words and I ought to get out of there in case I have a panic, but then he smiles at me. 'I'd like you to say an especial welcome to Anthony, who's come to stay with us, definitely for a little while, for longer, maybe.'

I'm trying to understand whether I've got to say something when the mother plays a chord on the keyboard, and everyone gives a little chuckle which breaks the tension.

'Now,' Keith says, 'as we've said before, we don't just expect God to look after us but we stand in solidarity with each other in the community of Jesus, and to express this we sing together, so all of us up on the stage, please, and Mabel will give out the songsheets.'

My guts feel bad going up the three steps onto the stage and I'm having to tell myself it's singing hymns or sleep out tonight, but then the young girl comes round with the songsheets and instead of a hymn it's You'll

Never Walk Alone.

The blokes are all looking at the words and shuffling about till we're standing in three rows.

I make sure I'm in the back row, hoping no one's going to notice I can't sing. I've even had geezers on the North Bank tell me to stop singing because I was putting them off.

It's the girl, Mabel, who calls us to order and starts the first verse solo to give us the tune. She doesn't look much: the beauty's all in her singing.

Everyone else joins in on the second verse but I'm back in Liverpool, my fourth professional fight. It sounded like the whole crowd were singing him on with their special song, but all he had was front. I broke his nose almost the first right I threw: I felt it go, he bottled it and didn't come out after the third, but the singing started to drop off when I did his nose.

We're more than halfway through by the time I'm back in the present.

I start growling along and then I'm wondering if it's just me a bit carried away, but we get to that last line and it feels like it's the same for the other lads as well.

Keith says, 'Now a prayer.'

I must be thick: I haven't even thought we'd have prayers, but as he starts reciting, I feel okay about having my eyes shut. It's not like at school when you hate the feeling and you want to get rid of it by mucking about with your mates. It's peaceful not feeling anything.

The prayer ends with the rest saying, 'Amen, praise be to God.' Then we get down off the stage and sit on the chairs.

Keith waits till we're settled down. 'Now let's go round in the circle and introduce ourselves to Anthony again by telling him our names and just a little bit about ourselves, but we won't test you afterwards to see what you remember, Anthony.' Everyone laughs, but not like they're taking the piss.

I'll start,' he says. 'I'm Keith. I became a Christian eleven years ago and started to set up this community with two others about eight years ago.'

Sally's sitting next to Keith. 'I'm Sally. Along with my daughter here, Mabel, I'm one of only two women in the community, but we don't mind, do we, Mabel?' And everyone laughs, because of the way she says it, only I can't work out why it's funny.

The girl says, 'I'm Mabel, and I try not to let my Mum speak for me all the time,' but she's giving her Mum a big grin.

Next to her there's a fat bloke in a polo neck who's wearing a home-made -looking wooden cross that hangs down from a couple of strands of fuse wire around his neck. 'I'm Douglas,' he says in a half-posh voice. 'I've been a Christian since I came out of prison three years ago.'

After that it's a little Scotsman and after him another half-posh bloke then a Welshman, but as I fix on whichever one's speaking I forget the name of the one before, although I try little tricks to remember, like thinking, 'Yeah, Jerry in the blue jumper and Sam in the shirt looks dirty.'

I'm about three quarters of the way round when it gets to me. I say, 'I'm Anthony. I'm an alcoholic. I used to be a boxer and life's been pretty hard since that finished, mainly my own fault.' Most of them look interested, and a few nod or smile as if they've been on the same road sometime.

Next to me there's a short guy about my age, dapper in a suit with a collar and tie. 'I'm Danny. Like Anthony, I'm an alcoholic too. Christ came into my life about three years ago, soon after I had my last drink, which was three years, two months and five days ago.'

As I look at the next bloke I'm trying to guess Danny's last drink – something flash, I reckon, like brandy and coke to go with a good suit, although inside I'm laughing at myself, because he probably ended up drinking Tennent's with his arse hanging out.

Thinking about that I forget to take in what the last three or four blokes say before we get back to Keith.

'Thank you, everyone,' Keith says. 'I hope that's made you feel a bit more at home, Anthony?'

I nod at him, even though I still haven't got half the names.

Now Keith says, 'Let's look at the Bible.'

Each chair has got a Bible beside it on the floor, and when everyone bends down to pick one up I do the same.

Keith says, 'We haven't looked at The Sermon on the Mount for a while, not since before some people here joined us, but as many of you have heard me say, it's a particularly important part of the Bible for us.'

As he gets to 'particularly', three or four of the lads join in saying the rest of the sentence with him, and there's smiles round the room, so I guess everyone's heard him say it a few times.

Most of them have got their Bibles open and look like they know where they want to be but he takes pity on the wallies like me. 'The Gospel of Matthew, chapter five, and let's go to verse 13.'

'Let's all read it together.'

Sally starts off, clear as a bell: 'Ye are the salt of the earth…' The rest of us try to keep up with the old-fashioned words and I don't do too badly because at least I've read this before in bang-up, although never out loud because people would have thought I'd cracked and gone schizo.

We do three verses then Keith says, 'Would anyone like to tell us what they think this means? Just the beginning of it if you like.'

'Aye, I'll give it a go,' says the Scots bloke. 'Mostly us Scots are the salt of the earth, but I have been called the scum of the earth as well.' I laugh along with the rest of them, and going by his smile he likes that.

'No, but,' he says, 'it's the decent hard-working people keep the place going. It's not the rich man who cannae enter the eye of the needle as the Bible says. Do ye not make me right, eh, Keith?'

'It's not me to judge who's right, Ronny, but I do agree with you about the working people being the people who do the work.'

'Well, if I may,' Douglas says, 'it does say, "Ye are the salt of the earth". Isn't it more likely that Jesus was talking to a more select group of people?' The half-snob way he talks I'm wondering if he means the roughs aren't included, but then he says, 'Aren't we like the salt of the earth, latter-day disciples that Jesus has chosen to salt the earth with his truth?'

Keith's nodding away as he carries on, and there's a few of 'em look like they really rate what he's saying, but a geezer called Jeff looks towards me from four chairs away, nods at Douglas and then down to his right hand resting near his crotch, clenches his fist and gives the 'wanker' sign.

I nod to let him know I've seen, then look away trying to kill the smile that's coming, because I've got to know what brought Douglas here before I agree he's a wanker.

Then Keith comes back and says something about Matthew writing in Greek and how 'if the salt has lost his savour' means something like being foolish in Greek.

I have to look at him carefully to see if this is another one of his little jokes but he doesn't look as if it is, which I can't get a handle on because I always thought the Bible started off in English from the olden days and that's why it's so hard to read.

Nearly everyone thinks of something they want to say, and I hear some of it but mainly I'm thinking about the Greek business, deciding that's one of the things I'm going to ask Keith about, but not till I get him on my own so I don't show myself up in front of everyone else.

I'm still thinking about that when we take a break for a cup of tea.

As we get in line, Jeff looks like he wants to tell me something but he's put me off and I sidestep him, stand by myself in the queue.

Everyone gets their tea and biscuits from Keith and

Sally behind the jump and stand around in twos and threes, except for four or five of them standing around Mabel looking like they're dreaming of a taste, but she doesn't look bothered, probably used to holding them off, although all the same I'm expecting it to be a bit different here without that sort of thing going on.

I've just turned away from looking at them when Danny comes over.

'Finding it a different from Fellowship.'

Without thinking, I say 'Yeah, well no one's pissed,' wishing I hadn't said it before it's out of my mouth but he's sweet as a nut, looks up at me twinkling.

'Has been known to happen in AA,' he says. 'That's because AA doesn't give you anything except sobriety,' he carries on. 'What's a drinker going to do when he gets bored of being sober?'

I nod that I make him right because I've seen that with plenty.

'Done many rehabs?' he says.

'Couple,' I say, then I smile at him. 'Mainly been nick that's dried me out.'

He touches my elbow. 'You've had it rough, mate. Still it's not like that here, here we've got God's love.'

He seems like a decent geezer who can take an idea so I want to explain how new I am and I'm not in God's love, although maybe it'll happen but people have started sitting down again so I just go, 'Thanks for talking to me, Danny.'

We sit down next to each other again and as Keith's calling us to order again Danny leans over and whispers,

'Fellowship tomorrow evening if you fancy it?'

I whisper back 'Yeah, okay, might do, long as I can get a lift,' only then I feel like a lemon because I look round and everyone else is quiet and the whole meeting's waiting, looking at me like I've said something hooky.

'Sorry.'

I'm still embarrassed when Keith kicks things off again and I miss about five minutes, thinking about how often meetings end up giving you a prat feeling.

Then I hear him say, 'Now the Lords prayer.' I look round then close my eyes like everyone else and join in, thinking about my nan, who taught me the words.

I think maybe that's going to be the finish, but Keith says, 'Now, I'm looking for teaching on this one, and some of you will have noticed when we come back to words from the Bible there's always something new God teaches us from our experience. Besides, its good exercise for us to try one that starts plainly enough but ends a bit more difficult. Luke Chapter 1, verse 51: "He hath shewed strength with his arm; he hath scattered the proud in the imagination of their hearts."'

Even I can see the first bit because you've got to have a strong God – what's the point in having a weak one, but loads of them are diving in with this and that so I keep schtum.

That dies down and Keith says, 'Any ideas about the second half of the verse: "He hath scattered the proud in the imagination of their hearts"?' You can feel everyone thinking, almost hear the strain of the thoughts and then I think of an example, at least I think it could be but

I don't want anyone laughing at me.

Then I see Keith looking at me and he must've seen I've had an idea because he gives me a little nod. When I still don't say anything he raises his eyebrows and it feels like he's saying, 'Come on, mate,' so I say, 'I might have got something.'

'Yes, Bomber?'

I don't know why he says that, because here I'm Anthony, and there's one or two looking like they want to snigger, but it's too late for me not to say anything, so I give it my best one. 'Well, perhaps it's like a boxer who beats the heavy favourite. He has a look at the other guy, realises the other guy thinks he knows how it's going to happen but he gives the favourite a fight he isn't expecting, punches holes in the favourite's game plan, going in at angles the other bloke isn't expecting, hooks instead of straight punches, uppercuts on the way out.'

I finish and sit back.

A lot of them are looking at me but I can't tell what they think and there's a few looking at the ground because they don't want me to see they think I'm a cunt, but then I see Mabel's got a big smile on her face. 'Well, I don't know anything about boxing,' she says, 'except I like the name Bomber,' and a few of them are smiling along with her. 'But I can see what you mean really clearly: God takes the proud who think they know it all and shows them they don't know anything about Him.'

Scots Ronny says, 'Aye, cannae quarrel with that, Keith,' and there's a few murmurs of 'Well done,' and 'Yeah, that's interesting.'

Keith says, 'Well done, Anthony. Sorry I called you Bomber. Perhaps it was God telling me you'd come up with a boxing way of looking at things.' Keith looks around the room. 'Lets all of us remember not to get too cocky about thinking we understand what God means.'

After that Keith goes through everything we've talked about tonight and once he's answered any questions we stand up and get on the stage, where Mabel leads us through a rehearsal of a gospel song, I'm on my way to Canaan, then once she's happy we do it for real, and the way Sally and her get going with the music it's better than at football when they're winning six-nil but I'd be flying anyway because of getting it right about that quote from the Bible.

Chapter Twenty Six

Keith's giving me a lift home, back to Tommy's after Bible study. It's three and a half weeks since they took me in.

He says, 'You've got a real gift for it – you know that, don't you?'

It's the second time he's told me that. The first time I said, 'Always thought I was a thick cunt.'

He said, 'That's because ignorant schoolteachers said you were. Know-nothings who'd closed their hearts to God and closed their hearts to God's people as well.'

Sometimes he sounds so fierce I have to look to see if he's putting it on for a laugh.

This time I don't say anything, just nod to let him know I've heard and sit there enjoying the compliment.

'His time in the wilderness, you've got to see it: it's like a boxer training for a fight, forty days and forty nights and all you're doing is getting ready, proving your strength, but the devil's looking for his chance. Bet your mates tried to get you to go out for a pint, expect they guessed you were dying for one as well – isn't that like the first temptation, when Satan said if you're the son of God, turn the stone into bread? Bet your mates tried that didn't they, they said one pint, what's the harm when you're the man?'

I say, 'Yeah, that's right, they did,' but I don't need to say anything because he starts saying the verses from

Matthew out loud.

I love listening to him, an ordinary working-class bloke like me, but the way he speaks he can bring out how much he loves the words.

He keeps going and after three weeks I can recognise what comes next: the Sermon on the Mount, Matthew Five. Near the end there's the bit I can't swallow about turning the other cheek. I haven't talked to him about it yet, haven't told him, 'not where I come from in the East End – wouldn't work,' but sooner or later I'll have to, ask him to explain it.

It's almost like Keith's timed it, he gets to the end, Matthew 5.48, as we turn off onto the track and he has to go quiet to concentrate on driving, but the atmosphere's he's made is still there, the night outside the van bringing us closer together, making the feelings he's brought up stronger.

We come into the yard and park. As he switches off the ignition he turns towards me. 'I mean it,' he says. 'You were good tonight, very clear with your meanings. So remind me: you've got AA tomorrow. See you at the community meal the night after?'

'Yep, that's right.' I shake his hand. 'Take care, mate.'

'And you, brother.'

I get out of the car, wait to wave as he drives off and then stand there hardly believing I can like the country darkness this much, black night wrapped round making me feel safe.

As I walk over to the outhouse Sheba must have recognised me. I can hear her in the farmhouse snuffling and whining to get out.

Keith paying me the compliment and thinking hard at the session tonight I ought to be content, but when I get into bed I'm still buzzing. I can't help thinking it through, making the argument to tell Keith why he's wrong about a fighter in training, because Jesus went into the desert to make himself ready to take away the world's pain and sin, but in boxing it's all about being selfish, making yourself so hard you'll kill the other guy if that's what it takes, maybe without noticing you're doing it, but Keith's already told me he hates pro boxing, so he must know that, was using the training as an example I'd understand.

I lie there a bit longer, imagining the conversation with Keith and him paying me more compliments, but just before I go to sleep I tell myself not to enjoy it too much and tear the arse out of it, because out of all the community I'm the only one God hasn't spoken to yet, and even good people can be jealous.

I'm still thinking about it when I wake up the next morning and lie there pondering, trying not to have pride because if I'm good at something it's for the faith, not for me, the exact opposite of when I was a fighter, even if back then I thought I was the good cause.

I look at the alarm and it's half eight. Often I'm up and out earlier than this for a couple of hours with Tommy, which is usually all he wants, but he told me yesterday, 'Have a lie-in tomorrow. I'm off into town.' So I stay in bed a bit longer, thinking about seeing Danny tonight at Fellowship, how we've become mated up and some of the laughs we've had, because that's what I like about him: he's deep into living with Jesus but it doesn't stop him having a joke. Some of the others are serious the whole time. It makes you think they reckon they're more Christian than you are.

I splash my face with cold water over the sink, smiling at the shock as it first hits, thinking how that never changes, even after a thousand punches to the mush, and wondering if you get a shock when Jesus finds you, whether it's like a punch you didn't see.

I asked Danny what it was like when he was chosen but he said he couldn't really describe it: he said he was sitting in a church on his own thinking his thoughts about God, waiting for Stuart, one of the guys who was supposed to be meeting him, and he saw an old woman, a bit like his old granny in Ireland, go past him on a horse and cart as if it was out in the country, and then it was like waking up and he thought he must have had five minutes' doze, but there's Stuart, and Keith and Sally and Mabel, sitting with him in the church, and they're saying, 'Take it easy, you've been out for nearly four hours, talking the Bible in tongues and praying. Stuart found you and then fetched us so we could witness with you.'

I look at myself in the mirror, wondering if God's close, whether I'm going to be called. I try prayers every day and when I do it's peaceful but I don't know if there's anything there except me feeling the quiet and the solitude.

I go over to the table where I put everything and count my dough as I pick it up. Along with a bit of smash there's forty quid, two weeks' pocket money from the community and a bit more, because Tommy gives me a fiver when I do a little job, says it's only the same as a packet of fags.

Sometimes he tries to give me more but I tell him to forget it, because him and his brother already paid me in kindness.

Time still hangs when Tommy hasn't got anything for me so I put on the secondhand trainers I found in a shop in Brighton and get ready for a run over the hill. After that I'll have a go at Solomon, see if it's really love poems, like Keith said, then I'm going to cook shepherd's pie for Tommy and me, because after the first week of takeaways I sussed he can only do fry–ups. Since then I've been trying out recipes from the cookbooks his ex-missus left behind.

The shepherd's pie tastes good and I even manage to get the broccoli and carrots done at the same time.

Afterwards we sit in Tommy's living room to watch the news before he drops me down to AA and then hangs around to bring me back.

The first thing on the local news is a new shopping centre opening up in Southampton. 'Just a way to get you to spend more,' Tommy grunts, 'puts all the little guys out of business.'

The programme goes back to a smarmy geezer in the studio, and as he speaks I almost know what's coming before they show the pictures. 'Brighton police were on hand this morning when bailiffs evicted the last of the squatters...' There's a woman reporter, hair blowing around in the wind, holding a microphone, standing on the pavement in front of the house Dove took me to, there's a couple of uniforms standing just behind the woman.

'It's all quiet now, but earlier there were scuffles.' The film changes: it looks like early morning, there's two big lumps throwing stuff out of the windows and Vic's little mate who's got Spider in a headlock, pulling him through the garden, then it changes again and on the pavement there's two guys, one with a Mohican, the other with locks, both of them holding a can, turning round to give V-signs to the camera while in the background there's Dove in the garden, too far away to hear, but looking as if she's screaming at one of the bailiffs.

The picture changes again and Dove's side-on to the camera talking to the woman on the mike. Dove's leaning forward from the shoulders like she's going to bite a bit out of anyone who gets too close. The woman's saying, 'Are you a spokeswoman for the squatters?'

Dove says, 'Yeah, whatever you say.'

The camera closes in on her and she's looking straight into it. Her eyes look as if she's close to tears. 'We don't have a spokeswoman, right, cos no one listens to us.' The woman moves sideways into view again, holding the microphone like it's a juju doll to keep off evil spirits, she looks like being that close to Dove is making her want to shit, then Dove grabs the microphone off the woman and the camera sweeps round to focus on her so the interviewer disappears again. 'Just tell 'em this: we don't care, we ain't moving no more, we're going down to the beach, come and find us there. Sod the lot of yer.'

The telly goes back to the bloke in the studio. 'A spokesman for the property developers said in a statement earlier "We are relieved to have possession of this fine building at last, and look forward to returning it to its former glory."'

Tommy says, 'Fuckin' state of that.'

I don't know why, but I say, 'I had my last beer with her.'

'You have anything else with her?'

I say, 'It was before the community took me in, before I changed.'

Tommy says, 'So you did have something with her?'

I look at Tommy, knowing I've got embarrassment all over my face, wishing I hadn't said anything.

He shrugs. 'Doesn't bother me. Hope she was a good turn?'

I stand up to go and get my jacket. I look down at him in his chair. 'It was before I changed Tom, before I changed.'

'Dirty dog,' he shouts after me with a laugh as I walk out to the kitchen.

Chapter Twenty Seven

I can't get started with the AA meeting that night.

There's only six of us there, including two herberts who turn up together, both of them a bit pissed. The chair doesn't know how to handle it when one of them starts a story about trying to rob a paper shop with a walking stick.

Danny gives me a look. We've heard all the stories and half the time we've got better ones. I wink at him, wondering if he knows I'm thinking of my favourite one of his, the time he was working at Heathrow, got pissed drinking vodka and orange juice in front of his computer, stopped a runway for twenty minutes.

He and I always go to a kebab house down the street for a cup of tea afterwards. The bloke who runs it has got used to us, doesn't mind we only have a tea. Most of his business is after the pubs close.

Tonight's the first time I've noticed the only light in there is from strip lights, makes the place look like it's always four in the morning.

I interrupt Danny, who's talking about a new plane coming out that he's read about in a magazine.

I say, 'You noticed the light in here, it's like the light in nick. It's there because it's got to be but it's not going to give you anything, like usually you expect light to be a warmth in the darkness, but in the factory either it's dull and cold or it's so bright it almost blinds you, reminding

269

you you're small and the system's big.'

Danny says, 'You're down tonight, aren't you? Thought you were, thought I could see it on your face when you came into the meeting.' He carries on, 'It's a bit cold, alright: nights are drawing in.'

When he says that I know what's up. All night under the surface I've been thinking about Dove and the tribe, feeling what it'll be like down on the beach, the cold coming in off the sea like a silent killer when they're akip.

I say, 'Did you see the news tonight?' but I've forgotten they don't have telly in the house so I start explaining about Dove. I do tell him we had it when I get to that part but I give him the hint it wasn't up to much.

When I finish I say, 'You reckon Keith could do anything for 'em?'

Danny says, 'You mean put a roof over their heads?'

'Yeah. Don't think they're up for Jesus yet.'

Danny says, 'Don't sound like it,' and the smile he gives me I know he's seen through me making out Dove wasn't all that.

I say, 'Like I explained to Tommy, it was before.'

Danny says, 'I'm not judging you mate, or them. Keith knows one or two people might be able to do something. That new Vicar at St Clement's, he's alright.'

As he finishes Tommy arrives, comes over to us with a bit more hustle than usual and stands by our table.

We're both looking up at him. Danny says, 'Want a cup…'

Tommy doesn't say anything, looks over to Dino

who's down the other end of the café, cleaning the grill, then looks at me. 'You got a black mate, about your age, scarred up around the eyes?'

I say, 'He on his own?'

Tommy says, 'Far as I could see, said he's been all over looking for you.' I give Dan a quick look across the table, trying to see if my face is telling him I'm wobbling now its come on top, but he just looks excited.

Tommy's saying, 'Saw him outside the hall where your meeting was, says he went to another AA first.'

Danny says, 'Could be Southview Hall, Hove. There's a meeting there tonight as well.'

'Wants to talk to you,' Tommy says. 'Waiting by the side of the hall.'

I start to get up. Tommy says, 'I'll come up with you.' His combat jacket opens slightly at the front and I catch a look at the top of a monkey wrench tucked into an inside pocket.

I say, 'See you back here, Dan. More than five minutes, have a gander out of the door without being too obvious.'

Dan gives a smile, half-funny, half-curious. 'Sure thing, captain.'

Tommy and I go out of the door, start walking up the street, I don't know why but I say, 'Everything's either up or down in this town.'

Tommy says, 'Best hope he's on the level then.'

I give a little smile at the joke.

Tommy says, 'He's in the recess leads to the side gate of the hall, if he's still there.'

Tommy sounds as if he's hoping Andy's still there.

I don't know what I hope. I'm clearing my head just in case.

I turn into the recess. Tommy's behind me a couple of feet, covering my back.

Andy's about six foot back with the side gate behind him. He's wearing a trilby and a raincoat over a collar and tie. 'Put it there, mate.' He comes towards me and we bump into each other trying to shake hands and hug each other at the same time.

'Where you bin, mate?' he says. 'Thought I told you to come into the shop.'

I look at him feeling stupid, don't want to give him the weak excuse I didn't know where the shop was, can't be many black butchers in a town like this.

'Caught up with some Christians, Andy, good people. They've been helping me out.'

Andy, says, 'You not down with the squatters then. Vic thinks you is, disappointed he never found you this morning, mate, wants his vengeance.'

'How do you know?'

Now Andy looks embarrassed. 'Go back there sometimes, have a lickle drink.'

I want to tell him he should have more respect for himself but what can I do: he's come here to warn me.

Andy says, 'Vic and his lickle mate, Nigel – but they call him Bormann, that's his nickname – they want to kill you, mate, tink you're with the squatters down by... what do you call them boats with the two bits in the water?'

'Catamarans.'

'Yeah, that's it: going down there, bout one o'clock,

going to splash everyone with a bit of petrol, then whoosh. Vic reckons Old Bill won't care. Good thing you ain't there, mate.'

I say, 'I got to warn them.'

Andy says, 'Sure thing, mate – you be the hero. Just doan tell no one old Andy tell you.'

'Course not.'

'I reckon this is goodbye then, mate. I done my bit, ain't I?'

I say 'Sure, big man. Give us a hug,' and we both try to squeeze the life out of each other for half a minute. I don't even mind the smell of stale drink coming off him: he probably thinks I stink of tea.

I say, 'You want a lift anywhere?' I give Tommy a quick look to see if that's okay.

Tommy nods, but Andy turns back towards me. 'Black man going to disappear into the dark of the night, won't be no one sees me,' smiling at me with his brown eyes, first time I've clocked his whites are yellow.

He turns back to Tommy, holds his hand out and they shake. 'Look after him. Good mate, that's Bomber Jackson,' he says, still laughing as he goes down the slope away from Tommy and me.

Tommy says, 'What do you want to do?'

'Got to warn them, mate. Just hope they're not too pissed.'

'What you going to do about Danny?'

'I'll tell him on the way to his, then maybe you drop me over towards Hove?'

'Sure,' he says.

We collect Danny from the kebab house and go around the corner to Tommy's jeep.

I give Danny the story as we drive along, leaning through the gap in the two front seats to tell him.

Danny doesn't say much in return, but when we get to the community house, he says, 'You don't have to go down there. You know no one's going to blame you if you don't.'

I say, 'I'm my brother's keeper, Dan. I got to.'

Tommy's rolling a fag. He looks like he's trying to concentrate so hard he can't hear us.

Danny says, 'You've remembered we're non-violent, haven't you? You're just going to warn them, right?'

I say, 'Sure thing, Dan.'

He says, 'Best of luck then, and you see you tomorrow night.'

We shake hands and I'm glad I can't see in the dark whether he believes me or not.

'Blessed are the peacemakers,' he says.

'Blessed are the peacemakers,' I reply.

Danny says, 'Good night, Tom,' and gets out. I watch as he crosses the pavement and puts his key in the lock, then opens the door to go into the house of holy men.

Tommy's got his window half-open. He's looking over the top, blowing his smoke out.

He doesn't say anything for a minute, then he throws the dog end out of the window.

'How much notice you want to give 'em? Don't want to waste it if they're pissed and going to forget?'

I say, 'Dove'll be alright.'

Tommy says, 'Late night caff round the corner from here. Want a soup?'

He closes his window and starts off. Five minutes later he's reversing into a tunnel that comes to a dead end fifty yards under the hill that the railway that runs on top of.

We're about thirty yards in from the turning, opposite the café.

'I'll get it,' he says. 'We can drink it in the motor. Place fills up with cabdrivers this time of night – the noise of their rabbit drives me mad. Tomato or Minestrone? That's all they do.'

I say, 'Minestrone, mate', hoping it's got as much flavour as I'm imagining.

Tommy reaches inside his jacket to take out the monkey wrench and puts it down on the seat between us.

'Just in case. Back in a few minutes,' he says. Tommy opens the door and gets out of the jeep.

At first I'm just looking out of the windscreen, noticing how the night's never much darker than grey down here in the town, wishing I was in the blackness of the night at the farm with Sheba looking after me.

Then I look down at the wrench and half of me thinks about picking it up, feeling the weight of it, working out what it could do, but the other half of me doesn't want to fight at all, wants to be somewhere else, still in my new life with the community, studying the Bible and asking God to find me.

Then I think about Vic: 'Always a winner, son, always a winner.' He's always said it like it was his catchphrase.

I'm feeling how much I hate him. I start wondering if I can have the fight then go back, convince Keith it was something I had to do before I could become a real Christian, turn my back on hatred at last.

Tommy comes back with a paper cup in each hand. I lean over and open the door to let him in.

'He's let me down,' he says. 'All he's got is Oxtail: that alright for you?'

'Yeah, of course.'

Tommy wriggles up onto his seat, both hands still holding the soup, then gives me one and closes his door with his free hand.

'Hot,' he says.

I take the lid off mine and let it steam. I sniff it and say, 'I'm enjoying the smell till it cools down.'

Tommy gets into a pantomime about taking his top off and not waiting. 'Fuckin' 'ell – burnt my tongue.'

We could be two geezers mucking about on a meal break.

Then we both wait for the soup to cool down, looking through the windscreen like a couple of holidaymakers in a car park.

I take a sip and then a mouthful. 'Yeah, it's good, thanks mate.' It's like Tommy doesn't hear me.

'Nothing happened when I was in the caff, did it?'

'No, nothing at all.'

'Dan's right,' he says. 'You don't have to do anything. I could even drive you up to London tonight.'

I say, 'I'm here now, I'm bang in it, wouldn't just be walking away: I'd be turning my back, maybe letting Dove and her lot get killed, and that's on me. Burning them is only in the picture because Vic thinks I'm tied up with 'em.'

'You know Keith ain't going to have it, don't you?'

I say, 'Well, you never know, do you?'

'Yes, I do know. He's never told you why, has he?'

'I don't know. Why what?'

'Why he became a Christian.'

'No, he hasn't.'

Tommy looks at me and then looks away. 'It was because of me. Geezer owed me money for months, a lot of money. It was a bit of business, something me and Keith had going, but we were both going skint. The old man was still alive then. He used to run the farm, didn't want to know about me or Keith. I hit the bloke when he wouldn't pay up, and he banged his head going over. Suddenly I was looking at a murder charge. Keith always was a bit churchy, especially when he was a teenager. He drove up to the Downs one night, sat there till it started getting light, and when he came back down he told me he'd done a deal with God, he'd give everything up for religion if I got off. Three months later I walked away with a slap on the wrist. My bit of the bargain was never be violent again, and I haven't been, can't do it, not even to help you out, mate.'

Tommy's still looking ahead, the emotions the story's set off flickering across his face.

'Keith started off running soup kitchens, then he fell out with a couple of priests. They got jealous of him because he got on so well with the dossers, and besides Keith reckoned the vicars were too friendly with the well-to-do people, what he calls the establishment, so he set up the community.'

Tommy turns to me. 'Now you know, mate. Still want to go down there?'

It's my turn to look away from him. I say, 'I've got to,' but the history he's told me is making me cold. I don't know how I'm going to fight, feel as if I've lost already. I say, 'I'll get out, Tom, walk it over there,' because if I get away from him then maybe I can warm myself up, but Tommy looks closely at me. 'Come on, mate, you've still got a ride.'

Chapter Twenty Eight

It's getting on for half twelve by the time we're driving along the sea front.

It's a windy midweek September night so apart from the traffic there's hardly anyone around except for a few walking along in front of the hotels and past the bottom of the squares and the big blocks of private flats further on. Most of them look like stragglers on the way home from afters in the pub, except for a few youngsters without enough clothes on, heading for a club.

We get to about level with where the catamarans are and Tommy slows down, but in the dark you can't see them, not even the masts. There's a wide pavement then a wider stretch of grass, then another wide path between the road and the sea.

'I'll go on a bit further,' he says, 'have a look.'

We go up to where the town ends near the aqua centre, then he turns round and we cruise back on the other side of the road. When we're back level to where the catamarans are I tell him to stop.

'Better let me off here, driver,' I joke.

'Okay, pal.'

Tommy turns towards me. 'Any of the squatters got a fight in 'em?'

'Probably not. Alright if I take the wrench?'

'Just be careful you hit the right geezer with it.'

'I might give it to the bird. She's a bit spunky.'

'Do what you got to do,' he says, and we shake hands. 'Thanks for everything.'

As I step down out of the door I remember my stuff – haven't thought about it before.

The height of the jeep means I'm standing looking up at him. 'Got a bit of gear at your place. Alright if I pick it up sometime?'

'Be expecting you, mate. Pity you never got a mobile. Give us a bell, whenever.'

I say, 'Later,' as I'm shutting the door and perhaps he says something else but I don't hear because I walk off, trying to keep feelings down, getting ready in case I can't persuade Dove and the rest of 'em to do one and disappear but knowing I've probably crossed the line already, that Keith won't let me back.

I stick the wrench in the right pocket of my donkey jacket and go across the road.

I'm about halfway across the grass when I notice flames down where the beach is and wonder whether I'm too late, half of me hoping I am but soon I hear drunken voices sounding like party time.

Now I'm out in the dark I can see a long way either side of me, but there's no one around except a couple of cyclists going in either direction.

I cross the path and then look over the railings at the campfire, down the beach from the catamarans, nearer the sea.

I'm looking for Dove but against the flames they're all just black figures, some of them standing, others moving about to music that must come from a portable, waving their arms around like the hippies, pretending to be aeroplanes coming in to land.

As I go down the steps I recognise Spider by the fire.

A movement makes me glance towards the catamarans, where I see the top half of Dove between two boats. I can't see her moving up and down as I walk over to her so I don't reckon I'm interrupting anything worse than a shit.

She's just standing up doing up her jeans as I get close enough to shout, 'Hello.'

'Who the fuck – oh it's you. Bit fucking late, Mr Boxer. Needed you this morning.'

I say, 'Yeah, I saw it on the telly.'

She climbs over the boat and stands in front of me, this close I can't help wanting her.

She starts to say, 'Yeah they didn't...'

'What the fuck's he doing here?'

I look round and Spider's crept up so he's standing beside me, about three foot away, looking straight at Dove.

I look down at the top of his head, trying to sound friendly. 'Alright, Spider?'

'What the fuck does he want?' he says to Dove.

I say, 'Calm down, mate.' If he wasn't so stupid he'd be afraid I might give him a slap.

I look at Dove. 'I've come to warn you: you got some more ag coming, the same people who threw you out of the house.'

'Fuck him,' says Spider.

We're both talking to her now, like she's the queen and she's got to choose between us. I say, 'They're after me an' all. It's a long story.'

Spider says, 'He's probably fucking tied up with 'em, Dove. Don't take any notice.'

Dove says, 'Now fuck off, Spider, and go back to the fire.'

Spider looks at me then down at the beach, then he mutters, 'Fuck you an' all.'

Dove shouts, 'Spider!'

'Yeah, alright.' And he turns around, starts weaving his way back to the others, looking like his legs are feeling whatever he's swallowed now he's not shouting at me.

'Sorry 'bout him, mate.'

I say, 'That's alright,' thinking Spider's done me a favour with his abuse, stopped me getting the horn when I should be concentrating. Maybe I'll have a laugh about it with her later, if there is a later.

I say, 'They're coming down with petrol, want to burn you out.'

I look straight at her, but maybe the drugs have got hold, because her face doesn't move, like she's not hearing me.

'They want to set fire to you.' I say it slowly, like I'm talking to a kid.

She says, 'I've been in fights before. I can be fucking vicious.'

I say, 'Yeah, so can I, but sometimes you've got to swerve.'

'No, mate, I haven't ever swerved,' which is about what I'm expecting but I don't say anything because my mind's wandering again, wondering why I'm risking everything for a bunch of lowlifes and wollies, then I

282

remember the verse where Jesus said it was the sinners not the righteous who needed him.

I say, 'You got anyone tasty here?'

'Not really,' she says. 'I'm better than most of them. Come on, though. You'd better talk to Bear and Jackal.'

I go with her over towards the fire. I reckon there's about twenty altogether, most of 'em sitting down looking into the flames. Half of 'em could be having visions, the rest are drinking their way towards it, everyone with a bottle or a can in steady motion up to the mouth, then down, then back up again.

Spider phlegms up as I pass him, just misses my boot.

The one she calls Bear is big, even when he's sitting down. Standing up he's like a concrete tower block, he must go near on seven foot and he's solid all the way across. Going by what he's wearing he started off with the Angels, biker boots, jeans, denim shirt and a leather waistcoat.

'Saw you the night you stayed,' he says, shaking my hand. 'Didn't introduce myself – looked like you and Dove was busy.' He smiles at me with rotten teeth half hidden by a gingery beard that looks wrong with his long grey hair.

I smile back at him, liking his lively eyes. 'Yeah, we were.'

Dove says, 'He says we got more aggravation on its way.'

I say, 'That's right. The bad guys from this morning, coming down with cans of petrol.'

Bear looks at me without saying anything. I let him see how relaxed I am just in case he's para, but he must decide I'm kosher or maybe the drink's slowed down what gets through to him. 'Want a mouthful of this?' He offers me the bottle of Southern Comfort he's holding.

'Given it up.'

He nods he's heard me, then he says to Dove, 'Go and get Jackal.' He nods towards the sea. 'He's down there with Mary.'

'She'll be back in a minute,' he says, a teasing look in his eyes as if he's not bothered who he has a fight with.

Dove comes back. 'You'll have to break 'em up.'

Bear nods to where she's just come back from and the three of us move off. The beach goes up in a slope: down the other side there's a couple lying on the beach kissing. He's half covering her but I can see he's got a hand down inside her jeans and from the way he's moving backwards and forwards she's giving him a wank.

Bear kicks him in the back just above the waist.

His head separates from their kissing. 'Fuck off.'

The girl looks up at the three of us, a pale white face with mousey-coloured hair pulled back extra tight in a pony tail but quite pretty for this lot. The bloke's still got his hand inside her jeans but it's stationary.

Bear kicks him again. 'Get up, yer cunt.'

The guy shrugs, says, 'Later, Mary,' and springs up.

He's shorter than Bear but only by about three inches, skinnier as well but wiry-looking. Straight off I see he's only got one eye: the left one's covered over with white flesh.

'What?'

Bear says, 'Man here says the cunts who turned us over this morning are coming back, probably on the way with petrol.'

Bear says to me, 'Don't know your handle.' I say, 'Bomber.'

The other guy says, 'Jackal,' shaking my hand. The girl's standing up now, tucking her top back into her jeans.

Bear looks at her. 'Best piss off Mary – this is business.'

Mary nods. 'Cunts,' she says as she walks past us back towards the fire.

The other three don't look as if they've heard her, probably how they talk to each other all the time.

I look round at each of them in turn so they'll listen. 'They'll come in motors, so most likely they'll park up near and come down from the promenade. It'll be quieter for them, less obvious than coming along the beach. How many of you any good?'

Bear says, 'Just Jackal and me,' then he smiles at Dove. 'Her as well.'

I say, 'You got tools?'

Jackal says, 'That's down to us.'

I say, 'Fair enough. You going to have a word with the rest of them?'

'We'll do our best,' says Jackal, not sounding bothered.

I say, 'There's a shelter just up the steps. I'm going to shove myself under the bench, come at 'em from behind as they go down the steps if they come from the left, on the path if they come from the right and they've got their backs towards me once they go past. You'll hear the noise.'

Bear says, 'We'll be near the bottom of the steps, catch 'em as they come down or come up to help you, depending.'

I say, 'Could be very soon. I'm going to go round that way, up the next lot of steps, then double back to the shelter. Good luck.'

The three of them say, 'Good luck,' and I start moving, glad I'm on my own again.

The stony beach is a slippery trudge to move across, difficult to have a fight on.

I find the next lot of stairs up to the prom and five minutes later I'm tucked away under the bench in the shelter. When I feel the wrench in my pocket I remember I was going to give it to Dove but if Andy was right Vic's boys should be here any moment, so it's too late to do anything about it.

I can still hear the voices around the fire so I don't reckon Bear and Jackal have got them to listen but I didn't think they would and I've done everything I could even if I still don't know why I'm here, because in the next half hour I could end up dead or in lock-up for double figures.

Then I think about Tommy and Keith and how they've changed me, like the week before when I've seen Tommy wobble going up the three-piece ladder so I've told him I'd do it instead, been glad to help instead of despising him for being a weak cunt.

I've been listening for them on automatic pilot and now I hear them, quiet but not silent coming from my right, whispering and muttering first then the rustling of clothes and then the sound of footfalls getting louder as they come near. 'Glove him up.' That's the worst time before a fight when the trainer says that. 'Our father which art in heaven…' The first time I've prayed before a fight since I left the amateurs: I can't stop myself, Keith's done a good job.

Three big geezers go past, about eight foot away, looks like petrol cans they're carrying, then there's the little cunt, 'Bormann,' another two lumps behind him. I thought there'd be more but they're all I can see or hear.

I'm out from under the bench like a snake, then I'm crouching, wrench in the left hand, now I'm moving, 'light on his feet for a big man,' loved it when Boxing News said that. I hit the nearest one in the back of the neck and he falls without a sound. His mate level with him turns, saying, 'What the…' and I've done him in the face but he hasn't gone over. Now I'm screaming, and there's six of them trying to grab hold. I nut one, get a big kick in the balls and then they're on me, going, 'Get him on the fucking ground.' Where's Bear and Jackal? I see Jackal coming through them from the back but I go over, Bormann coming towards me, screaming, 'Burn the fucker,' then Jackal's got him, pulling him back, then I take a big one and then they're kicking me, they're holding my left arm. I have to let go the wrench then the pain flashes through me. They're breaking that arm, boot on the chin and I'm sinking, waiting for the splash of petrol. This is it, all over trying to be a hero, and suddenly there's new shouting but I can feel the space around me: I'm going, waiting for the flames that are going to kill me, blackness, gone.

I wake up, still on the ground, someone holding me up from behind avoiding the bad arm. I spew half onto the pavement, half on me.

I hear, 'Stretcher over here,' from behind me, the arm holding me shifts and the pain from my left arm stops everything else happening. 'Okay, George, get some gas over here,' then a mask over my face. 'Deep breaths, mate.' Now I'm floating, Old Bill everywhere, Bormann cuffed up, Jackal on his face on the ground, two coppers on his back, Bear cuffed to the railings.

Easy up into the ambulance and a vicar's talking to me, squeezing my right hand. 'You'll be alright, Anthony,' then whispering quieter, 'You're Anthony Johnson, remember that: Anthony Johnson, my son.' Another mouthful of gas I'll be anyone he wants.

Chapter Twenty Nine

Later I hear one of the nurses talking about concussion and maybe I'm a bit doolally for the first few hours because I don't really remember anything until the morning when they tell me they're keeping me in for a few days to keep an eye on internal bruising from the kicking I took, which going by how the doctor describes it must've come after a boot to the chin knocked me out.

There's a few on the ward who are up and about and as they walk past some of them ask me how I broke the arm, but I just say, 'Mucking about.' Let 'em know I'm not feeling conversational.

I'm in and out of sleep a lot that morning and afternoon but every time I wake up my first thought is that Old Bill are going to walk onto the ward any moment and nick me for starting the affray.

Then Tommy blows in that evening and starts to explain things.

As soon as we dropped him off Danny was on the phone to Keith, who got on to the vicar of St Clements, who rung a senior copper he knows but calling me Anthony Johnson, because Keith's told him I was a bit of a dope who'd wandered into things without deserving to be bang in trouble.

Tommy doesn't know the whole of it, but he says he thinks the Old Bill were waiting for a chance to nick Bormann and his little team anyway.

He says he doesn't know what happened to Dove, but Bear, Jackal and about seven of the others were nicked as well. 'More unpaid fines on 'em than fleas on a donkey,' Tommy says.

'But your mate Vic doesn't figure in it, so better if you think about moving on, Bomber.'

I want to explain that stuck in hospital you can't help feeling like a kid and wanting someone to look after you, but all I say is, 'Yeah, makes sense,' because Tommy's done his bit and it sounds like Keith's saved me but he isn't forgiving me.

The doctor comes round again the next morning and reckons I'm making good progress, although I still sleep a lot of that day.

Tommy comes in again that evening with my carrier bag with all my gear in it. When he says Keith's got another wayfarer who needs the outhouse I know I've definitely been outed for breaking the no-violence rule.

Maybe Tommy's embarrassed because he doesn't hang around long, and after he goes I have a few hours feeling bitter and twisted, laughing to myself like vinegar at all the verses I've learned where Jesus preaches forgiveness.

The thing Tommy hasn't told me is that gathering up my gear he's found my notebook and rung the only two numbers in there.

Dorothy's first: she rings the next morning. They bring the telephone round to me on a trolley.

'Hello there,' she shouts. 'Hear you had a close scrape. Glad you came through it okay.'

I say, 'Good to hear from you, Dorothy.'

'Now,' she says, 'no good at hospital visiting, can't ever think of what to say, terrific strain all round, but got a little news for you, most it from the local paper. Chap I think you may know, Peter Edward Moxon, nickname Moxy, just been jailed for eighteen months, burglary. I'm keeping mum, of course, but local gossip says you might be pleased to hear that, and the girl, Maria, she's in rehab but further down the coast somewhere. No one knows where, but don't suppose you mind not knowing, do you?'

I say, 'No, that's right, Dorothy, I don't mind,' but after she's said good luck and rung off I spend the rest of the day full of sadness for the poisoned happiness I had with the girl.

The next day the doctor says, 'Good news, Mr Johnson. You'll be going home tomorrow.' I try to make it look like he's making me happy, while underneath I'm wondering how far forty quid is going to take me with a broken arm, some dodgy ribs and a moody surname.

Cynthia turns up that afternoon. She's wearing jeans that have been out of fashion a few years and a jumper in a kind of green I don't like, but straight off I'm having to make sure I look at her the right way so I don't have those man-woman feelings she used to give me.

Perhaps she should've been a brief, because I can feel those clever blue eyes working me out as tell her about the situation, and it can't be long before she realises I've got to be away a bit quick, even if she doesn't let on at first but changes the subject instead, starts talking about the letters I sent her when I was inside. 'Believe me, Bomber, you've got real talent as a writer.'

I tell her about the story I haven't finished, set in the drinking club.

She says, 'Even you must have been frightened, Bomber. How did it feel when one of the brothers held a gun against your forehead? Did you have an accident, I mean lose control?'

'Thought I was going to, Cynthia, had to try not to.'

'Oh, Bomber, you should definitely put that in. Don't be embarrassed – we want to know how it feels.'

I don't know who 'we' is, but I let it go.

'Nice of you to be so enthusiastic, Cynthia.'

After that I tell her a bit about Keith and my few weeks with the community and how they sort of changed my life. As I'm talking to her I'm trying to work out how I feel about the way they've made me feel like a leper. I get a bit carried away and I say, 'I don't know why they call it heartache, Cynthia, because it's more like the pain you get in your gut when a bird – sorry, Cynthia – a woman, lets you down and there's nothing you can do to make her suffer or bring her back.' She's looking straight at me as I'm telling her that and her eyes are lit up like flood-lights. She says, 'Yes, Bomber, I do know what you mean.'

She never asks if I want to come to her in Dorset. Perhaps it's obvious I haven't got anywhere else. Instead she steams straight in, 'How bad is your arm, Bomber? Do you need an ambulance, or would you rather a taxi?'

I tell her a cab'll be lovely, and she laughs in a happy way.

'Well, I'll go home tonight if that's okay with you.

I'll get the spare room ready.'

I say, 'Yes, of course, that's fine, Cynthia,' because with her class of person it's manners to make out what you think matters, even when you know it doesn't.

After we settle that she phones Tommy on her mobile to tell him the plan, and then says she'll see me tomorrow.

When she leans over to kiss me on the cheek I'm worried she'll knock the bad arm but that doesn't stop me remembering the perfume from the letters she sent me inside.

Once they've brought the dinner round I'm hoping that maybe one or two from the community might have heard it's my last night and come in to say goodbye, perhaps Danny or Mabel, because they were the two I got on with best, and I wouldn't even mind seeing Douglas. He could put his hand on my good shoulder and tell me in his half-crown accent, 'Self-education, the best kind there is,' although with this bruising I could do without him trying to feel my bollocks. But when no one shows I know they've gone along with Keith, made me a sinner.

Tommy comes in the morning to say goodbye and hang around waiting with me for the cab to make sure nothing happens.

I've seen before he doesn't like hugging other blokes and I can't anyway with my left jab in plaster, so when the cab turns up I shake his hand. 'Thanks for everything, Tom. Won't ever forget, mate.'

Tommy shakes his head. 'He had very high hopes of you. You know that, don't you?'

I wink at him, 'Could've been a contender,' and then I'm in the cab.

There's still a lot of miles to go by the time the cab driver's finished on football, but I have a doze, real and pretend most of the rest of the way, although I still feel a bit of a ghost when I get there.

Cynthia's says I look tired, and she'll show me my room straight away.

This time she doesn't have to help me up the stairs, although I let her bring my carrier so I can hold onto the banister with my good arm.

'Afraid it's not much more than a box room,' she says, and with a wardrobe one side, a desk up against the window at the far end and a single bed on the other side there isn't a lot of room, but I've been in cells and hostel rooms a lot narrower, and none of them had a desk you could sit at looking out of the window at the sea, which is the first thing I do after she says, 'Come down when you're ready Bomber. We'll have tea at your convenience.'

The sea's the colour of an acid drop with no more than a few white ruffles. There's a red lightship out on the point of the bay and a ship heading up the coast, but so far out all I can see is the dark shape against the sky.

I could sit there and let it hypnotise me, but thoughtful Cynthia's put a notepad and biro on the desk, and there's things I want to get down before all the punches I've taken make me forget them.

I flip open the notepad and pick up the biro, making sure I'm in a position where I won't knock the bad arm.

I start writing this.

ACKNOWLEDGEMENTS

I was lucky enough to attend two inspiring creative writing courses while working on 'Bomber', the first in Ty Newydd, taught by Patricia Duncker and Jim Friel, at the start of the novel, and 'Stuck in the Middle', taught by Sara Dunant and Gillian Slovo at Faber nine years later when I needed help finishing the book. I also had the pleasure of several terms of Linda Leatherbarrow's course at the Mary Ward Centre. The book has recently benefited from the rigorous attentions of Bobbie Darbyshire and the other members of the Writers Together group. The novel gave birth to two solo plays on its way to completion, Bomber Jackson Does Some and On The Out. My friends Nick Revel and Tony Green were both generous beyond the call of friendship in helping me stage the two shows and Dominic and Steve Conway provided the music. Ruth Nicklin produced and directed me as a version of Bomber in the short film, On The Out. Nick Sweeney sorted out typos, spelling, paragraphs and formatting.

Becky Morrison let me exploit her design and compositing skills ruthlessly. Mark Reefer is a boxing trainer extraordinaire, and I hope I've lavished as much craft and love on the book as he does on his classes.

My partner Jane and daughter Tali kept me going with their enthusiasm throughout the ten years it's taken me to write the book. Jane Conway has often been keener on Bomber than I have and was also kind enough to be the first person to read the almost final draft, which was also read and commented upon by Marek Kazmierski. My thanks indeed to the following friends in particular for their many words of encouragement: Lesli Godfrey, Jenny Landreth, Hannah Lindsell, Paul Lyons, Eddie Nicklin, Roni Rossi and Mark Thomas. Lastly, my grateful thanks to The East Finchley Book Group for discussion and wine.

For further information or to order additional copies of this book please contact heavybagbooks@gmail.com